Dedication.

To all the ladies of the UK, who dream of the *filthy* mouthed cowboys of "Booktok", this one is for you....

About the Author

Hello readers.

Thank you, for showing an interest in my debut novel, a Cowboy in Yorkshire.

I appreciate you, giving me, your time and I hope you enjoy the book.

Allow me to take this opportunity, to tell you a little about myself. I live in a Yorkshire city, with my husband and daughter, but the Yorkshire countryside, has my heart and always will, wherever I am in the world.

As you can probably tell, from the previous statement, I am a proud Yorkshire lass and wanted to put our beautiful county, on the map, with this book.

I stay at home, through the day, as a carer and home educator, to my daughter. Although, I love doing this and it is my entire world, I wanted to add something, that would challenge my creative side a little, hence, deciding to write.

I'm an avid reader and dedicated "Booktoker", so I set my sights, on putting my own work out there, to the world of Book lovers.

As a big fan, of cowboy romance books, Elsie Silver, being my favourite Author, I wanted to bring one of those Cowboys, here, to the UK.

I am already planning, the next two books in the series, so please keep an eye out, for more work from myself, in the near future.

Thank you again.

May I introduce you to, Carter and Sammie…

Carter and Sammie's Playlist

- Country's cool again- Lainey Wilson
- Watermelon Moonshine- Lainey Wilson
- You in a Honky Tonk- Randall King
- I had some help- Post Malone and Morgan Wallen
- The right kind of wrong- Leann Rimes
- Worst way- Riley Green
- A bar song- Shaboozy
- Man I feel like a woman- Shania Twain
- Thinkin' 'bout me- Morgan Wallen
- I'm the problem- Morgan Wallen
- Beautiful Crazy- Luke Combs
- Save a horse, ride a Cowboy- Big&Rich
- Wind up missing you- Tucker Wetmore
- Stargazing- Myles Smith
- Your Man- Josh Turner
- Dancing in the Headlights- Dustin Lynch
- I'm gonna love you- Cody Johnson and Carrie Underwood

Prologue.
Carter, how I was.

I'd never had a healthy relationship with most of my family, but Pops was a different story.

Even though, I'd always been the black sheep, a bit of an outlaw- hell, a lot of an outlaw is more the truth, he never gave up on me. Showing me, from a young age, how to live life on the ranch.

The ranch stood proud, among the trees and the mountains of Vinemont, Alabama, and although the view was stunningly beautiful and serene, it was hard fucking work out there! The days long, the work grueling, but the rewards and the sense of achievement, made it all worthwhile.

So, from the age of eight, I had been helping around the land with maintenance work, upkeep and livestock chores. There was always a fence somewhere, that needed fixing, or a calf that had gone missing, so I was kept busy and my troubled mind, welcomed it most of the time.

My grandfather, always the hardworking, strong minded, gruff rancher, was my hero and I thought he was invincible. But nobody ever is!

My world and dreams were shattered, when Pops was diagnosed, with Cancer of the Bowel.

≈≈≈≈≈≈≈≈≈≈≈≈

Over the year, since Pop's diagnosis, my responsibilities on the ranch, had piled up, and as well as the maintenance work on the grounds, that I carried out, with a count of four other cowboys, I found myself training horses and buying and selling cattle.
I felt honored, to be given the extra responsibilities, but I knew it would only be a matter of time, before I screwed it all up and let my grandfather down.

I tried to be a good Christian man, like Pops and my father, but it never worked out that way.
This one particular Friday was spent breaking in the newest member of the family- a Mustang Mare.
I've gotta say, I never usually had issues with the ladies, but this one was a bit of a Broom-Tail. She really did not want me on her. Again, not a problem I'm used to, when it comes to the females in town, but after chewing gravel too many times and probably being black and blue, under my button down, from being thrown into a metal gate over and over, I decided I was done with her for the day, and after managing to take my life in my hands one more time and get the little shit into her stall, I headed out for a drink.

The friends I had growing up, had started to drift away, I never admitted out loud, that I had realized they'd grown sick of my regular shit, but I had realized it, I really had! Did I miss them? Yeah!

Did I find myself feeling alone most of the time, and needing to speak to people, who would understand how the news of my grandfather's health issues were affecting me? Of course! But enough to give up the endless stream of women, or putting an end to my drunken antics and bar fights? No! I was a lost cause!

      I headed into the "Lucky Horseshoe" bar, to the sound of Morgan Wallen playing over the speakers, neon lights galore, people singing and dancing along, the string of regulars, that had seated themselves on bar stools- their permanent assigned seats.

On one of those bar stools, sat Clay, one of the cowboys from our ranch, so I headed over to him, and ordered us both a double bourbon.

Before long, the drinks were flowing, the bar was packed out, and I could feel the electricity that I craved, I knew something was brewing and there would soon be a sign of trouble.

I always found myself in the middle of any trouble, fuck, who am I kidding? I was at the forefront of it all, because it's the only thing I knew. Well, it's the only thing I thought I knew... and I did it well!

      I had come to find, that a mix of strong proof and women, was a concoction for a bar fight and that is exactly, what rolled out that night!

One of the local buckle bunnies, Cassidy, was being hit on, by some guy who was just passing through, he probably saw the ripped denim shorts that barely covered her ass, the cropped man's shirt and cowboy boots and thought she was a one go, good time girl.

It didn't help that she had taken his fucking hat and put it on her own head!

The problem was, she knew what she was doing, but she was *my* one go, good time girl and this guy's hands were all over her.

To cut a long story short, I saw red and threw the first punch.

I'm not gunna lie, the guy gave as good as he got, he fought back, so I had to end it well, and there it was, a beer bottle, right next to me on the bar, you can guess what happened next.

The blood was running, the sirens were sounding and because of the severity of the injuries I caused him and the fact I couldn't keep my ass out of trouble, with a few bar fights and a couple of DUI's under my belt, *which I may add, was always complete with an impressive buckle*, I ended up being incarcerated for three fucking years!!

I thought I was slick, thought I was the big cheese and at the time, I was enjoying beating the shit out of that guy, but what I didn't think about, was the consequences, the fact that I had been locked up in this shit hole for the last three years, but I could handle that. I was a big boy, I knew what I was doing and could take care of myself.

What I couldn't deal with, was the fact that I couldn't help my grandfather, I wasn't on the ranch, I wasn't helping him with his morning shave, when he couldn't manage and more importantly, I never got to say goodbye.

≈≈≈≈≈≈≈≈≈

Since the loss of Pops and finally realizing that I had let him down, let my family down and let myself down, I spent my last year in jail, trying to turn things around. I wanted to improve myself, I wanted to have faith, so I turned to God and tried to better myself, so that I could have a fresh start on the outside.

A big part of that change was writing to a woman. I know what you're thinking, he's in jail and still at it with the women, but it wasn't like that, she was actually good for me.
The hoosegow was running a program, where inmates could be linked up to a pen pal, as part of a self-help service and getting used to people on the outside again. Obviously, all mail was vetted and read, before we could get our hands on it, or send them out, but that didn't bother me, because for once in my life- I was being decent. I was talking about wholesome subjects and about, how I wanted to improve my life once I got out, how I wanted a whole fresh start.
I had picked up some skills in jail, but I would always be a cowboy, that's who I am.
But I wanted to be a good one and to help others.

My pen pal was Sammie, from the UK. I had never spoken to anyone in England before, and we had a little bit of fun with each other, about the different words we used. It was all good, *clean* conversation.

She was sweet, kind, funny and although there was nothing questionable, at all, about our letters to each other, it didn't mean I wasn't starting to feel something for her.

We made plans for my release, and I was heading to stay with her and her family for a while, to help on their farm.

I was used to land work and livestock responsibilities, and this was the perfect chance for a whole new start, on the other side of the globe.

I had nothing keeping me in the States, after all.

My family took over the ranch, wanted nothing to do with me. The last fight and being incarcerated, was the last straw for my friends, who were already disappointed in me, anyway…so if I was somewhere else, across the pond, maybe I wouldn't *realize* I was lonely.

Chapter 1.
Sammie.

Nothing particularly exciting, ever happens in my day-to-day life. Don't get me wrong, it's far from boring, living on a farm doesn't allow for boring.

Today is Saturday, it's the last Saturday of the month and we have a busy week ahead.
With Spring in the air, you would think that I'd open my curtains, to lovely blue skies and sunshine, hitting the beautiful panes of green... but no, it's 4am and it's still very much dark! I really should be asleep, but no rest for the wicked!
Who am I kidding, the only wicked thing I have ever done in life, is lie to the man I have been writing to for the past year or so. But I will get to that later!

After my normal morning routine; showering, styling my hair in a very fashionable ponytail, dressing, et cetera. I head downstairs to be greeted by my family, for preparation of breakfast, which we will eat, after we have started some of the chores.

I love our family home; we all live together and are extremely close. We have, my dad, Frank, my mum, Elsa, my older brother, Carl and my gran, Clara.
In the farmhouse we share, we are often accompanied in the mornings, by our staff, who work on the farm with us, including my boyfriend of two years, Jake and his dad, Miles. We have a work force, of five paid

employees, that doesn't include family. My best friend, Hannah, also used to help on the farm, before we sadly lost her, to Cancer a couple of years ago.

The guy I have been writing to, Carter, lost his gramps to Cancer a bit back too, so that, alongside our love of farm life, animals, and country music, was something we shared and bonded over.

I think it really helped, having someone to talk to, who was feeling the same grief.

I was so nervous, because he was actually coming to stay with us on the farm, to help out and to help himself also. He wanted a fresh start and to "better himself" as he used to put it, in our letters.

My mum and dad knew all about him, and although they were worried about him being an ex-convict, they were intrigued to have a western cowboy come stay on the farm- there would, undoubtedly, be some clash of procedures there, and it would be interesting, to see the differences.

The conversation with them, was obviously, very nerve wracking, especially seeing as I had gotten carried away with Carter and made plans for him to come over, before discussing it with anyone, so the conversation had to happen fast.

At first, my family were worried, just knowing he had been locked up. I had explained that he wasn't a danger, he had just made some stupid decisions in life, and because he had a record, he had received a longer sentence than usual, for a bar fight.

The injuries were bad, but not life threatening, and after telling them he had been handy with his fists, but only in actual fights, not just randomly hitting people and that, in his world, it wasn't unusual to have punch ups, but that he was, in no way, dangerous and he wouldn't cause any issues with the business, they agreed to give him a chance. Thank God!

We obviously, also, took the correct steps, in getting him over here. Usually, if an American ex-convict, was coming to stay and work in the UK, they would be refused, if their sentence was longer than 12 months, but because Carter received a longer sentence due to him previously getting into trouble with the law, rather than the one case, and due to him coming to stay and work, on a private farm, we managed to get the correct paperwork done and accepted.
It also helped that he had really turned things around in prison and gained a couple of degrees.
He obviously had to keep himself out of trouble now, too.

I hadn't, however, told Jake about him... and now that I mention it, I didn't tell him about Jake either. I didn't lie to either one of them, really, I just didn't tell them the whole story. Not that I needed to tell them anything, Jake was my boyfriend and Carter was just an ex-convict, that I had been writing to… I didn't need to tell Carter that I had a boyfriend, because it was none of his business and I didn't need to tell Jake, that the guy who was starting work on the farm tomorrow morning, was a cowboy from Alabama, that I couldn't stop thinking about.
Okay, maybe that's something I should really own up to. Or is it? People think about others, right?

With all that said, there was a lot of work to be done, so after feeding and watering the cattle, I left Miles and Jake to get them set up for milking, whilst I went over to the stables.

Usually, my dad would be around for the cattle too, but he had some paperwork to be getting on with.

That's one of the things I thought Carter could help with when he got here, although he is a cowboy at heart and is used to all the manual work there is to do on a farm, he had done a business and accounting degree whilst he was inside. So, he had a lot to offer, I was quite proud of myself, for finding someone who could help us, in so many ways.

The stables were at the other end of the farm, and it was quite a walk, but it was my favourite job. We didn't really use horses much, for agricultural reasons, although, we did try incorporating them on the farm, when we could and they definitely came in handy, but the stables we had, were used for livery.

We had a couple of Geldings of our own, but we rented out the stables to other equestrians, and that was just another way to make money, here on the farm.

Today, I was aware that one of the owners couldn't get up to the stables to see to her Mare, so I was going over there to feed her, along with mine and do the mucking out. I wouldn't usually come up here first thing, but it depends on what needs doing at the stable and on the rest of the farm. I'm usually here, a while after the sun comes up.

It wasn't often, that we were hands on with the care of the other horses, but there were times, where something had crept up, and the owners would call on a favour, and whilst I was up here seeing to our own horses, it didn't hurt to check if anything was needed for the others.

  The sun had risen, and it was a lovely, clean air this morning. Wasn't overly warm, but comfortable, and I loved taking this time, to myself, to look at what we had around us.

Not only, was the farm and our family home, our pride and joy, but the surrounding lands we had here, always made me happy.

Not many people around the world, would know of the county I am from, it's not very well known, but it is the biggest county in England, so everyone in the UK, knows of the beauty that is, God's own country-Yorkshire.

It is beautiful and I am blessed.

≈≈≈≈≈≈≈≈≈≈≈

I spent a bit too long with the horses, I had done everything necessary, but then when it came to grooming, I always spent so long making their coats shine.

  Our two Geldings, Max and Otis, loved being brushed and I loved to see the shine that was left. Max was a beautiful Chestnut and Otis a Palomino, and their temperaments were fantastic.

Well, Max was great with me, and he was a good horse generally, but he didn't like being ridden by anyone else.

Otis was so laid back, I'm surprised he didn't fall over, if it wasn't for the four legs, he probably would.
He was like a horse on marijuana.
As much as I loved standing here, brushing and talking to them, I had other things to do, before Carter arrived.

I'd already passed my gran, at the chicken coop, so I knew today's eggs had been collected and her and my mum, had probably started baking and making breakfast for the rest of us, but I needed to head back to the parlour, to see if Miles, Jake and probably now, Carl, needed any help with the cows.
I also needed to make sure things looked presentable, including myself and try and find the time to tell Jake about Carter and why, I had suddenly, become stressed, about how I look such a mess.

After getting the cows in one field and the horses in another, we all head up to the farmhouse for breakfast. Gran and mum have outdone themselves, like they do every morning, putting on an incredible spread of full English breakfast, baked goods and cereals.
Along with tea, coffee and juice.
They always say that they must provide enough, to keep us all going for the rest of the day, working out on the land, with anything else that needs completing. I do think, they overestimate the portions though, unless they are planning on feeding the whole village.

After filling up, to the point where I don't think I could move without being sick, we head on outside, to finish up what needs doing. I don't think it is fair to ride a horse, while I feel like the size of a house, or run the risk of being sick on the poor animal, so I help out, on the cattle side, for a while and leave the horses roaming in the paddock, for a few more hours.

The cows are being taken to the milking parlour at the moment, so they will need moving back to the fields, when they're done.

Once all the cows are attached, I head over to the stables and leave the men with the cattle.

Nothing much needs doing at the stables, right now, it was all done this morning and because I've eaten too much and I'm nervous, so that will be a factor too, I am feeling a bit nauseous, therefore, I don't feel like riding. Sitting on the fence of the paddock, where the horses are roaming, I just stay and watch them for a while, running around, playing, they're like a herd of foals. I'm sure they're showing off, they keep coming up for cuddles.

Whilst I'm watching Max, Otis and Flash, one of the other owners- Connie, comes to the stable, to do what's needed for her horse, Clover.

I don't know if she's here for Zara too, I hope so, because I can't stand her owner and would rather, not be around when she comes.

Connie brings Clover to the paddock, so she can muck out her stall.

"Hey," she says.

"Hi, you alright?"

"Not bad, they're having fun, aren't they?" she laughs.

"Yeah, I'm going to be the bad guy now though, they need to come in because we have a visitor coming, I need to get back to the house and can't get back up."

"I'll get them in, I'll be here for a while yet, you get back to what you're doing."

"Are you sure?" I ask.

"Yeah, go, are they groomed?" she asks.

"Yeah, yeah, they just need putting in their stalls, everything is done. Thanks Connie, you're a lifesaver."

She waves and heads back to the stables.

As I walk back towards the house, I see the other farmers, also heading in the same direction.

I meet them all, on the way back, and I am just about to pull Jake aside, to tell him why my mood has suddenly changed, when my dad pipes up with,

"When is your cowboy arriving? I thought he would be here by now."

If ever the ground could open up and swallow me, I would want it to be now.

Jake turns, to look between my dad and I, with both confusion and annoyance written all over his face!

"Cowboy? Your cowboy? I didn't know anyone owned a cowboy."

Yeah, he wasn't happy!

Dad pulls a face, that was somewhere between *"oh shit"* and *"I'm sorry love"*, before scurrying off, like a dog, who had been caught ripping to pieces, its owner's favourite outfit.

"Yeah, thanks dad!" I call, before turning back to Jake. "Firstly, the guy who is starting work here tomorrow and who probably should be here already, is a cowboy from Alabama. Secondly, he's obviously *not* my cowboy and lastly, he's just been released from prison."

I then also, turn and walk, very quickly, in the same direction as my dad just did.

Drop a bomb and run away- the apple doesn't fall far from the tree!

After heading back into the house, and seeing my dad, half hiding behind the newspaper, I am just about to tell him, how much I appreciate him just dumping me in it, when Jake storms in, with a little bit too much enthusiasm.

We all turn to look at Jake, who was obviously, just about to tell me what he thought of this idea, after almost ripping the back door off the hinges and causing my gran to jump out of her skin, when the front doorbell sounds.

Saved by the bell.

Chapter 2.
Sammie.

We stand, staring at each other in the kitchen, before my brother, Carl gets up, out of his chair.

"I'll get it shall I?" Looking at us all, in pure disbelief.

A couple of minutes later, I can hear two male voices coming back from the front door, through to the kitchen, where we are all still stood, staring at one another...

One of those voices being American, not just an American twang, no!! A thick and sexy southern drawl, I have to stop myself from drooling shamelessly.

After all, my boyfriend is stood right here!

Carl comes back into the kitchen, introducing us to Carter, who looks round us all, with a smile and a nod of his head, until his gaze falls on me... His electrifying, sapphire blue eyes land right on me, shooting through me like a damn bolt of lightning!

I can barely breathe.

There he was, after only speaking to him, through vetted letters, to and from a prison house in America and not even having the slightest clue what he looked like, because we never asked one another and we never sent pictures (that probably would have been taking it too far after all!) he was finally stood right here, in my family home, in the heart of my family home!

We had talked about so much with one another, had really deep and meaningful conversations and I felt we really knew a lot about each other, but seeing him stood here, in the flesh, I felt like I didn't know him at all. I take a few seconds, which probably feels like uncomfortable minutes to everyone else, to take him in.

Tall, over 6ft tall for sure, he stands taller than everyone else in the room, with broad shoulders that are accentuated by the t-shirt he is wearing… a tight black t-shirt, stretched over his shoulders, his muscular chest, his arms… his god damn arms!!

Bless me father, for I have sinned!!

My eyes rake over the strong, tanned biceps, complete with black ink, trailing all down his veined arms to his hands, his big hands… is it hot in here?

"Howdy," he finally says to me, to which I reply with,

"Nice jeans, are they Wranglers?"

And they were nice jeans.

Yes, I was now looking at his jeans and how well he fills them, what the hell was wrong with me?

Look up Sammie, I silently will myself.

But that isn't any better, because he has removed his sexy, black, buck skin cowboy hat, to reveal his tousled, sandy coloured hair- the man looks like he has been carved in Calacatta marble, by the likes of Aphrodite, Eros and Kratos.

I HAVE A BOYFRIEND!

Daring to have another look at his face, I notice he looks confused, answering,

"Yeah, they're Wranglers."

I shake my head.

"Sorry, Hi Carter, it's great to meet you, we were expecting you earlier on," I say, extending my hand out to shake his and then immediately regretting it, because I really don't think it is a good idea, to touch this man.

As though he can read my mind, although, I am glad he actually can't, Jake steps in and stops our handshake from happening, offering his own to him instead,

"Hi Carter, how do you do? I'm Jake, Sammie's boyfriend."

Kill me, kill me now, another silent plea.

After a quick gaze in my direction, Carter takes Jake's hand.

"It's nice to meet you, it's nice to meet all of you," he offers, looking around the room, to my family.

≈≈≈≈≈≈≈≈≈≈≈

After the very intense time, I leave all the men talking inside, while I step out into the evening air, with my mum and grandma, who are sat on the decking out back, having a glass of wine.

"Want a glass?" My mum looks up at me, with a smile- a mischievous one at that!

"Sure?" I almost ask back.

Sitting down on the garden furniture we had bought, just a few weeks ago, I look around at the trees against the deep blue and purple sky, and sigh.

"That was quite a sigh, is everything okay?"

"Yeah Gran, I'm fine, just been a long day and I think, the last hour or so, feels longer than the rest of them, put together."

"Yes, you have seemed a little tightly wound today, is it just nerves? I thought you was going to have an aneurysm in the kitchen earlier."

"You're such a drama queen Mum, I can't think where Carl gets it from! I wasn't that bad!"

"Wasn't that bad? Time stood still; I was a nervous wreck!" My gran pipes up, gobby when she's had a wine or two!

I just laugh at the memory of how ridiculously dorky I was, "I don't know why I reacted the way I did, we knew he was coming, it was just everything with Jake, leading up to it too! Bad timing, I suppose."

"Yes, I guess if Jake hadn't thrown a hissy fit, you might have handled the devilishly handsome American cowboy stood in our kitchen, a whole lot better," my mum winks.

Damn, looks like I didn't hide the fact I was a walking hormone, very well.

Hopefully, Jake managed to skip that bit, I'm hoping he was too busy being angry at the way Carter looked, to notice the way I wasn't angry about it at all.

"I take it, by the look he gave, both you and Jake, when Jake introduced himself, that you never told him you had a boyfriend?"

"Oh gosh, Mum…no, I didn't, and I need to face that with both of them. It isn't that I told him I was single or anything, there was never any need to, our conversations were always on a friendship level, but I

should have mentioned it. You know, as a woman, writing to a man and telling him things about her life, worries, fears, dreams- real deep stuff... our situation could easily be misread and in hindsight, I should have told him I had a boyfriend, I told him practically everything else, what am I going to say to them?"
"Just be honest and upfront," they both reply at the same time.
"Yeah, I'll talk to them about it tomorrow, they're drinking in there, we are drinking out here. I don't need to be trying to explain the inner workings of my mind, to either of them tonight."
With that, we sit in comfortable silence, finishing off the bottle of red.

Chapter 3.
Carter, My New Start.

I've hardly slept, in the last week, anticipating my release from jail and second guessing what I was planning.

Was I crazy? I was goin' thousands of miles across the world.

With no direct flights, I had to do a layover, which only made the journey more stressful and tiring. I hate airports! But there was no turning back now. With the complete travel time, over three airport locations, the layover, the waiting around and the time difference, I had no idea what day I was actually on when I finally landed in Manchester, England.

I still had to go through baggage claim and all the checks, before I even got out of there!

Let me tell you, for an American ex-con, that was no fun! But I got there in the end, and now I had to find a cab. I hope the people in the North of England aren't friendly, I'm too tired to have to talk to a cab driver, I just wanted to get to my final destination.

Suddenly, I was smiling at the thought of that, the thought of finally meeting Sammie, after we had been writing to each other for over a year.

I didn't even know what she looked like, I only knew what she had portrayed in her letters, but I had never been more excited about meeting a woman in my life... and there had been a lot of women.

"Are you here for the country music festival?" the cab driver disturbs my thoughts.

"Oh, no, I'm here to work, from Alabama... what country music festival?"

"Oh, a real cowboy, are you? You'll feel at home over here, it seems the country and western scene has hit big, it's very popular and only getting bigger every day! They are holding a big music festival this weekend and I assumed with the way you are dressed, that you were attending."

"No, this here's my everyday duds, well it used to be and now, let's just say, I'm back!"

I guess Lainey Wilson called it- Country's cool again!

I didn't realize how far the farm was, from the airport, apparently a different county!

The damn driver doesn't shut up, telling me about his family and the fact he never wanted to be a taxi driver, but now couldn't see himself doing anything else, it was goin' to cost a fortune and it was getting late.

≈≈≈≈≈≈≈≈≈≈≈

"Here we are."

I look up and out of the window, to see the drive up to the farmhouse, surrounded by nothing but fields and trees. It was starting to get dark, but I could still see the never-ending spread of greenery. I wondered if they owned the whole lot and I strangely felt at home.

The gravel drive leads up to the main house and off to the right, I could see a few other buildings, couldn't make out what they were from here, but I knew from

Sammie's letters that they had cattle and horses, so I was guessing they were barns.

The main house, which I know they call, the "Farmhouse" over here, stands in the center of it all. It was a good size, definitely big enough for her large family, who I was looking forward to meeting, and the stone was a light sandy color.
It looked different to the main house at the ranch, back home and it wasn't as big, but still impressive.
Even though it was large, it had more of a homely feel to it, rather than a working farm. It probably helped that there was a soft warm glow, coming through the windows and I could hear people talking.

I couldn't work out whether it was coming from inside the house, or around the back somewhere and suddenly, I became nervous, about the fact that I was goin' to be around a real family, a family who love and support each other. That, with the exception of Pops, was foreign to me.
I was here and it was too late to change my mind, not that I wanted to, but I probably would have tried to talk myself into it if I waited any longer, to walk up the stairs out front and knock on the door.
So that's what I do.
Shit, I didn't mean to knock so loudly, then, as if they wouldn't have heard the ridiculously loud bang, I saw the bell and continued to press the button.
What the fuck Carter? They're goin' to think you're an impatient dick.
A few seconds passed, felt like minutes really, but surely not!

Then suddenly, the door opens, and I am faced with a guy, a young guy, probably a couple of years younger than me, maybe.

This must be Carl, Sammie's brother, but I don't say anything, just incase.

He's fairly tall, not as tall as I am, probably just under 6ft, with dark hair and, I'm not going to comment on what color eyes he has, *he's not my type!*

"Hi, you must be Carter, come on in, I'm Carl." He sticks out his hand and I shake it, as I am entering the house.

"Nice to meet you Carl, sorry, I'm later than I thought I would be, it took forever to get here."

Carl just nods, as he closes the door behind us both.

"We were just in the middle of… a discussion…in the kitchen, Sammie is through there with everyone else. Come through. Nice boots by the way."

Was I, his type?

I don't think I've ever told a man he has nice boots personally, maybe a cultural thing.

The only time I've ever admired what is on someone's feet, is when they're paired with a nice short skirt or some ass hugging jean shorts and even then, I'm only ever wondering what they would look like high up on my shoulders.

As we walk towards the warm glow and the amazing smells of the kitchen, I hear whispering and hushed tones, before finally, standing in the doorway, to the heart of the home.

I didn't immediately look at Sammie, for a moment, stepping into all those eyes staring at me, I forgot why I was actually there and who I was there to see.

Carl was the one who introduced me to everyone scattered around the kitchen, apart from two of them.

Looking around the room, to the people he pointed out, I smile and nod a hello to Sammie and Carl's parents, Frank and Elsa, their grandmother, Clara and one of the employees, Miles.

They were all smiling and greeting me, with friendly faces and happy voices, looked like a great group of people to be around... good people, I could tell.

Then suddenly, my brain catches up with the rest of me, and my eyes land on Sammie.

Fuck! I wanted all of me on Sammie! Shit!

I stare way too long, but she stares back and the longer we look at each other, the more I notice her eyes raking over me and the more her eyes dance around my body, the more she blushes. My mind has a little chuckle to itself and then finally, I put us both, hell, all... out of the silent misery.

A simple, "*Howdy,*" is what I decide to go with, just to put an end to the silence that has blanketed itself over the entire room.

"Nice jeans, are they Wranglers?"

Hhmmm maybe it was a sibling thing? To notice people's items of clothing.

I can feel the rest of the room are as uncomfortable as I am.

"Err, yeah they're Wranglers."

Finally, she actually says hi and puts out her hand, to shake... I think she says something about the time and me arriving, but I can't be sure, because some annoying asshole pushes her hand out of the way, before I can touch her and replaces her hand with his own, introducing himself as Jake, her boyfriend!
Her fucking boyfriend?

I have no right to be annoyed at the fact she has a boyfriend, we are only friends, well actually I don't know if we are classed as friends really, we were pen pals and now, I suppose, she is sort of my boss?
Fuck that's hot!
Well, it would be if I wasn't the dominant type, but I wouldn't mind her topping from the bottom every now and then.
Fucking hell Carter, some guy has just introduced himself as her boyfriend!! Have some respect!
"It's nice to meet you, it's nice to meet all of you," I offer, while I look around the room, at the people staring at me, and shake his hand, while silently wanting to break it.

≈≈≈≈≈≈≈≈≈≈≈

A bit later on, after sharing sneaky quiet glances with Sammie, where none of us spoke but just kept catching each other looking and smiling, I settle onto one of the chairs, and the atmosphere in the room lightens and lifts a bit. I no longer feel like I am on a stage, or in a fishbowl. We are all talking between ourselves, and Sammie slips out back to join her mom and grandmother, who had left the room after Carl and Jake got a bit loud with their stories, having had a few drinks.

I watched her walk out the door quietly, as though she had managed to slip away without me noticing. Let me tell you, since I looked at her for the first time and took in everything about her, there was no way I would ever not notice.

She's beautiful, with deep chocolate hair and her milky smooth skin, her beauty shines through from the inside too. She has a warm smile,

I have seen snippets of it being cheeky at times too, but whichever one of those smiles she gives, I've noticed that it reaches her eyes every time.

She is fairly tall for a woman, above average and it looks like she has a killer body under the jeans and t-shirt she's wearing. I have noticed that she keeps holding herself in a way that would say she might be insecure, wanting to hide away at times. I hope that's not true, because she is striking and I'm goin' to make sure she knows it.

As we sit, just the men, drinking and talking, I am building up a picture in my head of the family around me.

By now, I know Miles is Jake's dad and a good friend of Frank's. The two men are probably a similar age and I learn that Frank had inherited the farm from his mom and dad, Clara and her late husband, Harold.

I wondered where Sammie's other grandparents were, on her mom's side of the family, whether they were still around and just didn't live on the farm, or whether they had lost them too.

Listening to Frank and Miles talk about Clara and Harold, had me thinking about Pops, teaching me the ropes when I was a kid.

Both Frank and Miles, had grown up on this farm, helping out after school and learning all the ins and outs of Dairy farming, so they could then go on to teach their kids and keep it running as a family business and a family home.

From their story, I realized that Jake and Sammie had probably known each other their entire lives and that Jake was probably good friends with Carl, I began to feel incredibly jealous.

Jealous of the depth of the relationship, between the guy, I had no real right to hate and the woman I couldn't stop thinking about.

Chapter 4.
Carter.

Frank grabs another few beers, and hands me one, over the table.

"Sammie tells me you have a degree in Business and Accounting, is that right?"

I welcome the distraction, from my own thoughts, that Frank has just given me, with that question.

"Oh yeah, I thought it was best to actually get something positive out of the whole jail situation," I smile back.

"Well, I hope you learned other lessons too!" Miles jumps in, "We don't want any trouble on the farm or in the village at all, for that matter."

Who put 50 cents in that fucker?!

"Of course," I say with a smile, an almost sickly smile. "I don't plan on going back there anytime soon."

"Or at all," Carl raises his eyebrows in my direction.

I just nod back with a thin, tight-lipped smile. I wasn't sure how much personality these people had. Better not make a joke of anything just yet.

"What were you in for?"

I knew that was coming and I knew it would be fucking Jake who asked it, so he can look down his goody two shoes nose at me, well that guy will never be big enough to look down at me!

"Jake, we don't need to ask that. My daughter trusts him and that means I do too, let the man leave his past in the past."

I appreciated Frank saying that Sammie trusted me, especially to her dweeb of a boyfriend, but I was fine answering any questions.

"No, it's okay, I agree- y'all should know who's goin' to be staying and working with you. I know what goes into building something like this up and keeping it running, you don't want some guy, an ex-con, coming in and not knowing for sure, if you can trust him, not to screw things up for you."

Frank nods for me to talk.

"To cut a long story short, there was a woman and I got territorial," I glance over at Jake when I say that and neither Frank or Carl miss it,

"A fight broke out because some guy touched her, there was a smashed bottle involved and I caused quite a bit of damage to his face. The severity of the injuries and the fact I had a record, didn't go down too well with the judge and I was sent down."

"What did you have a record for?" Miles asks, while sitting forward in his seat and looking extremely interested in the bit of gossip I was bringing to town.

"Fighting and a couple of DUIs… I have an ongoing issue with drink and other substances, it's a work in progress."

Frank suddenly looks frighteningly embarrassed and concerned, looking at the bottle of beer he has just handed me, as though he has led me into dangerous shark infested water.

"This is fine," I hold up the bottle slightly and smile at him, seeing him instantly relax and sigh a little.
The guy is a nice guy.

"So, after being in there and serving your time, coming out with a couple of degrees and obviously learning your lesson, although at the time, I imagine you were pretty pissed off! Are you glad of the time you got to spend in there and serve out your punishment?"
I wasn't sure If Carl's question was a stupid question or not. I mean, who the fuck would be glad to have been in jail? But my honest answer was, "Strangely yeah, at the time, obviously I would rather have gotten away with it! But I have done my time, learned my lesson the hard way, learned a few other things and I would never have written to Sammie, if it wasn't for me being inside."
With that last statement, I look directly at Jake, and I actually didn't mean to piss him off with that, this time, but I did anyway.
"Yeah! What was it you wrote to my girlfriend about by the way? Anything exciting?"
This guy was goin' to learn in time, that I wasn't the type to be fucked with, but it had been a long day, and I was tired.

I was suddenly aware of how long, we had all been sat around talking and the women were still outside, it was past sunset now and the sky out the window was deep blues and purples.
"No, nothing exciting, but I won't lie, it was insightful most of the time. We just got to know each other on a deeper level." I was now wanting to piss him off, "She

told me about her dreams, her wants, about her interests and things she loves. We talked about the loss of Hannah and the loss of Pops, sorry, my grandfather. Both of them had passed from Cancer, so we sort of bonded over the understanding we both had, of how hard that was."

"Did you know she had a boyfriend?" He came back with, probably thinking about the *"things she loved"* part of our conversations.

"No," I answer honestly.

The mood was a little sour then. Everyone else was fine, but they probably felt bad that Sammie hadn't told me about Jake, and he was sulking about it like a big fucking baby.

"Jake, why don't you show Carter to the guest room in the attic?"

I don't know why Frank had suggested Jake show me where I would be staying, maybe to try force us to have a conversation on the way to the room, to sort things out before work started on the farm tomorrow.

I wasn't sure, but I was sure that I didn't want to go upstairs without seeing Sammie again tonight.

"Sure," Jake sighed, and we both stood up in unison.

"I'll just head out back and say goodnight to the ladies if you don't mind?"

I directed that question- statement towards Frank, as I was already heading to the back door. I could feel all their eyes burning into the back of my head as I opened the door and stepped outside, to where Sammie, Elsa and Clara were drinking wine and looking up at the sky.

All three of them turn around at once and look up at me, Sammie standing up almost immediately and stumbling slightly on her way up.

I'm not sure if it was because she stood too quickly or had drank too much of the red, that had spilled out of the glass and down her hand, wrist and arm, causing my eyes to track it and tongue wanting to glide over her skin and lick it off.

Yeah, my mind didn't need to go there!

All the same, I reach out my hands and gently catch her elbows to steady her. We are close now.

Looking down into her eyes, I realize they are green.

Do you know, only 2% of the population have green eyes? They are like emeralds. Stunning!

"Woah, are you okay?"

"Y-yeah, I just stood up too quickly- head rush!"

I just smile at her.

      After a couple of beats, I realize we are just staring at each other and not doing or saying anything, although there is so much, I want to do and say to her, none of it suitable when her mom and grandmother are sat looking at us with twinkles in their eyes!

Women!

"I just came out to say goodnight to y'all, poor Jake has been given the job of showing me to the guest room, much to his disgust." I smile down at the two ladies still sat, staring up at us, smiling like the Cheshire Cat.

"Oh, I should be the one to show you, I invited you here, sorry- I haven't been great company, have I? I will jus—"

I stop her before she can start to feel worse about leaving me to talk to her family and boyfriend. "Don't worry, you finish the drink that's managed to *stay* in your glass, I've had a good talk with your dad, brother, boyfriend and his dad- it's all good. I'm sure Jake can manage showing me to the attic, he will probably have visions of throwing me out of the window up there, falling to my death," I wink and smile. "Night ladies, sleep well."

And into the house I go.

"Ready?" Jake asks, when I re appear into the kitchen.

"Sure," I nod, "Goodnight y'all, see y'all in the morning."

"Night Carter," they all say at once.

The guest room is right at the top of the house. Obviously, it is the attic after all and I wondered if it would resemble a guest room or an attic, would I be sharing the room with roof rats and spiders? Not that any of that bothered me, but I'd spent over three years in a cell with a steel can for company, I was hoping it was a bit nicer than what I'd been used to lately, I'd settle for an actual bed.

When Jake opens the door and I step inside, I am pleasantly surprised.

I actually wasn't expecting to be sharing it with rats and spiders, but I wasn't expecting this either.

I had grown up with luxuries, being from a wealthy family and maybe if I hadn't have screwed everything up, the ranch would probably be owned and run by me now.

But lately, I had been living in a dive, I deserved it, but it still wasn't nice- so this is like a palace right now. Not that I know what a palace looks like!

The window was bigger than expected- Jake probably could get me through it if he tried hard enough.

The bed was big too, maybe a king- I'm not sure on the sizes over here, but I could sleep mighty fine in that, for sure. Even the bedding felt luxurious, I had been sleeping with itchy blankets for long enough and this didn't feel itchy at all.

With a closet at the other end of the room and a nightstand at the side of the bed, with a lamp on top... complete with... holy fuck... a bible!

I had tried to find God again, but I'm not gunna lie, he's got lost a few times since! I can't have a bible there, next to me, when I'm thinking of Sammie, stroking my cock, which I undoubtedly will be doing, often!

I'll put that out of the way at some point.

It looked very comfortable and home like.

"What's through there?" I head towards the door adjacent to the bed and opposite the window.

As I open it, Jake answers, "En suite."

I can't remember the last time I had a shower by myself, let alone the whole room, privately.

Set out in the bathroom, were towels of different sizes, male toiletries, toothbrush and toothpaste and even a trash can! A trash can!

Jake points at a basket in the corner, "That's for your washing…. Laundry! Clara does all the washing every

Friday and it will be washed, dried, ironed and put back in your room by the following Saturday evening."
I couldn't quite believe that statement, so I just blinked at him.
"You good?"
"Erm, yeah, thanks. Goodnight Jake."
"Hhhm," was his answer, as he walked out the door backwards, closing it behind him.
I just smiled.

Chapter 5.
Sammie.

Wow today has been a long day. Probably not as long as Carter's, but I have been a bit of a mess throughout!

The nerves, earlier on, were a killer and I am a nervous person at the best of times anyway.

We had finished the wine before coming back inside and by then, there was only my dad left downstairs. Gran was a little tipsy, so she sailed through the house without even saying goodnight to anyone and retired to her bed. I look around the kitchen at the glasses and empty bottles lying about.

"Wow, you lot have had fun! Where is everyone?"

"Your brother has gone to bed, Miles has headed home and your boyfriend hasn't come back downstairs after showing Carter to the attic."

I bite my lip and must look worried.

Dad comes round the kitchen table to me and puts his hand on my shoulder,

"Don't worry love, he will get over it. I wouldn't want to be him either with the way Carter looks at you."

I can feel myself blushing, "What do you mean? He doesn't look at me any sort of way, I'm just the person who invited him, that's all."

"Yes, and if none of them are in any fit state to work tomorrow, I'm holding you responsible! Goodnight love," he kisses me on the forehead and takes my mum's hand, as they head upstairs.

"Night Mum! I'll clean the rest of this up, shall I?" I call after them.

To be fair, I welcome something to keep me busy downstairs for a bit, hopefully, that way, Jake will be asleep when I go up and I won't have to talk about today.

After cleaning up the mess that the men folk have left, I lock everything up and turn out all the lights, letting the dogs outside. Although the dogs are pets, they do sleep outside on an evening because they are actually, guard dogs and they have to protect the livestock and the properties. Heading upstairs, I stop outside the bedroom door and look up the next flight of stairs that leads to the attic.

I can hear a faint sound of running water which I just know is the shower.

Damn! Now I'm thinking of him in the shower!

Shaking my head, I open the bedroom door, my hopes of Jake being asleep are shattered, when I see him sitting on the edge of the bed, still dressed and scowling in my direction.

I wasn't in the mood for this, but I suppose I wasn't going to have much of a choice. Great!

"Okay, go ahead..."

I sit down next to him, and he moves away.

Wow! Childish. My back is up.

I just stare at him, waiting for him to talk.

"Seriously? A fucking cowboy? Who looks like that?!!! Do you not care at all, how I feel?"

"What are you talking about? I was writing to someone in prison, someone who, I had no clue who he was, I didn't know he was a cowboy at first, we were just having a written conversation about all the things I wanted to talk to a stranger about. Someone I didn't know, someone impartial, who would not judge what I ever had to say and would never know me or my family."

"Well, that turned out well, didn't it? He's upstairs for fuck's sake! He's here, in the flesh- a fucking mountain of flesh and bastard muscle!!"

He was shouting at this point, and he was right, he was upstairs, and he was a fine mountain of a man, but it was never meant to be this way when we first started writing to each other.

"Look, I didn't know what he looked like, and it doesn't matter," *who was I kidding?!* "Because he's just a friend, he's an employee of my dad's and he's an ex-con, I don't feel we are going to have *that* deep of a friendship in person! What do I have in common with someone who has been inside for three years? He can help on the farm, it will be interesting to see what he can do, but that's it!"

I was of course lying; he was a fucking dream!

But I did have a relationship and really, the only thing I was guilty of, was not knowing how the hell to tell Jake the whole story when it came to Carter.

I hadn't cheated, I wasn't going to cheat. I had no idea he would be like this.

I didn't want to put Carter down in that sentence, because I'm proud of him and how far he has come, but Jake seemed to need building up and needed validation.

I hated this situation.

"Carter isn't a threat to us or our relationship, the only thing that is, is the way *you're* speaking to me right now. Yes, he's a good-looking guy, yes, he's a cowboy, does that really mean anything? You are my boyfriend, and he is a friend, you can think what you want, I'm going to bed."

With that, I go to the bathroom to get ready for bed, get into bed and turn off the light, leaving Jake there, standing in the dark, to decide what he is doing for the rest of the night.

Turning over to face the window, I just lay here, unable to think about anything but that damn cowboy.

What the hell was I doing?

I just wasn't expecting him to look that way. I didn't know *anybody* looked that way.

Not only is he insanely good looking, but he is confident too, I could see and feel how cock sure he is. I don't know why Jake is worried. It doesn't matter if I find him attractive, it's normal to find other people attractive. What matters is, it isn't reciprocated, it never would be.

Carter was a god, made by several other gods, obviously! He was never going to find someone like me attractive.

I wasn't slim or stunning, I had hips, I had boobs, things moved when I moved. I never look glamorous, I live on a farm, I don't have time to look glamorous. The only thing I ever really did with myself, is put my hair up, usually in a messy bun or ponytail and stick some mascara and lip oil on!

He will be used to hot American blondes, with skinny bodies and tanned skin.

Girls who can ride a mechanical bull, moving their hips like a stripper on speed!

That's who he would be into, plus, he would want a sexual person and that is far from what I am.

I hate sex, I could live without ever having it again.

I have questioned being possibly A sexual, but if I thought I was before tonight, I know I'm not now. Apparently, A sexual people don't find anyone actually sexually attractive, and I definitely find Carter sexually attractive. He's gone way past attractive.

So no, I'm definitely not A sexual, but before I saw Carter, I had every other trait of being so! Definitely would have explained a few things.

Like now, Jake has crawled into bed, while I've been wondering about my sexuality, or lack of! And I feel physically sick at the thought of him being there, dread feeling creeping in, just incase he touches me.

So, if I'm not A sexual, what am I?

Chapter 6.
Carter.

The alarm sounds at 3:50am, I used to like laying around for a bit before actually getting up out of bed, that was my 10 minutes to myself, before the day started properly.

That shower last night, I can't tell you how good it felt to actually feel the water.

The showers in jail were quite pathetic, it would have been quicker and felt cleaner to have people spitting on me. Dehydrated people at that!

It was also nice, not to be showering with 20 other men at a time... not gunna lie, I was close to making the most of it and giving myself some relief after seeing Sammie and thinking about those rose colored, plump, soft looking lips of hers, but I refrained and got out of the steaming shower instead, to get settled down for what turned out to be the best sleep I have had in so long.

I've not slept that good since, well before Pops got sick. Not only was the bed the right level of firmness, but the sheets were so soft, and they had the same scent, that Sammie had, when I went to keep her upright last night. Fresh, clean and pure.

Being tucked away in the country, with no one else around, no lights, no sound, made for a very quiet peaceful night.

It was so dark, and I was out like a light.

That was of course, after the shouting had ended below me.

When I came out of the En suite, ready for bed, I had heard a few loud outbursts, coming from one of the bedrooms below.

I'm guessing it was Sammie's room, as I can't imagine Frank and Elsa arguing like that. I felt bad for getting at Jake that much, that Sammie had to put up with his tantrums.

The second alarm went off at 4am and I was up and out of bed, quickly goin' to brush my teeth, skipping the shave and grabbing a quick cold shower to wake everything up and get my blood pumping.

After getting dressed in my black Ariats, dark blue Wranglers, a white t-shirt, with a black open shirt over the top and my signature black buck skin, I head off downstairs to meet the others in the kitchen.

I bump into Carl on the way downstairs.

"Morning."

"Good morning, Carl, how's your head today?"

"Too early to talk about that."

I just smile back, and on the way down the second lot of stairs, that lead to the kitchen, Carl turns back around, towards me.

"No chaps?"

I laugh and tell him, that I felt that might be pushing it a bit.

"Oh, I don't know, I think my sister would—"

He stops talking when he sees Sammie glaring up at him from the kitchen table and I just smirk. *Noted!*

"Good morning boys," Elsa sings, "How is everyone this morning?"

Carl, Sammie, Jake and Clara, all give her a look, that would cut ice.

I'm guessing they are suffering.

Smiling, I wish everyone a good morning.

"Coffee?" Frank hands me a steaming cup. "Help yourself to milk, cream and sugar," pointing over at the side, where someone has left everything out, ready.

"I'm good with black thank you and I'm sweet enough," I smile.

Jake sniggers and Sammie looks up at me with an apologetic look and a small smile, I throw her a wink in return. That gets me a little blush.

I wonder how many other things I could do to make her blush.

Carl and Jake head outside.

"Sleep well?" Elsa asks, looking over at me, while she's beating the shit out of some dough.

"Like a baby, thanks," looking at what she is doing, with a bit of concern for the safety of it.

"Baking bread," she smiles.

I lift my chin in acknowledgment and smile back.

At this point, Miles and three other men, walk into the kitchen, the buzz of the morning was upon us quickly and everyone was fueling up on coffee.

I came to find that the three other employees, that had joined us, were Steve, Johnny and Malcolm (who was also a vet).

"I'm off to get eggs," chimed Clara.

"Mum, why do you insist on going to get eggs this early in a morning? just wait until the sun comes up, at least, and help Elsa with the baking. We have a full house today and we will all want feeding a feast, when we get back from the pre breakfast morning chores."

"Son, I love you, but don't ever tell me what to do again, I'm old enough and daft enough to make my own decisions!" she says, as she taps the side of Frank's face, on her way past him and out the door.

Frank turns around to the rest of us, we are all smirking at him for being scolded by his mom.

He clears his throat, "Right, after that little episode, I am now going to assert my authority."

We all laugh.

"Malcolm, we have a couple of heifers that are calving any day now, so I'm going to need you available at the pens today please."

"Yes boss."

Frank looks at him in time to catch the fake salute and rolls his eyes.

"Carl and Jake are out in the barn now, feeding and watering the cows, when that is sorted, I need Johnny to join them and get them down to the parlor for milking. Steve, if you could head over to finish off that wood chopping you started and get that all loaded up for log sales, that would be great."

Steve and Johnny both answer with a simple, "Yes sir."

"Sammie, you're going to be spending the morning with Carter. I don't have any jobs for any of you, but the horses will need seeing to and I thought you could also show him round the whole farm and tell him about what we do here, all in all."

She answers with a quiet and very unenthusiastic, "Okay."

I'm not gunna lie, I was pretty disappointed by her reaction.

"That good for you Carter? Once everyone has done what I ask of them, we will all come back here and eat the feast these two ladies," he gestures to Elsa and Clara, who was just coming back in with a basket full of eggs, "Will make for us, and we will all reflect on the morning together and talk about any issues."

I nod a "Yes sir, sounds good."

"Okay, everyone- off to work."

We all drain the last of our coffees and head out the door to join Jake and Carl on the farm.

Everybody heads off, to the areas, they have been told to work and to get on with what's been asked of them.

I follow Sammie to the barn area, where the cows were being led from there, down to the parlor, by Carl, Jake and Johnny.

This is where I felt at home, after all, what the hell does a cowboy do? Although they do things different around here, to what I'm used to!

Sammie heads towards Jake, so I hang back slightly and proceed to pet one of the cows, I briefly look up to see if there is any sign of her coming back this way, just in time to see a pretty gut-wrenching kiss being exchanged between the two of them.

Yeah, that sucks!

She obviously feels the need to put on some sort of show, so I give them their moment and walk out towards the edge of the drive, just outside the farmhouse.

It was only last night that I was left here by the cab driver, but it felt like a lot had happened, in such a short time.

Chapter 7.
Carter.

Sammie comes up behind me, as I turn to look over my shoulder at her and give her a little smile, she just shoots me a brief glance and storms her way past me, towards the other end of the farm.

So, I just follow suit.

"I feel like I've pissed you off somehow?" I was almost running to keep up, was this girl on speed?

"I have a lot to do, and I don't know why my dad thinks I have time, to play tour guide."

Ouch! She is a bit of a brat! I like it!

When I finally catch up, with the little windup toy, I try to find out why, I had travelled across the other side of the world to be more or less ignored, but as I start to speak, she stops in her tracks, causing me to almost collide into the back of her.

"Jesus! … what the hell are you doing? I nearly ran into you!"

She spins around on her heel and squares right up to me, tipping her head back slightly, to look up at me.

"You have caused big issues in my relationship, I hope you know that! Now I'm left having to constantly step on eggshells whilst trying to reassure my boyfriend that I do not find you attractive in the slightest."

"Firstly, all I have done is come here, after you asked me to! Secondly, I haven't said or done anything to make your boyfriend doubt you or your relationship and lastly, I thought you had stopped with the lying! Saying you're not attracted to me? Like I said, I've not made your boyfriend doubt you, you've done that all by yourself, by the way you were more or less, undressing me, with your god damn beautiful eyes!"

Her mouth drops open, as she looks up at me.

"Careful darlin', if you keep your mouth open like that, someone might have to fill it!"

I wink and walk past her, to the stables, I could now clearly see in the near distance.

Now she was the one running, to keep up with me.

"Hey!" She catches up and grabs my arm, to pull me around.

Fighting the urge to pull her towards me and crush my mouth to hers, is the biggest fight I have ever had.

Out of breath from the running, she looks up at me with a slight curl, to the corner of her lips.

"You can't say things like that! … creep!"

Then she just starts laughing, I'm beginning to think she's a bit crazy.

"The stable," she says, whilst taking the lead and walking in front of me again, not trying to get away this time though, "Is a livery stable, we rent out the room to people, who can't house their horses. So, most of them aren't ours. We only have two horses, come meet them."

She shoots me a look that I can't quite read, but I think friendly helpful Sammie, was making an appearance.

"Most of the horses will stay locked up for now, it's only early and we haven't had any news of people not being able to come see to their own, so I will just introduce you to ours and check that everything is okay over there. We will come back later to muck out et cetera."

"Sure," I was glad we were walking at a steady, friendlier pace now.

"This is Max and Otis," she glides her hands over the necks of each horse, as she says their names- lucky horses!

I step forward to pet the pair and she just watches; I think I caught a glimpse of contentment in her eyes.

After checking in all the stalls and seeing all the animals in the stable were good, we head back over to the rest of the farm. The stables, for some reason, stood away from everything else.

"You have a lot of land here, what is it, around 350 acres?"

"That's exactly right! That's all in all, but yeah. It's a large area, but I'm guessing you were used to bigger?"

"A little," I smile, both, at her and the memory of growing up on the ranch.

"I'm sorry."

I turn to look at her, "For what?"

"The way I have been treating you, I must seem a little *crazy*."

"Slightly," I smile.

She nudges my arm with her shoulder, "Shut up!"

We both glance at each other. This is more like it.

"So, you have the cows, for Dairy farming, it's obvious how you make money there, the Stables that you rent out… what else happens up here on the English farm?"

She looks up at me and decides, at that moment, that we were sitting down on the wet grass.

We sit here, the sun still not quite up and already having had a bit of a run around the farm and an argument.

"Well, we have the chicken coop. My mum and gran bake and make jams…sorry, jelly," she smiles, "We sell everything they make, along with eggs, chickens, milk, cheese, butter and the logs that Steve is currently chopping up over there," she points towards an area of thick trees, "At the farmer's market, which is held in the village, every first Sunday of the month… so a week from today."

"Do you grow anything on the land?"

"Only what we use ourselves, there's a lot of home cooking and home baking goes on here, as you will see. You'll never go hungry, that's for sure!"

"So, when we are not looking after the cows, which we try to do in the morning, we prepare for the farmer's market for one week out of the month. That's a busy week and you've arrived at the right time for that. Our afternoons are then used, taking care of the land… maintaining grounds, fixing things, making sure no one or nothing comes onto the farm that doesn't belong here," she starts to play with a plane of grass between her fingers, "Then there is, of course, all the outside work- the finances, the shopping, the budgets, housekeeping and ensuring everything runs smoothly, whilst adhering to the correct laws and procedures. I don't need to tell you any of that though. I can imagine it's a lot like ranching but with less riding and… *roping.*"

Her swallow is actually audible, and I don't miss it!
"Yeah, I guess. We use our cattle for meat and leather too though, probably much sooner than you do over here."
I look around the farm, as the sun is on its way up, it's a quick sunrise and all of a sudden, it seems to go from darkness to bright light.
"We break in horses too, so we will take a horse that's never been ridden and train it to follow commands, that we need them to recognize for herding."
She looks at me and smiles.
"How many times have you been thrown off a bucking horse?"
"Too many to mention, sometimes on purpose and by choice and sometimes whilst trying to get them to do the opposite."
"By *choice*?" She looks at me like I'm insane.
I chuckle, "Yeah, Rodeos are big where I come from."
        There seems to be a lot of noise coming from behind us now, people finishing up what they're doing, before breakfast. We both look over our shoulders at the same time, to find Jake watching us, sat on the grass, talking.
Here we go again!
"Well, that's our cue to go inside for breakfast. I promise I won't be a bitch anymore," she smiles and stands up, to walk towards the house.
As she looks back at me and catches me openly staring at her ass, she smirks and shouts, "You coming in?"
What an invite!
I stand up and head into the house with everyone else.

Chapter 8.
Carter.

When I walk into the house, following everyone else, the aroma hit me, and I suddenly realize how hungry I actually *am*. I also realize that I can't remember the last time I ate, with the long travel getting over to the UK and all the messing around, between airports, planes, baggage and other forms of transport, passing through so many time zones, it felt like I was in and out of a parallel universe.

It dawned on me that I hadn't had any food since leaving the Motel, after being released from jail and I definitely can't remember the last time I had anything like this to feast on!

The sheer volume of food could feed the entire village, Sammie was right, I would never go hungry!

I was overwhelmed with it, all the cooked goods set out on hot plates on one side of the kitchen- bacon, sausage, eggs in all different forms, baked beans, tomatoes, hash browns, mushrooms and toast.

Then on the other side there were croissants, a selection of fruit, an array of cereals, syrups, jelly, peanut butter (it made me smile that it had been placed next to the jelly) chocolate spread… there were jugs of different fruit juices and two big pots of tea and coffee... and as if that wasn't enough, Elsa was stood at the stove frying homemade bread and scooping batter into a pan to make pancakes.

I don't know how her, and Clara pull all this off, especially having farmers coming in and out all the time, getting under their feet, not to mention the three dogs that were running around like raging bulls.

There are 11 people and three dogs in the kitchen at this moment and no one was arguing, I look around at everyone just helping themselves to the amazing spread and talking about all different sorts of subjects.

The kitchen was loud and even though I was pretty over stimulated right now, I felt a real warm feeling about being here.

I was happy I came, especially now Sammie and I were getting along.

"You hungry?" Elsa asks, looking at me.

"I didn't realize how hungry I was, this looks—"

"They always go over the top, but get stuck in so it doesn't go to waste,"

Frank kisses his wife with a mouth full of croissant. She acts as though she is disgusted, but her smile says otherwise.

I grab a plate and help myself, to the selection of food on offer.

"All local produce you know!" Miles says, while leaning past me to grab another slice of toast.

"These women know how to take care of us," he winks in my direction.

"Speaking of women, not seen Sara around here in a while Carl, what's going on with you two?"

Carl turns his attention to Steve, "Yeah, we are good, she's studying at the moment, so she's busy, she will be around at the market I would imagine."

"That girl is too smart for the likes of your dumb arse."
"Fuck you Steve," Carl gives him a playful punch on the arm.
I guess I'm not Carl's type after all and he really did just like my boots!
I sit at the table, opposite Sammie and Jake and everyone else takes their seats and tucks in.

≈≈≈≈≈≈≈≈≈≈≈

After a while of light chat between everybody, Elsa cuts through my quiet thoughts.
"Is everything okay with the food love? You've hardly eaten anything."
I look at Sammie, who is just picking at little bits of her food and pushing the rest of it around the plate.
Jake speaks before she can open her mouth, "Yeah, you don't usually have any issue with your food, you feeling okay?"
I notice the look she gives him, I can see both, the embarrassment and the annoyance at it being brought up, but also his comment about her liking her food every other day.
"I'm fine!" She's blushing a little, now that everyone is looking up, darting their eyes between her, Jake and the plate of unfinished food.
"I'm just not hungry and I still have to get back to the stables, it was too early to do much earlier."
I look at Sammie and think of the fact she has been messing with her food this morning, and also other little things I've noticed about her, the way she stands with

her arms wrapped around her stomach when she is talking to someone, her body language is very closed off, but I feel it's to do with low confidence.

She also pulls and tugs at her t-shirts too, as though she feels they're clinging to her.

They're not by the way- but they ought to!

She looks up at me, noticing my staring, only with concern at this point.

Giving me a pointed look, she clears her throat, drawing everyone's attention back to her.

"So, as I was saying, it was too early to do anything at the stables this morning, so I'm going back there after breakfast. I introduced Carter to Max and Otis, has anyone heard anything from Mollie, Louise and Connie? I don't know if they're coming to see to their horses or not today."

"Not heard anything love, so I would imagine they're coming up to the yard themselves, so just concentrate on Max and Otis and just water the others if they need it," Elsa smiles at her daughter lovingly.

"Sammie showed me around the rest of the farm too, told me about everything you do here and at the farmer's market. Do y'all attend that?"

Frank looks up at me and says, "No, we go as a family. Jake and Miles usually go to the pub, Malcolm usually goes to the market, but as a customer with his wife, Jane and I don't want to know what Steve does with his spare time."

We all look at Steve.

"Yeah, you don't want to know," he winks and smiles at us all.

"Sunday is everyone's day off, like I say, we do the market as a family, my mum joins us when she feels like it," Frank concludes.

"I like to sit and read my book after church," Clara says.

I just nod and wonder where I fit into all that, is Sunday my day off? Am I classed as part of the family that would be helping out at the market?

I guess I will soon find out. I might go to the market either way, just to see what it is like and meet some more locals.

Carl, who is sat next to me, turns and asks how I'm liking the farm so far and how it compares to the ranch.

"Yeah, it's great out here, I like how y'all work together and get on really well, whether you're family or not. It has a lot of similarities to the ranch really. We don't usually milk on the ranch though, there are Dairy farms that we use, where the farmers come to help out sometimes, and it's done by hand. The work we do with cattle is more breeding, herding and taking care of the cows. They're usually used for meat and leather. It was strange to me, seeing y'all this morning, moving the cows to and from the barn on foot."

"Yeah, well if we were moving them over a large area, we would obviously use a livestock box, but the barn and the parlor aren't far from one another and it's a safe practice, they're used to it."

I glance around at everyone in their own little bubbles of conversation, looking over at Sammie, who in that moment, glances back at me.

She looks more relaxed now.

"Right, everyone," Frank taps his palms on the table, grabbing our attention, "Jobs for the rest of the day are," he looks around us all to make sure we're listening. I like this guy.

"Carter, can you go with Steve and help him on the last leg of the log haul? Sammie, you're going back to the stables, aren't you? You do what you need to up there and then come back to the house and help your mum and gran. Malcolm, if you can just stay around the pen today, unless you're called away, and wait for these calves to make an appearance. Carl, Jake and Johnny, you get back to sorting the cows and after you've finished there, leave them in the paddock while you head over to fix that fence on the stable side. The yard is getting to a point where I feel it's almost unsafe and we don't want to be losing anyone's horses."

Everybody nods and stands up, putting their empty plates and mugs on the side that Elsa and Clara are stood by.

I smile apologetically at the two ladies, feeling responsible and guilty for the heap of plates everyone else had just put on the side for them to deal with.

They both smile back at me, appreciatively.

"Have a good day all," they both call, waving us out the door.

Everyone is heading off in front and I'm behind Sammie.

Before we go any further out, I grab her gently by her wrist to check she's okay.

Chapter 9.
Sammie.

I'm heading back out, towards the stables, when Carter grabs me by the wrist.
Damn!!
The electric bolt rushing from the contact of his strong fingers, wrapped around my arm, travelling all over the rest of my body. I've never felt this before and I don't like it, it's uncomfortable and foreign, and makes me feel uneasy.

I get the sudden urge to drag my walls up and revert back to snappy bitchy Sammie- the one who isn't really me, the one Carter never got in our letters, so probably doesn't understand why I'm being this way.
I don't understand it either, but I think it's fear.
"God, I'm fine! Why do you feel the need to check on me, to stop me from falling over... to talk to me all the time? Just get on with your work!"
I didn't even give him a chance to talk back, all he did was ask if I was okay and I snapped at him and now I'm speed walking across the damn farm, to get far away from him and everyone else.
I don't look back, but I can imagine he is wondering what the fuck is wrong with me.

I walk for a bit longer, slowing down now and thinking about what had happened over breakfast.
I didn't mean to snap there either, but I do wish my mum hadn't noticed I wasn't eating much and even more so, I wish she hadn't called me out on it.

My real annoyance was with Jake, what the hell was with his comment about me not usually having an issue with food?

Yeah, that is going to make me feel fucking great about myself! So, I'm usually a heifer, am I? Have I to go join the rest of them in the barn? Prick!

Yeah, I like my food, it shows too! I'm hardly skinny!! But I don't need it pointing out, especially in front of Carter, who was sat there for the first breakfast with my family, already making me feel anxious about eating in front of him. I feel self-conscious about eating in front of people I don't really know anyway, especially the first time and you'd think my boyfriend and family, would know that about me.

I did relax a little, once everyone started talking between themselves in smaller groups and I was happy not to have the negative attention on myself.

It was nice seeing Carl and Carter talking too.

Carter- I just keep being nasty to him, I don't mean to. At this point, almost at the stables, I sneak a look back and see him heading out over the main field, with Steve, towards the tractor.

I welcome the large expanse of distance between us, and I head into the yard, to get to the stables, starting, by watering the three other horses in there and keeping them in their stalls.

Heading over to Max first, because he is the most impatient, I open up his stall, attaching a head collar and leading him out to the main stable.

I secure him with a lead rope and start by cleaning his hooves, then take out my frustrations by currying and brushing his coat, I find it soothing, the motions of brushing him, especially when it comes to brushing out his mane and tail. That's my favourite bit.

I grab the comb and start detangling, starting from the bottom and working upwards.
Once the hair is smooth, I brush lightly through it, while telling him he's an impatient git, he is always trying to get going! But not before I clean his eyes, ears and nose.
Then he can go!
I unhook him and lead him to the paddock, outside of the stable yard, before going in and collecting the other three horses, to put them in the paddock too, leaving only Otis in the stables.
After letting the four horses have a little freedom and securing them in the field, I head back in to see to Otis.

Letting him out of his stall, and securing him, in the same way I did Max, following the same procedure, I start the grooming process. I spend a little longer brushing out Otis' coat, tail and mane, talking to him about Carter. Telling him that, I feel like the worst person ever, because I invited him here to stay and work, it was harder than people realise too, with all the correct paperwork for permits that were needed, there was a lot to look into and do and now he's here, I'm jumping between being nice and being a right twat to him.
He must have whiplash!
But the worst thing, is, I'm treating this guy like crap because I'm feeling something for him, and I have a boyfriend!

My feelings are causing all sorts of issues that can affect everyone.

My multiple personalities are affecting Carter, if it got out how I *really* feel, it would hurt Jake, which would then in turn hurt Miles, who is my dad's closest friend and longest serving employee on the farm.
Jake is also my brother's best friend, so if I end up hurting him, that will piss Carl off too and make things awkward, because we all work together.
"I don't know what to do Otis, I'm trying not to hurt anyone, but however I act or whatever I do, it's going to cause either hurt, or problems for somebody."

I give him a cuddle and apologise for loading my depressing crap on him, sigh and take him out to live his best life with his brother and friends, onto the green, green grass of home.
While all the horses are out in the paddock, I use this time to muck out Max and Otis' stalls and wash down the main stable.
I start by removing any messed areas, sifting through the bedding and separating the wet and soiled stuff, from the clean stuff and disposing of the dirty bedding, using a wheelbarrow.
I leave that outside the stable, in the yard, for now.
Going on, to level out the clean bedding in the stalls and add more, fresh to it, making sure it's even and comfortable for both horses.
Max prefers a thicker layer than Otis.
I then, replenish the feeding and water buckets for both and sweep down the length of the main stable, before

hosing down the whole floor to remove all the bits from the earlier groom.

I don't do the same for the other three used stalls, because, as far as I know, the horse's owners are coming today, and I only do it when they can't get here. Finishing off, by securing all the tools, I head out to the yard to dispose of the full wheelbarrow, which has already been done and was now back and empty. Putting it back in the main stable, I head back out of the yard and away from the horses, for now.

Chapter 10.
Sammie.

On my way round to the front of the yard, in the field, I notice Carl, Jake and Johnny fixing fences over this way, so I head over to them before going back to the house.

"Hey, I didn't know you lot would be over this way yet," I greet them all, they look up and smile. Carl seems a little bit worried, I look at him a little longer to try and work out what the expression on his face is.

"I'm going to the House now to help mum and gran, is there anything you need before I go?"

"I'll walk back with you, these two can finish off here."

"Wow, his dad is still alive and he's already cracking the whip! You're not our boss you know!" Jake pipes up.

Johnny laughs and adds, "No, but his sister is!"

I just smile and tell them I would never make a good boss, I'm too much of a pushover.

"Pppfft," Johnny makes a noise that says he doesn't believe that.

If only he knew that I was a massive people pleaser and was only being a snappy bitch right now, because I was so confused about things.

Carl and I head back towards the house, leaving Jake and Johnny to finish the fencing.

"It's okay, I didn't want a kiss or anything," Jake shouts after me.

I ignore him, because I am still upset with him for what he said over breakfast.

"You alright?" Carl asks.

"Why wouldn't I be?"

"Well, as you know, horses aren't my forte, so I'm not sure if it's normal to talk to them about the fact that you would rather be with the cowboy that's staying on our farm than your boyfriend, or not and that you're only trying to keep everyone else happy right now."

The more that came out of his mouth, the more mortified I must have looked- I definitely felt it!

"Don't worry sis, I won't tell anyone, but if you want to talk to someone who can talk back and give their opinion and support, you know where I am."

"I'm sorry, I know Jake is your best—"

"You're my little sister and as much as I love Jake, I love you more than anyone, your feelings come first."

I had to look away from him, to hide the tears that were welling. He understood and just gently touched the top of my hand as we walked.

Whilst avoiding my brother's gaze, I clock Steve and Carter across the field, bringing all the logs in.

That's what I need right now, seeing Carter driving the damn tractor!

He has also taken his shirt off, that was over his t-shirt earlier.

God help me!

As we all close the gap and head towards each other, Carl grabs my arm.

"I don't know how I feel about him," he says, "Carter. I don't know if I trust him, I know he has a past and a lot of people do and I know he's trying to change, but the way he looks at you sometimes- it's like you're a piece of meat and I don't know anything about him. Knowing how you feel is worrying me, only because of him and the fact that I'm not sure about him."

I smile at my brother and tell him that he has nothing to worry about, I am with Jake, and I have known him a long time, we were going to be fine, and Carter was just an interesting shiny toy on the farm, the novelty wears off, it always does, because there is nothing real there.

"Nothing is going to happen, but it would be great if you maybe spent some time with Carter, to get to know him a bit, just to put your mind at rest about the type of person he is, nothing to do with me."

He just nods and we carry on walking towards him and Steve.

As we get closer, I see that his white t-shirt that was mostly hidden by the black shirt he had over it, was all full of dirt, and so was his face!

Full of dirt and sweat, wearing a cowboy hat and driving a tractor.

Yeah, I was going to need more than God.

"Hey," they both call over to us.

"Do they even have tractors in America?" I ask, while trying not to drool at the sight in front of me.

For crying out loud- he smiles, he smiles!! And assures me that they do indeed, have tractors in America.

"Carter, do you fancy having a drink tonight? At the local pub, you and I? I think I need to get to know the guy staying on our farm because my sister invited him to."

Carter looks at me and I look back at him, oh 'eck! Carl just made that sound like a bigger deal than it is, and I think I'm blushing again.

"Sure, just let me know when and give me enough time, to not look like this," he gestures down his body, and my eyes can't help but drag down it too!

At that moment, gran heads over to us,

"Taking a break, are we?"

"Slave driver!" Carl whips back.

We are all smiling, when she looks at Carter and tells him, "Frank wants to talk to you at the house!"

With that, she heads over to the chicken coop.

We all look at each other and I don't miss the worry in Carter's eyes.

"I'll walk back with you, I need to help my mum and gran with housework anyway."

Carter nods and we smile at the other two, while we turn and walk back to the house together.

"How's the rest of your day been so far?" he asks me.

"Yeah good, just been sorting the horses out, was wondering if you wanted to go for a ride sometime, we have plenty of land for it, although not as exciting as I imagine your trails to be."

He looks surprised that I'm asking this, so I carry on, "I used to ride with Hannah but nobody else really does it, they all can, and they have. But it's not in their bones and I'm guessing riding is probably a massive part of your whole being."

He smiles warmly and says, "You've got that right. Is everything okay? Do you feel okay?"

I look at him, puzzled by what he means.

"Breakfast time and then after breakfast, when I tried to check on you, I was wor—"

"Oh! I'm sorry about that, *again*, I was a bitch and I snapped at you, this really isn't me and I don't understand why I'm being this way but the real me, is the one in our letters."

He smiles, not sure why, but it's a genuine smile anyway, so I carry on, "I'm fine, I just get a little weird eating with new people, it's a strange fear I have, it's nothing, it doesn't mean anything."

"So, you don't want to talk about anything? Nothing is on your mind? You're not feeling a certain way that you might feel better about if you said it out loud?"

I try shrug it off, and not face telling him, how I hate how I look and have extreme self-doubt and low self-esteem, why would I do that, so I just answer with,

"Wow, that's a lot of questions," on a laugh and carry on walking the last few steps to the house, but just before I open the door he calls, "hey!"

I look round at him and he smirks at me before saying, "Just so you know, your ass in those jeans is impeccable." *chefs kiss*.

I roll my eyes and turn back towards the door, letting myself enter the house quickly, into the cool kitchen to try and rid myself of the crimson blush creeping up my neck and onto my face.

This man is going to kill me, but I'll die happy!

Chapter 11.
Carter.

I was goin' to let her know that she looked good, just incase she needed to hear it.

That woman should be brimming with confidence.

She was, not only beautiful, but fucking sexy as hell!

Since I laid eyes on her, I've wanted my tongue and cock to be buried, deep inside every part of her, into every fucking hole she has to offer.

It annoys me that she has no idea how fucking hot she is! She could quite easily have any man begging on his knees for her, while worshipping her pussy, which I can imagine, tastes sweet as hell.

When we get into the house, Sammie heads on up the open staircase, that leads from the kitchen to the upstairs rooms.

That fucking ass, I would love that to be bouncing on my dick.

I watch her walk all the way up, making sure she knows that my eyes are on her. I'm not fucking around now, this girl is goin' to know that I can't keep my eyes off of her. She watches me too, through the gaps in the banister, until she is out of sight.

I look over to the kitchen table, where Frank is sat, looking highly stressed out and surrounded by papers with his head in his hands.

"Everything okay?"

The way he looks up at me, he doesn't have to say anything.

"I'll just go get my glasses and I'll be right back."

I run upstairs and take off my hat, put on my reading glasses and head back down to the kitchen to help Frank out, before he throws himself under a moving tractor.

"What's up?" I say, sitting down next to him.

"I can't make it add up, there's something missing."

"What's missing?"

"I think 10k is missing!" He says with a huff.

"Jeeez, okay, don't worry, $10,000 can't be missing, we will find it."

"Pounds."

"Sorry?"

"Pounds, £10,000."

"Oh right, yeah, sorry. Well, it's a lot of money to lose, it won't be lost, we will find it."

Frank looks at me as though, he loves my enthusiasm, but he isn't so confident.

"I've looked and looked, I don't know how I've done it, but my budget is blown and I'm going to leave us in the minus."

I put my hand out to him, as a gesture for him to hand me the bills he is holding in his hand, so tight, his knuckles are drained of all blood.

≈≈≈≈≈≈≈≈≈≈

Spending the last few hours, looking at all the bills and paper, sifting through the evidence, we updated a lot of lines in the finances. There were small mistakes along the way, which I'm hoping will add up to some of that 10k, and I had managed to convince Frank that, at least a big bulk of it, is goin' to show up by the end of the records. We did, still have a long way to go, but all the farmers had come into the house, to say the work was complete and there was still no sign of a calf.

There were only the horses to sort.

By that time, Sammie was heading downstairs, "I'll do that now, are they still in the paddock?"

"Max and Otis are," Jake walks over to give her a kiss. *Asshole.*

"Okay, are you leaving too?"

"Yeah, I am going to head home now with my dad. I'll see you tomorrow."

"Okay. See you all tomorrow- dad, I'm going to get Otis and Max into the stable and lock everything up."

"Okay love," he holds his hand up but doesn't look at anyone, "See you tomorrow boys, thank you for another good day out there."

"Bye everyone," they all reply.

By this time, Clara and Elsa had come downstairs too and Carl was just coming into the house, crossing paths, with everyone else leaving.

They all say their goodbyes.

"Carter, you still up for going to the pub?"

"Oh, I don't know man, we still have a lot to go through here and it's getting late, I'm still in my work clothes."

"No, you boys go have a drink, get yourself ready, you both deserve it. I'll incorporate finishing the finances into tomorrow's workload," Frank sits back and rubs his eyes.

"You sure?"

"Yeah, go get ready, have a few drinks."

I stand up and look at Carl, "See you back down here in 15?"

"Last one ready buys the first drink."

"You're on," I say, darting up the stairs ahead of him.

I am in a race against time to get a quick shower, wash my hair, brush my teeth, get a shave and get dressed.

After being in jail, I am an expert at working quickly. There ain't no way I am buying the first drink!

I go with my other set of Ariats- brown dress boots, Levi's, a beige Coors Rodeo hoodie and a ball cap, settling on a beige and brown Stetson.

Throwing on some cologne, I quickly make my way down the two flights of stairs, to see if I am goin' to have my first drink bought for me, courtesy of my new boss.

When I get downstairs, I'm glad to see Carl hasn't made it down yet and Sammie was back from getting the horses secured.

I stop at the foot of the stairs, and everyone looks up at me from the table.

"No cowboy hat tonight?" Asks Frank.

"No, I don't often wear it out unless it is an affair where hats are part of the main attire, it's usually just a work thing."

"What affair would that be?"

I look at Clara and tell her that they're usually worn at a country music gig, a Honky Tonk, a country wedding, a Rodeo, places like that. Otherwise, it's worn at work, to protect against the elements and because it's part of our culture.

"It's the job we do, so we wear the hat, sort of like a uniform."

"Ah, I see. I'd like to go to a Honky Tonk! Be two stepped around a dance floor by a handsome cowboy."

I smile back at her and look over at Sammie, who is rolling her eyes at her grandmother.

"What about you? Would you want to be two stepped around a dance floor?"

I see Frank and Elsa look at each other out of the corner of my eye.

"Oh erm, I can't dance," Sammie shrugs.

"Right, I guess the first drinks are on me then?" Carl heads down the stairs.

"What took you so long? I've been down here ages, already arranged to take your grandmother, on a date to a Honky Tonk."

They all laugh.

As we head out the door, I turn back to give them all a parting smile and notice Sammie staring at me, biting her lip.

I'm goin' to bite that one day!

That fucking does something to me! Drives me insane!

I'm guessing it's not just the cowboy hat that does something to her either! It seems she likes a backwards ball cap too!

Chapter 12.
Carter.

The bar is quite full, not overly hectic but busy enough to get a good feel of the place, the atmosphere is right and it's definitely a local sort of venue, Carl had warned me that I would be noticed as someone who isn't a regular and that people would likely stare.

We head over to the bar, and Carl reaches over to be served, he looks back at me and shouts, "beer good?"

I nod back.

A couple of minutes later, he steps back towards me with two bottles of beer- lager they call it, and we look around to find a table.

We settle on a small four seater in the corner, where it is a little bit quieter. I suddenly felt a bit, uncomfortable being here sat in a corner, with another man, a man I don't really know, it's not like we are friends.

"So, what made you want to get this drink?"

"Sammie!"

I look up at his face, he has my attention.

"Sammie? She wanted us to go for a drink? Why?"

"Well, you know, you must realize that I am a little wary of you, you were writing letters to my sister for over a year, then you get released from an American prison, to here. I don't even know anything about you really."

"What do you want to know? I'm an open book and I have sisters, I don't see them, but I understand what it's like. I understand you feeling the need to protect her. I do want you to know though, I'm the last person you need to protect her from."

Carl looks at me suspiciously, with narrowed eyes, as though he's sizing me up, but also trying to think of something to ask me.

"I know from the conversation in the kitchen when you arrived, that you both talked about pretty deep stuff."

I nod.

"So did it just start that way, or did you start off with questions like favorite color and favorite foods?"

I Half laugh, "No, I never asked her what her favorite color and food was. I don't remember off the top of my head, *how* it started if I'm honest. I do have the letters though."

"You saved the letters?"

"Yeah, of course I did. So, I *could* look back and see how it started, but we seemed to get straight into a steady flow, it just sucked having to wait so long for replies."

Carl is still narrowing his eyes at me.

"Look, I know you're worried and I know you probably think I have some sort of motive with your sister. I don't, we are friends, she's in a relationsh—"

"Yeah, but you didn't know she was in a relationship, did you? Not until you arrived here. So, you were writing to a woman for over a year, to the point where you had planned to travel across the world, to her neck of the woods, telling her all your deep emotions, thinking she was single, and you only ever had the hope of being friends?"

Woah, I felt like I was being attacked here, but this was Sammie's brother, and he was right, there was something.

So, falling out with him and reacting the way I usually would, wouldn't be a good idea.

"I never knew what she looked like, neither of us knew. We just talked and got to know things about each other and our lives, and yeah, I'm not going to lie, she was often the first person I thought of when I woke up and the last thing I thought about when I went to bed. She ended up being the only thing I cared about and I was developing feelings I wasn't used to having-for someone I had never even seen. But now I'm here and I *do* know she is in a relationship, so it doesn't matter what I did and didn't know, I know now."

"What do you mean you wasn't used to having? Are you a one night sort of guy?"

What's the point in lying to him?

"Yeah, I have been known to be very casual in the past. She made me feel something else, she was the most beautiful soul I had ever gotten to know, and then when I turned up here, I saw that her inside beauty was matched by her outside beauty too. Am I attracted to your sister? Yes I am."

Just as Carl is about to answer me, two women come over to the table, one of them sliding in next to Carl and giving him a kiss on the cheek, the other just stands there smiling down at us, brightly.

"Carter, this is Sara, my errrm,"

"Girlfriend, much better half, love of my life. Take your pick," she finishes for him.

He just smiles at both Sara and then at me.

"Carter," I say, putting my hand out to shake hers.

"This is Louise," he gestures up to Sara's friend who is still stood at the end of the table, and I look up at her. "She has a horse at the farm."

"Nice to meet y'all," I look between them both and then focus on Louise, "Are you gunna sit down?"

She sits and smiles at everyone. She seems shy.

"I'm goin' to go to the bar, it's my shout, what's everyone drinking?"

I stand up and look around the table at them all.

"Beer please."

"Two white wines please."

I nod and start to walk away.

"Hey Carter, you want a hand?"

"No, I've got it."

I walk towards the bar and leave them all talking for a bit.

By the time I have been served the drinks, I have had a woman putting her tongue in my ear, another woman grabbing my ass and I'd been given a handful of telephone numbers. I look over at Carl, Sara and Louise at the table and they're all watching what is goin' on, smiling.

I roll my eyes.

Heading back to the table with the drinks, I sit back down.

"Thanks," they all say in unison.

"You not going home with any of those women feeling you up?" Carl laughs.

"No, I like a bit of a challenge, a lot of the fun is in the chase," I say.

"So, Carl tells us you're a cowboy and you're working on the farm, how long you staying for?"

I look across the table to Sara, "I'm not sure really, that was never discussed. Now I'm here, I'm beginning to think it was a bad idea," I answer her honestly.

All three of them look at each other and back at me.

"What do you mean? You not enjoying being here?" Carl looks confused.

I'd had enough of being polite, I was fed up with Sammie's split personality, never knowing what side of her Jekyll and Hyde was gunna come out, I'd been incarcerated for over three years, today had been another long day, I was warm, tired and fucking horny.

"It's not that I'm not enjoying it, I'm just extremely frustrated. If I'm honest, sorry ladies, it's been too God damn long since I either had a fight or a fuck, and I just want to do one of those things tonight, seeing as though I don't want to go back to jail, I'm goin' for the latter."

They all swallow their drinks, way too hard and just stare at me.

I look around the bar, at the women that are in here, none of them my type really, definitely no buckle bunnies in here and the tongue in my ear, did nothing for me.

My gaze lands back on Louise and I smile at her, looking between her lips and her eyes, watching the blush creep up from her chest, over her neck and to her cheeks.

I need to get Sammie out of my system, and this is the only way

≈≈≈≈≈≈≈≈≈≈≈

Looking up at the clock, I see that I had been talking quietly to Louise, for the last hour.

I glance over at Carl who gestures that he's goin' to the bar.

I excuse myself to walk over there with him. "What do you want to drink?"

"I'm not goin' to have another drink, thanks, I think we are gunna get out of here."

"What? Where to? What do you mean?"

"I'm goin' to go back to Louise's place. Have fun with your girl," I grin.

"Woah wait! You're just going to go home with her? You've only just met her and she's a customer."

"Yeah, I'm just goin' to go home with her," ignoring the other two points he made, I finish with, "Tell your mom and dad not to wait up, I'll see y'all tomorrow."

I head back over to the table to say goodbye to Sara and take Louise by the hand, leading her out of the pub. She looks back at Sara and Carl as I'm dragging her out of the bar.

Looking back myself, I give a quick wave to Carl and Sara, who are both now stood at the bar, staring at us, wide eyed and jaws dropped.

Chapter 13.
Sammie.

Everyone has gone home, after another long day on the farm, including Jake, which surprises me, because he never leaves.

I was, however, pleased about it, I can have a little pamper and some time to myself for a change.

I decide to have an *"everything shower"*.

You might be confused by this term, I know I was, because why would you not have an *"everything shower"* all the time?

Were people just washing selected parts of themselves on a daily occasion?

But no, I looked it up, so you don't have to!

For an *"everything shower"*, you take your time going overboard with shampooing, conditioning and soaping, making sure you wash areas thoroughly that you might not usually care about, you know, like your bellybutton!

It's also a time to fully exfoliate everywhere, double cleanse your face, pluck and shave.

It then extends, to making sure everywhere is dried properly, don't forget to dry between your toes!

So that's what I did, a full body pamper!

Steamed up, squeaky clean and smooth as silk, I leave the bathroom before I pass out.

Gosh it was hot in there!

I put on a face mask, one of the peel off ones, whilst I am filing and painting my toenails.

I don't really ever bother with my fingernails, why would I? I'm a farmer's daughter and I graft hard out there! Then once that has set and the nails are dry, I peel it off. Definitely no more dead skin left!

I then proceed with the rest of my skincare routine. Brushing through my hair, I then put on a leave in hair mask, to let it dry naturally.

I have naturally curly hair so I need to use some sort of product, otherwise I would look like Monica from friends, when the humidity hits her.

Finally- looking over at my choice of PJs, do I go with a slinky silk short and tank top, my jersey set, or do I advertise the fact that I love cowboys and wear the western set I picked up from the local supermarket? They're selling country and western wear all over the UK now, Carter might not even stand out in certain places!

I decide on the jersey set, simple, comfortable and no one is going to take the piss.

Heading downstairs and going through to the living room, I find that gran has gone for an early night and my mum and dad were sat on the sofa.

It was strange to see, because whatever time of day it is and whoever is around, we tend to always be in the kitchen.

Everything happens in there.

That's something that never really dawned on me until this moment either.

It was nice to see someone using this room- it's a comfortable, classic room, with wood furnishings, plump cream carpets, warm glows of the lamps, a roaring fire and the couches are soft, the kind you just sink into, surrounded by cushions.

"Movie night?" My mum looks round at me with a smile, while my dad holds the remote in the air, which I think must be the universal sign language for, *"movie night."*

"Depends on the movie, I'm not watching anything about cars or war."

"You ladies choose, I'll probably fall asleep halfway through anyway!"

I smile and head towards the other sofa and jump down into the soft upholstery.

"Don't bounce in the furniture!" my mum glares at me.

I roll my eyes, "Yeah now I remember why no one uses this room, too many rules!" I give her a pointed look back.

"Come on girls, choose a movie, otherwise I will put on Hacksaw Ridge," my dad knew how to stop the two hormonal women in his life, before anything ever started.

My mum snatches the remote off him and looks over at me,

"What we going for then?"

I look at the first page of movies on the list and decide to go for a Bridget Jones movie, I knew I wouldn't be able to concentrate anyway, and I had already seen all of them movies.

My mum selects, *"Bridget Jones Baby"* and we all settle down to watch it.

Suddenly, my dad stands up, we both look up at him and he just says, "Popcorn," in reply to our stares.

He comes back in the room with two bowls of popcorn, a larger one for my mum and dad to share and a smaller one for me.

We start watching the movie, and I was dragged into it to begin with, but then my thoughts drift to Carter. I knew they would, but it's nothing to worry about- I was only looking forward to talking to him properly, without anyone sulking about it.

Things had been up and down with us since he got here, and I felt bad for the way I had spoken to him a few times. I always feel on edge.

I'm trying to push down the fact, that I know him quite well, I do if everything he wrote to me was true, I mean and really, considering the fact that I do think about him too often and I do have a boyfriend, I don't have the right to know him as well as I do.

I also snap at him to cover up the fact that I seem to blush every time he looks at me.

What is with that? It's not like I'm not used to being around blokes!

I work in a predominantly male environment, I have male relatives, I have a boyfriend that I've been with for over two years and known more or less my entire life, but when Carter is around, I turn into some sort of pathetic schoolgirl, who has to go against everything that is natural and be a total bitch.

I'm usually so passive and... well, nice to be honest.

So yeah, I want to apologise properly and hopefully put a stop to how I've been acting around him.

Stop making the poor guy dizzy!

I also wanted to speak to him alone, to desensitise myself around him and try fight this blushing!!

To see if I can somehow, mask all that and come across as an actual adult woman, who doesn't melt at the sight of some *damn cowboy*.

He does look good in that hat though, but what about tonight?! The backwards cap!

I've seen a lot of men wearing backwards baseball caps before, but it never looked like that. Do I now have some strange thing for a baseball cap?

I don't know what has gotten into me.

I realise I had spent too much time thinking about Carter, we were about a third of the way into the movie and I had hardly touched my popcorn.

The back door opens, and we all look towards the archway, separating the kitchen from the lounge and my mum calls out, "We're in here."

Carl and Sara come into the lounge, not drunk but definitely a little *"fresh"*.

"Oooh Bridget Jones. Oooh popcorn!"

Sara sits down next to me and digs into my bowl with a wink, I smile back at her and put the bowl onto her knee.

"Where's Carter?" I look up at Carl with a furrowed brow.

Sara answered, before he could say anything, probably with less sensitivity than Carl would have, knowing how I feel about him.

"Carter, my darling, is probably getting laid!" She giggles like a schoolgirl.

I look at Carl, trying to put on a brave face, who is actually wincing, in response to his girlfriend's choice of words, then my gaze drops to my parents, who are looking at me with concern, then we all look back at Sara, who is stuffing her face with popcorn and watching tv like she hadn't dropped a bombshell.
"Elaborate?"
She looks back at me with a slight, glazed over look, then her eyes snap open wide.
"Oh!! Yeah, so Louise and I were having a drink and a girly chat, I was actually telling her, that there was going to be someone new on the farm- someone you had invited over from America. Never told me he was a cowboy!"
She winks at me and nudges me suggestively with her elbow, "Then I looked across the room and saw my handsome boyfriend sat at a table, with, sorry baby," she glances at Carl, then back at me, "The fittest man I have *ever* seen! I tell you what, Louise is having some fun right now! But then again, I've seen her ride Flash, Carter is probably having fun too!"
Then, she turns her attention back to the tv and carries on eating the popcorn.
Carl rests his hand on my shoulder, I look up at him and stand up.
"I'm going to go to bed. See you all tomorrow."
Carl and I exchange a small smile and my mum and dad quietly say, "Goodnight love."
"Night everyone."
Sara waves at me but doesn't take her eyes off of the tv.

Chapter 14.
Sammie.

I walk up the stairs, like I have lead for feet.

Feeling totally deflated, but not because he's with Louise, well at least I don't *think* that's what it is. I mean, am I jealous? Probably just a tad, but I have a boyfriend, and it's one thing looking at someone else and even thinking about somebody else, we all do it, it's actually normal, but that's all it is.

I have been with Jake for two years and I do love him. Just like I'm with Jake, Carter has the right to be with someone too and I want that for him, I want him to be happy.

I think I just feel, because I had expected to be able to speak to him properly tonight, that I had been tossed aside in a way, the moment he got off the farm and clapped eyes on a different woman.

On the other hand, he has been locked up for quite a while and he has told me in his letters that he's been a bit of a ladies' man before, so you know, by the standards he's used to, he's probably by now, really... let's just say... gagging for it.

That makes me feel even worse.

I get into bed, part of the self care evening I had planned, was to read a book before going to sleep, but I don't feel like doing that anymore.

Turning off the light, I face the window and lay there in the darkened room, looking out at the moon. I've been laying here for a while, before I realise, that I actually have tears, burning hot tears, streaming down my face.

Holy crap! I am *full* on ugly crying!

What the hell is wrong with me?

Am I actually heartbroken right now? Over a man I'm not even with? That I have no intention of being with? It's just a crush, that's all.

"Get over yourself Sammie," I whisper.

It is now 2am, and I've just laid here in the dark, the tears have dried up, but I've been silently willing Carter to come back tonight.

It feels worse to me, that he's *actually*, spending the full night with Louise.

I'm such a jealous cow!

My alarm sounds at 4am, I'm usually up a bit before now, so I'm ready for this time, but I don't actually have to get up until four, and today, I needed those extra few minutes.

I feel like I've been hit by a train, actually, no, scrap that! Let's go with a plane.

Yes, I feel like a plane has smashed right into me, right through me. I feel like shit!

After brushing my teeth and having a quick shower, after all, I scrubbed and shaved myself within an inch of my life last night, I throw on some clothes, without any thought of what I look like.

I put my hair in a messy bun, on the top of my head and almost roll down the stairs to the kitchen.

None of the employees are here yet, it's just my mum, gran, my dad and Carl downstairs.

"Morning love," my mum greets cautiously, they all look at me with annoyingly sympathetic smiles…. I just scowl at them all.

"Why are you all looking at me like someone has just made me shoot a kitten?"

They dart their eyes away, sensing I maybe shouldn't be spoken to much today.

I get a coffee and prepare myself for the others arriving, including Carter and Jake.

"Where's the bearer of good news?" I say, sarcastically. Carl looks at me from across the room with a tight, thin-lipped smile, "She's in bed, suffering a little."

I just shrug as though to say- *"serves her right."*

Everyone pours into the farmhouse and looks around nervously, they must sense something is wrong. Jake immediately realises, that Carter is missing and with an annoyingly happy tone to his voice, obviously thinking we have gotten rid of him, he asks, "Where's Carter today?" And smiles.

Carl looks up at him from under his lashes just as Jake's gaze lands on him, and he gives a silent and slight shake to his head, warning Jake to be quiet.

He follows his best friend's lead and shuts up, grabbing a coffee and kissing me on the cheek as he comes to stand next to me.

Do I flinch? Does he notice?

"Okay everyone, I think you probably all realise that Carter isn't here, I don't know what's going on there, I don't know if we are a man down or not, so we will have to see if he turns up. For now, can everyone do what they were doing yesterday apart from Sammie, Steve and maybe Carter."

Steve and I look at my dad, and everyone else nods silently.

My dad looks at Steve, "Can you start loading up the trucks for the market? We need the logs you've chopped, bagged up into fifteens and loaded up to sell. We also need two stall tables and the marquee putting on there too."

"Sure thing."

"Actually, Johnny, you can help Steve. Carl, Jake and Miles can manage the cows."

My dad looks over at me, "I need you in the house prepping for the market, doing whatever your mum and gran ask you to do."

I nod in reply.

"And if and when Carter decides to turn up,"

I feel sick!

"I need him here, to help finish the books. See you all at breakfast."

Everyone walks out almost silently, to do what they've been asked to do.

My dad goes into the lounge, to set up the laptop and gather his papers. Probably silently praying for Carter to turn up, before he has to start finishing off what

Carter started yesterday, got to hand it to him, he seemed to be sorting it out.

My mum and gran start on prepping for breakfast, and I take a load of art things up to my room, to get out of the way and on with some market prep. Nothing that will spoil, just crafty things, like making eye catching signs, price lists et cetera. I also sew up any rips and tears in the cow mascot costume that someone always ends up wearing at the stall (usually Carl), maybe this year we will make Carter wear it! I hope it's a hot day!

I smile to myself.

Okay that was devious, and I promise I'm not having those thoughts because he spent the night with Louise. It's totally because he seems to have stood my family up!

He should be here working, and he's decided not to even bother telling any of us what is happening, and I'm furious about it.

≈≈≈≈≈≈≈≈≈≈≈

After finishing my jobs, I stroll downstairs and pop my head into the lounge to see my dad.

"How's it going?" I ask.

He gives me a defeated look, "It's not!"

He stands up and heads towards me, reaching out for a hug. I smile and crash my head into his chest and squeeze my arms around his waist.

"Oooh not so tight," he exaggerates shallow wheezy breaths, and I roll my eyes and smile up at him.

My dad isn't that much taller than me, but he always seems it. I guess he has such a big presence, not just in my life, but in everyone's.

We head into the kitchen, dad grabs a coffee and steps outside the back door, I think he needs a breather. I automatically get on with helping mum and gran cook breakfast for the farmers, they will be in soon, for their break and there's still a fair bit to do.

"Sam?" My mum is approaching carefully, I can feel it, and I feel awful for making people think they can't talk to me properly.

"I'm okay," I say, with forced enthusiasm.

My mum comes across the kitchen and stands behind me, puts her hand on my shoulder and says, "It's okay not to be, it's okay to be confused and feel upset about a bomb being dropped, like it was last night. He's your friend and something big happened last night, something that doesn't usually happen around here, and whether you have a boyfriend or not, you're allowed to feel what you're feeling right now, but just remember, like all of them, he's just a man."

I nod in response, and we all go back to cooking and setting out the breakfast, drinks, cutlery, plates and mugs.

The last place matt goes on the table, just as they all enter the house.

Chapter 15.
Sammie.

The mood has lifted a little and there's the usual buzz in the air, of those who have already started work, whilst most people are still fast asleep.

We dish up our choices for breakfast and get seated at the table to eat.

Some of us are already tucking in, and others are still piling their plates, when suddenly, the back door opens, and in strolls Carter... well, he didn't stroll actually, he almost stumbled in the door.

Our eyes snap up to him, at once, as he looks around the room with a blank expression and it's nice to see that he almost looks like shit!

His hair is a mess, that's not a problem, but he looks like he might still be a little drunk and that is a big problem.

His eyes are all red and he looks like he could drop any minute. Then suddenly, it hits me!

His hat is missing!!

My dad looks up at Carter and I notice the look of disappointment on his face... when Frank Jenkins looks at you in disappointment, that's a bummer, that everyone understands and we all wince at the reaction.

All, apart from the person getting the look.

"You look like shit!" Carl says, "You need coffee."

Carter just nods once and walks across the kitchen to the coffee pot.

"You had better be in a good enough state to sort them books out," my dad looks over at him.

"I'm all good, I'm just tired, I'll get the books finished today," he glances over at me and suddenly looks ashamed.

I just look away from him and talk to Malcolm, who is sitting next to me.

"When do you think the calves will arr—"

I'm cut off, by Sara, coming down the stairs and noticing Carter in the room.

"Oooooh, good morning, Casanova, have fun last night?"

I roll my eyes, and look over at Carter, so he can answer that question while I glare at him.

He looks at me and swallows, hard. My eyes track his Adam's apple bobbing.

"Hhhm yeah, was fun. Sorry I'm late y'all," he sits down on the closest chair to him and rubs his forehead.

Shaking my head, I stand up,

"I'm going upstairs for a bit, I'll see to the horses later."

I leave, before anyone can answer.

≈≈≈≈≈≈≈≈≈≈≈

Coming back downstairs, a few hours later, I see my dad and Carter, now sat in the kitchen doing the paperwork.

Who has the right to look that fucking good in glasses?

Does he not know I'm trying to be angry at him.

He doesn't look half dead anymore that's for sure.

"Where's mum and gran?"

They both look up and I just ignore Carter, looking straight to my dad.

"They've gone into the village for an afternoon tea they booked a while back."

"I'm going over to the stables."

I walk out the house, without saying bye.

On the walk over to the stables, I see everyone hard at work. I don't let on to anybody and I try not to think too much, I just want to go sort my horses out and not speak to another person for at least two hours.

That wasn't going to happen though, because as I approach the stables, I hear music playing.

Who the hell is playing music over there? Otis doesn't like music!

I storm the rest of the way, ready to smash up the radio that's blaring out.

Where has this fury I suddenly have, come from?

Wow! I need to calm down!

Heading round the corner, to the entrance of the yard, I see a shadow of someone in a baseball cap on the stone floor, from the open stable door.

I walk into the yard and see Louise sweeping up the main stable floor. I sigh and she looks up.

"Oh hi," she smiles brightly.

"Hi, that's a little loud don't you think? You know Otis is sensitive."

"Oh yeah, sorry I forgot he doesn't like loud noises."

She turns it down, and from one of the stalls inside, there's another shuffle noise. Not unusual in a stable of horses, but it doesn't sound like a horse… then out steps Mollie.

Great! Neither of them has bothered to come see to their horses for a few days, asking either Connie or myself to do it for them, and then on the day that I really don't want to be bothered with them, they're both here, listening to loud music, around my nervous horse, in *my* stables.

I don't actually mind Louise, she's Sara's best friend, she's a fairly decent horse owner really, a nice, quiet person, polite and friendly and I would call her a friend myself, well, until last night.

That's not fair, it's not her fault Carter probably talked her into bed, with his fucking southern drawl.

I don't like the fact she definitely had sex with Carter last night and she's wearing his fucking hat today.

I wonder if the same rule applies to baseball caps, as it does to cowboy hats.

Yes, I know the rule!

But then again, she's skinny, she's petit in every way, long blonde hair, piercing blue eyes, doesn't have a fear of sun beds like I do, so she has a nice beach glow to her skin, and Carter is… well, he's *alive,* so of course he would be interested.

The woman could turn me, I don't blame him!

But Mollie on the other hand, I can't do with her!

I never told my family about this, because her renting a stall from us, is money for my family and it's all making a living, so I would never tell them why I dislike Mollie so much. We went to school together, she was the best mean girl around! Was a natural at it!

Real nasty, sly, evil bully and she made Hannah's and my school life, miserable.

I wasn't the type to answer back when I was younger and even though, before recently anyway, I'm still fairly quiet and non-confrontational now, I'm not like I was back then.

Especially this week, I seem to be murderous lately.

So maybe, Mollie would finally get a piece of my mind today.

"Why have you turned the music down? I liked that station," Mollie always has an attitude in the way she speaks.

"It's okay, it's still on, it's just not as loud that's all." Louise is trying to keep things calm; it's no secret that Mollie and I don't get on, just nobody but Hannah knows the whole story.

"It's turned down, because it's a stable, not a damn night club and my horse doesn't like loud sounds, especially loud sounds that are going to echo in a space!" I throw back at Mollie.

She rolls her eyes at me, and I suddenly have the urge to remove them, with my own fingernails, *I'll wait until they're dirty first.*

"Seriously Sammie, you really didn't do a good job with that one did you? Did you not even *try* to desensitise him?"

I really wanted to hit her right now, but I had to stay calm.

"First of all, he had full training, but he's still sensitive, just like your mum and dad probably *tried* to bring you up properly, but it didn't stop you being a *complete* bastard! Second of all, the only reason I'm not sticking your head in that bucket of shit over there, is because my horse wouldn't like the screech you would *undoubtedly* make! Today is *not* the day to piss me off!"

She stands with her arms crossed over her chest and smirks at me.

"Oh yeah? Why's that? Is it because our lovely Louise here, was riding the man you brought over, all night last night? Green isn't a good colour on you Sammie."

With that, I see red, and I just lunge for her.

Her eyes widen in a second of shock, Louise jumps back out of the way, but before I could reach Mollie, to tear that look off her poisoned little face, I had arms around me, lifting me off the ground.

They were like a vice, and I didn't realise what was happening at first, so I just scratched my nails at the arms, which didn't slacken up, kicking my legs about, trying to kick the legs of the person holding me.

I was spun round, still in hold to see Carl, Jake and Sara all looking at me with shock on their faces.

Suddenly, I calm down a little, my hair has broken free from my messy bun, no idea where the scrunchie has gone and I realise, I am still up in the air, with very strong arms wrapped around my waist and my back pressed against an extremely firm chest.

I look down and see the hands that are clasped at my stomach, are big, strong and inked, with veins popping from the hands, all the way up the tanned, inked forearms.

I freeze, chest heaving, with my heavy laboured breathing.

"P-put me down Carter," I say, calmly.

"Are you gunna behave darlin'?"

His voice was right at my ear and seemed, deeper for some reason. I felt his cool, minty breath on the side of my neck.

"Yes!" I say, calmly but slightly annoyed.

He sets me down and I look at everyone, turning to look back at Louise, who looks scared and Mollie, who looks shocked.

I suddenly clock my scrunchie laying on the floor, so I go pick it up and neaten up my hair, slowing my breathing down.

Looking back at Mollie, I calmly say, while pulling two bits of hair down, to frame my face, "Find somewhere else to board your horse and get the fuck off my property."

I turn and walk away, leaving everyone stood there, shocked, by my behaviour.

Chapter 16.
Carter.

It's now Thursday and I'm looking forward to seeing what the market is like on Sunday.

Things on the farm have been really awkward, people have taken sides after the fall out at the stables, they've fallen out with people they didn't need to argue with, others that weren't even there, have been dragged into it.

It's a nightmare.

There are people not on speaking terms, there's scowls and the evil eye being thrown around, the group breakfasts have felt like hell. It's bad!

However, Elsa, Clara and Frank don't seem overly concerned, the way they see it is, the jobs are getting done and everything else will blow over.

The only thing they had an issue with, was Sammie telling Mollie to get the fuck off her property and find somewhere else for her horse. Apparently, that was goin' to knock them back about 500 bucks... sorry, pounds, a month.

Frank and I did manage to find a large bulk of that 10k though, so that's good.

A mistake was made months ago and that then threw the whole thing off like a bit of a domino effect.

But it wasn't as bad as he thought and ended up being manageable and would be able to be pulled back, although, once Mollie comes to pick up Zara, it would be made harder, and they'd have to find money to replace what she was paying.

I had been staying at Louise's for a few nights, just so I wasn't on the farm all the time, but Sara had been calling Louise and filling us in on the bits we didn't see and some of the reasons for people not speaking to each other.

"Is Sammie into you?" She had asked me one night, after we had had sex.

I had a rule of not talking about other women, when I was in bed with someone else.

Was I picturing Sammie, being the one I was filling? Yeah! But Louise didn't have to know that!

"Why do you ask that?" I replied.

"Just something Mollie said, it doesn't matter," she answered, as she reached up to kiss me.

I was still on the farm during the day, but we have all been keeping our heads down and getting on with our assigned jobs, I'd been working up at the stables a bit more often, joining Louise up there when she's with Flash on an evening and then goin' back to hers with her, when she leaves.

Sara has told us, that Sammie had really been acting out of character lately, as we all know, and that her and Jake are arguing a lot more now, she thought it was over what Mollie had said to her, about Louise and I sleeping together.

Of course, by that time, Jake and I, as well as the others, were up at the stable to hear that last bit, right before Sammie nearly ripped her head off.

So, I knew exactly what Louise meant, when she asked me that question.

I had to stop her, from lashing out at Mollie, I didn't want it to lead to the cops coming around, which I knew it would. The last thing anyone needs right now, is Sammie getting done for aggravated assault.

I still have the scratches on my arm, where she was trying to break out of my grip.

I'm not gunna lie, I hope they scar, that's a massive turn on that I have her marks on my skin.

    The arguments between Sammie and Jake, had apparently now started to cause an issue between Frank and Miles, after Miles told Frank that his daughter was a spoiled brat. I can agree on the brat part, to be honest. I was goin' back to the farm full time today, it had been fun staying with Louise, I won't lie, and the sex was great, but I didn't want her thinking that it was ever goin' to lead to anything serious. I didn't want that with her. Don't get me wrong, she's beautiful, she's nice, but I don't feel the urge to, own her.

Yeah, I know that might seem strange but when I'm with the right woman, I want her to give herself up to me, submit her body and soul, be wholly mine.

I didn't have that with Louise. But I wasn't goin' to say no to a bit of fun, I'm single after all.

    I walk into the farmhouse kitchen, after missing breakfast, but things are a bit more relaxed around the farm, it was 9am by this point and most of the farmers were out doing their jobs on the land.

Louise had decided to come with me, she had a day off work and knew that Sara was still at the farm and wanted to hang out, maybe go for a ride.

"Morning," Clara said, as we both entered the house.

"Morning," Louise smiles.

"Sara is studying upstairs if you want to go up," she's looking at Louise, who nods, kisses me and goes up the stairs.

"Things are going well with the two of you! She's a nice girl," Elsa tells me and Clara nods in agreement.

"Yeah, she's great, where's Frank?"

Elsa motions her head towards the den.

I walk in, to see Frank and Miles, sat having a coffee and talking.

They both look at me and I instantly feel bad for coming in, I know they had been arguing, so it was nice to see them talking and I hoped I hadn't disturbed them making up.

"Everything alright?" Frank asks.

I head over to the pair of them.

"Sorry to disturb, I just wanted to apologize."

"For what?"

I look at them both, and Miles looks down at his coffee, but obviously wasn't goin' to leave us alone.

"My actions have caused a lot of trouble this week. I know Sammie had another argument with Jake and that caused you two to fall out and I feel, well I've been told, that their argument was something to do with me."

"It always is!" Miles looks up at me.

"I'm not meaning for it to be, I'm just here, I'm trying to be friendly with everyone, but Jake doesn't like me, and I never know which side of Sammie I'm goin' to get, from one day to the next."

"Don't worry about it son, it will be fine," Frank stands up and puts his hand on my bicep.

"Go help out with the work, just use your initiative."

My mind stopped functioning after he called me "son", I know it's just an expression, but my own dad doesn't call me that.

I just nod and leave the two friends to it.

Heading outside, just in time, to see Mollie driving up the road with a horse trailer on the back of an SUV.

Oh great!

Louise comes out of the house with Sara.

"Hey," they both call from behind me.

I turn around and smile at them.

"Is Sammie up at the stables? Mollie is heading up there now."

"Oh shoot, come on we had better go up and keep the peace," Louise throws me her keys so I can drive us all up to the stable, we wouldn't make it in good enough time on foot.

When we get up there, Mollie is just opening the trailer and Sammie comes out to see what's goin' on. Her face is set when she sees Mollie, she turns to us and gives a small, closed mouthed smile and walks back into the stable. We follow her, and meet Mollie at the entrance to the stable, where Sammie is grooming Otis, and Jake is on the other side, copying her moves with Max. I feel a bit of jealousy, at the sight of them doing that together, because it's evident from Jake's fear, that it's not something they do often, we might even be here for their first time.

"Can't we swap horses? Max hates me."

"My baby doesn't hate anyone, he just knows you're going to ride him after this and that's what he doesn't want, you have to face him sometime."

Jake's eyes widen, but Sammie ignores it.

He carries on brushing his coat.

"I'm not going near his tail, he will kick me."

Mollie sniggers and we all look over at her.

"What's so funny?" Sammie stares at her with pure hatred.

"Well, I'm beginning to see the reason, apart from the obvious," her eyes look over at me and trail up and down my body- *I actually feel violated,* "That you would rather be rolling around in the hay with Carter than this dork."

I raise my voice louder than intended and it clearly surprises Jake.

"Shut the fuck up Mollie. Stop trying to cause arguments between them, the next time she flies at you, I won't fucking stop her. Just get your damn horse, out of here."

Louise takes hold of my hand, and I interlace my fingers with hers, I don't miss Sammie's eyes watching that action, and as bad as I feel, I'm not goin' to show Louise up by letting go, just because Sammie has noticed our hands.

Jake looks pleased and I don't know if it's because, I half stood up for them as a couple, or if it's due to me holding hands with Louise.

"Fuck you all," Mollie flips us the bird and goes in to get Zara from her stall.

As Mollie leaves, Louise let's go of my hand and goes in to fetch Flash.

"Where is she?" She looks at Jake and Sammie. "We've already done her, she's out with Clover on the paddock, Connie couldn't get here today so we just did all the horses with it being the two of us, he needs the practice."

She glances over at Jake, who is still struggling with Max, and we all laugh.

"Thank you, I'm going to go for a ride, does anyone want to come? There's five of us here and four horses, four of us could ride, I'm sure Connie wouldn't mind if we took Clover, and one of us could muck out."

"Well, I'm meant to be, *"using my initiative"*, so I'll stay at the stables. Y'all go for a ride," I say, while I walk toward the tack room.

"I'll help you tack up."

"I'm not riding!" Jake looks panicked.

"Yes, you are," Sammie calls back at him, while goin' out to the paddock with Louise to get Clover and Flash.

I watch them walk out, over the grass and my eyes are drawn to Sammie and not the woman I've been sleeping with.

Watching her hips sway, as she walks toward the paddock, I lick my lips and realize in that moment, I absolutely *have* to have her.

Chapter 17.
Carter.

The three girls tack up a horse each and I show Jake how to tack up Otis. Sammie realized that Max wasn't goin' to let Jake put a cinch on him. I've got to hand it to him; the change of horse has relaxed Jake a lot and he's not doing too bad at picking it up.

"Can I ask you something, man to man?" He looks at me out of the corner of his eye and he's leaning in, so he can speak quietly.

I frown, "Erm sure?"

"How the fuck do I stay on the horse and not show myself up in front of Sammie? I've known her forever and we've been together for two years, but I've never ridden a horse and they're her life, I don't want to show myself up."

"I don't think you're goin' to fall off of this guy."

He doesn't look convinced.

I sigh, "Horses are like dogs, they're very in tune with other animals and he will read if you're nervous, and that will then make him nervous. So just stay calm, relax your body language, don't hold on for dear life, move your hips like you want Sammie to move hers," I wink at him, and he looks shocked, so I laugh.

At that moment, we turn around to see Sammie is standing close enough to hear everything we have just been saying.

And she's blushing, again!

≈≈≈≈≈≈≈≈≈≈≈

By the time they all get back from their ride, I have
sorted the stalls, replaced everything, arranged all the
ropes, cleaned the tack room, swept both the main
stable and the yard and hosed everything down.
I was finishing hosing the horse trailer, when they all
rode up. Even though it was late afternoon, the sun was
still hot, so I had been to get my hat.

"Hey cowboy," Louise waves, and I smile and
put the hose down, walking up to them and helping her
dismount.
She comes up on her toes and kisses me.
I glance up at Sammie, in reaction. She looks down,
then jumps off Max.
We are just removing the tack from the horses and
putting them in their stalls, when the commotion starts!
But this was commotion I was goin' to love.

We hear a lot of hollering, over near the
farmhouse and as we walk over to the edge of the yard,
to look at where the sound is coming from, we see Carl
and Steve, trying to chase a cow that has bolted.
I look around at the others, who are all trying not to
laugh, then we hear Frank shouting something that
sounds like, *"Be gentle with her."*
"Did he just shout be gentle with her? It doesn't look
like they're getting anywhere near her at all," laughs
Jake.
"They won't catch her, she's twice as fast as they are
and much stronger, it's going to take more than a person
to get her back in," I reply.

I look over at Max.

"No way! You can't ride him," Sammie gets hold of my bicep, I don't miss the way her eyes shoot to where her hand is, then back to my eyes.

"He will buck you off, he doesn't like strangers."

"He's the only one still tacked and trust me, I can handle him, this horse was made for this."

I run over to the wall and slip the lariat off the hook, that I had noticed when sorting the ropes, then head over to mount Max.

The fucker tries rearing, but I force him sideways, which pulls him back down, and then a good squeeze of my legs to his side, has him darting off to where I am steering him, straight towards the cow.

As I get closer to where Carl and Steve, are still playing tag with the cow, I shout down to them, "Go back to the house, get out the way, you'll get hurt."

They both stare at me in shock for a few seconds, then head off the field.

As I get closer to the cow, she suddenly starts darting around in different directions, I hope that Max can read what I need him to do.

He does really well, reacting to my strong commands and reading my leg and rein cues well.

When we manage, to get the cow moving away from us, slightly to the side, I can then lasso her.

I spin and throw the lariat, looping it securely around the cow's neck, causing her to stop and in turn, I slow Max right down.

He reacts perfectly to every command, both verbal and non-verbal, he is a natural at this.

I knew when I first met him, that he was a wild spirit, he's energetic and he needs working.

I then use Max's strength, to lead the cow back home with the rope.

She wasn't gunna argue with him, that's for sure.

As I am leading her back towards the barn, I see the entire workforce stood watching me.

Clara and Miles are walking from the barn to the farmhouse to join Elsa, Steve, Carl and Frank. They are, then, also joined by Sammie, Jake, Louise and Sara.

Malcolm and Johnny were now heading over from the pen, where they had come out from waiting for the calves, to see what all the shouting was about.

When I see everyone stood by the farmhouse, staring up at me, I change direction and head towards them, but hand the rope out to Malcolm, as he approaches, so he can take the cow to the barn, on his way back to the pens. He stares at me as he takes the rope, I just smile down at him with a single nod.

Making the rest of my way, to the front of the farmhouse, I dismount, as Max is still moving and lead him to Sammie.

Handing his rein over, I make sure to brush my fingers against hers, she bites her lip as she stares into my eyes. My eyes jump from her eyes, to her mouth and back again. Everyone just stands staring at me, all their jaws dropping.

"You'll swallow flies!" I say, while looking at them all.

"That was pretty impressive," Carl says.

"That was hot as fuck!" Both Sara and Louise say, together.

I just smile at them in response.

≈≈≈≈≈≈≈≈≈≈≈

We're all sat in the kitchen, when Sammie gets back from putting Max in his stall.

Frank grabs the bottles of wine and some bottles of beer.

We are just about to get a drink, when Malcolm comes crashing into the kitchen, making us jump.

"They're here!" He exclaims, "We have a male and a female."

Then he runs back outside, followed by Frank.

I head over to the pens to see if anything is needed.

"No son, Malcolm will stay with them to make sure there's no issues after birth and I'll check on everything before bed."

I nod and go back inside.

A few minutes later, Frank comes in and looks at Elsa, "They're grand! Malcolm will stay and make sure everything is okay and then he's going to go home, I've given him tomorrow off."

"Okay love," she smiles warmly and gives him a beer.

Miles, Steve and Johnny stand up, to set off home.

"See you all tomorrow," Johnny waves.

"See you tomorrow son," Miles says, squeezing Jake's shoulder.

"See you all tomorrow," Jake taps his dad's hand in reply.

"Goodnight, everyone, good work today, Carter," says Steve finally.

I smile.

"Bye," we all call to the three men heading out.

I sit down next to Louise, who straight away leans into me, draping both arms over my shoulders.

≈≈≈≈≈≈≈≈≈≈≈

After a couple of hours drinking and talking, about all the events of the day, I yawn loudly.

"Sorry," I laugh, "Bit tired."

Everyone smiles back.

"It's getting pretty late now, maybe I could stay here with you tonight? Plus, I've had a drink."

I look back at Louise, and by the look on her face, I obviously look as horrified as I feel, at that moment.

"I mean, I don't *have* to, I just thought..."

"You know, if this was *my* place, it wouldn't be an issue, but I don't feel—"

"Oh, that's okay! We don't mind."

My head whips around to Elsa.

"What?!"

"Oh, come on Carter, we are all adults, Jake stays over, Sara stays over. You're a grown man, we don't mind you having an overnight guest."

Was I blushing?

"Thank you, Elsa," beams Louise.

≋≋≋≋≋≋≋≋≋≋≋

Everyone is in bed now, and I come out of the shower, to Louise laying on the bed in just lingerie, looking up at me, with a sexy smirk on her face.

"We can't!"

I walk over to the bed and sit next to her.

She sits up, "Why?"

"Look, Elsa said she didn't mind a woman staying with me, but just because they said it's fine, doesn't mean we can get up to anything, it's disrespectful in someone else's home. It doesn't feel right, these walls are not very thick, I heard Jake and Sammie arguing once… and you're not the quietest!" I smile at her.

"That's your fault! I'm never usually that loud," she crawls toward me on the bed and straddles my lap.

Man, she wasn't making it easy.

"Fuck it!"

I stand up with her legs around my waist and lay us both on the bed.

Kissing her nose, I tell her, "You've got to be quiet, otherwise we will have to stop."

Knowing full well, there was *no* way I was goin' to stop.

Chapter 18.
Sammie.

Jesus! What the hell is going on upstairs?!

There's no way anyone is going to be sleeping tonight, with the creaking, squeaking and fucking banging!

I mean, yeah, I've heard people having sex before, but this sounds like they're either going to go through a wall or come through the ceiling.

What the hell is he doing to her?!

I look over at Jake, who looks back at me and whispers, "What the fuck?"

I shrug and turn over.

Then, I get the pillow and shove it over my head, trying to drown out the noise.

"Should I bang on the ceiling?" Jake asks.

"No, they probably won't hear it anyway, this is ridiculous."

After a few more minutes, Jake throws the cover off us both and sits up.

"What are you doing? I'm naked!" I drag the covers back over me.

"I'm going upstairs to fucking pound on the door."

"Just leave them, it has to stop soon."

He lays back down and we just stay there, in silence…

5,10,15 more minutes pass and there's no letting up.

I have gone from feeling a bit sick with jealousy, over Carter having sex with someone else, right where I can hear it… to actual worry!

Because now she is screaming. I don't mean sex screaming, as in moaning!! No no!! I mean *actually* screaming, like she is being murdered.

I really am worried. Maybe he was locked up for murder or something, or forced sexual acts?

Maybe he is a sexual deviant and is *extremely* dangerous! It would make sense, judging from the noises keeping the whole house awake.

It's been nearly half an hour, why are they still going?!

"Maybe you should go upstairs and just bang on the door after all!" I look at Jake.

He looks back at me, and I can see his facial expressions soften, in the moonlight coming in through the window. Sometimes I don't close the curtains, it's private up here, so I like to keep them open and look at the moon and stars.

"What?" I ask him.

"Seeing as though no one is getting any sleep and that's going to drown out any other noises, why don't we have a little fun of our own?"

Oh, for fuck's sake! This is the last thing I want.

This is not normal, I should want this but what do I ever get out of it?

I hate sex.

I try and think of a reason why I can't … he knows I'm not on my period, so I can't use that. Whenever I say I have a headache, he comes back with the fact that, an orgasm can help clear a headache.

Well yes, that's all good and dandy, for the people who get that happy ending!

I don't feel, as his girlfriend, when someone else is in the house, obviously enjoying their sex life, that I can say no, but I can't bring myself to say yes either, so I just nod.

This really is not normal, because my boyfriend is visibly enjoying himself and I am just laid here, under him, *crying*! Why am I crying? Have I gone from feeling sick with jealousy, to worried, to now upset? Was I crying because, I hate the fact that Carter is up there with someone else and they're *still* at it? Was I crying because everything was catching up with me all of a sudden? Because I'm not normal and don't like sex? Or is it because I've realised, I don't love, or even like my boyfriend anymore, yet, here I am, laying down and just taking it because I can't say no?!

I'm just glad that the room was dark enough to hide my tears and if he felt them, at least they could pass for sweat, considering the current activities.

This is so boring, I can't wait for it to be over. Finally!! He's done and I can hopefully try and get some sleep, well, when that noise upstairs stops, I can. It's not as loud now, but there's definitely still creaking going on.

I would quite happily run myself over right now! It's not possible, but I would make it work!

Jake starts snoring next to me, the annoying freight train sort of snoring.

Fuck my life!

I slyly boot him in the leg, to make myself feel a bit better, and turn away.

The bed upstairs is still making some sort of rocking noise, but nothing as aggressive as it has been, I'm guessing she's in no danger because every now and then, there's little chants of *"yes! Yes! Yes!"*
I roll my eyes, at the thought of it all, and will myself to go to sleep.

Chapter 19.
Sammie.

I am just drifting off to sleep, after the noises remained quiet enough for the last half hour, what the fuck?!
It's been over an hour and a half now, but I'm glad I can finally drift off, then BANG, yes literally bang.
   I sit upright in bed, jolting myself out of the early stages of sleep and look around, I'm shaking with the sudden shock.
Had I just dreamt it? No one else seems to be bothered by it. Jake is still asleep, and no one is coming out of their rooms. I must have dreamt about something making a banging noise.
Damn, I was just getting comfortable, fucking hell!

≈≈≈≈≈≈≈≈≈≈≈

I managed to fall asleep at some point, early this morning and now the alarm is sounding and I, *actually* cry.
   I don't usually have a problem waking up, I'm used to it, early wake ups have always been a part of my life, even when I was in school, but this morning, I was quite emotional about it.
Jake stretches his arm across me, "Morning babe, last night was fun."
I look at him and he opens his eyes, wide!
"What's wrong? Why are you crying?"

"I'm fucking tired! I'm so tired and I'm going to *kill* Carter! I'm actually going to kill him!"

He half smiles and wipes my tears, "Don't cry. It was a bit much, but you know… good for them and all that."

I scowl back at him.

"I'm sure your dad won't mind you resting for a bit, there's enough of us to do what's needed."

"So, you're not supporting me? You're not going to give me an alibi?"

He laughs and gets out of bed to get dressed.

I'm deadly serious!

Then I look at him, really look at him.

After feeling how I felt last night and realising, I didn't like him anymore, in the way I should, I wanted to study him and see what it was I didn't like.

So, for the first time in, ever, I really look at my boyfriend, while he's walking around my bedroom, naked.

I don't even blush! I don't blush!!

That's the first thing noted.

He's a good guy, he really is- one of the best, but I've never felt a real spark with him and until Carter arrived, I didn't realise how important that spark was.

I was comfortable with Jake. But comfortable isn't enough, is it?

He's a bit taller than I am, probably the same height as Carl and he has a decent body. He's lean, you know, there's a bit of definition there, but he's not a machine, who could throw me around a bit, or even lift me up and stop me from fighting a gobby little bitch at the stable, *now* I'm starting to blush! I shake it off.

He has a decent head of hair, keeps it very short though, so there's never any style to it, he has black hair... which is strange, because anytime I had a crush on a celebrity, they were always blonde.

He does have lovely eyes though, like chocolate, but again, I prefer blue.

He's a good-looking guy, he's a nice guy, but he's just the safe option.

I had been safe all my life, working with all these men, I would actually say, I had been *over* protected, probably why I ended up dating my brother's best friend and also my lifelong friend... I didn't *need* any more safe options, I needed to *feel* something.

I look at Jake's face, which was staring back at me in confusion.

"Why are you staring at my naked body? You planning to jump me later?" He smirks.

I just give him a quick smile back.

"I'll see you downstairs, just going to get a shower and that."

That's another thing, he doesn't get a shower every day! He works on a farm, and we had sex last night, yet, he hasn't had a shower.

I shiver.

Chapter 20.
Sammie.

I come downstairs to everyone in the kitchen as normal, for coffee. Everyone apart from Carter and Louise.

"Morning everybody," my dad greets us all, without his usual chipper voice.

"Well, while we wait for Carter to come down, let's just fuel up on coffee, lots of coffee and I'll go over the plans for the day, when everyone is here."

None of us have any energy this morning and we're going to need all the help we can get, none of us, apart from the employees that went home last night, that is.

"Oooh you all look rough," Steve says to us.

"Were you drinking late?" Adds Johnny.

"No, we weren't late, we went to bed not long after you lot left, couple of hours maybe, but then, well, I don't even know how to explain the noises coming from Carter's room," Jake says.

"Murderous!!!" I blurt out.

"Murderous? Fuck! was he hurting Louise??" Asks Miles.

"Well to be honest, I thought he was at one point! Jake and I were debating whether one of us really should go see if she was okay."

"She was okay for fuck's sake!" Carl adds, then goes on to a very poor impression of Louise's voice, *"yes! Yes! YES!"* and everyone starts laughing.

I look around at them all laughing, even my mum and dad are visibly trying not to laugh.

"It's not funny!" I shout, "I've never *been* so tired!!"

"I've got to say, even Frank and I were blushing."

"Did Sara say anything?" I look at Carl.

"She just laughed and said, "get in!""

Sara nods.

I roll my eyes, and everyone laughs again.

The laughter stops abruptly, when we hear someone coming down the stairs.

"Oh, here he is! The vampire! Obviously doesn't need sleep!" Jake says, as he comes into view.

Carter looks round us all and does actually look apologetic and embarrassed.

He comes down the rest of the stairs, walks across the kitchen to the coffee and pours a big mug full.

We track his movement and keep looking at him, until he sits down.

"Where's Louise, she too sore to move?" Asks Sara with a chuckle.

He ignores the too sore part and answers, "She's still in bed… I have a problem."

He looks at my mum and dad. They look worried.

"Oh no! You've hurt her! We are going to have the police here, aren't we?" I say, staring at Carter.

"What? No!! No of course I haven't *hurt* her! She's fine… the problem is, which, of course I will deal with, but I just obviously need to tell you… the bed—"

"What about the bed?" My dad asks.

"Oh shit, judging by your reaction, the bed is like a family heirloom, isn't it? Please tell me that bed doesn't mean anything and that it's not been in the family for years and you use it, in the guest room to *protect* it? I mean, even if it's a lie, please tell me that's not the case."

My mum looks at Carter, "What is wrong with the bed, Carter?"

He winces… "It's sort of broken."

"Broken? The bed is broken. A wooden bed is broken?" My dad is having a hard time believing it.

"Well, I don't know, it might not be broken, it might be something loose, I've not looked properly yet but it… crashed and we sort of spent the rest of the night, sleeping almost upside down. The head of the bed is more or less on the floor."

"So, you *are* like a Vampire!" Jake says, "You sleep upside down like a bat?"

"Well, they needed the blood to rush back to their heads," Sara chuckles and we all laugh with her, including me.

I'm enjoying my people grilling Carter.

"This isn't funny, please tell me the bed is just a bed, and means nothing to anyone!"

My dad wipes his eyes of laughter tears and puts his hand on Carter's shoulder, "It's fine son, it's just a bed, we will sort it. Just be careful in future."

He laughs again.

"Oh dear, right children, let's all calm down and listen up!" My dad addresses the room.

"Malcolm is off today and as you all know, we have two new arrivals. Two cows gave birth last night, a male and a female, so I want the majority of you guys around the barn and pen today. I'm going to keep mums and babies in the calving pen for a couple of days."

Our calving pens are not just a metal enclosure, with the rest of the cows, it's an area we have off the side of the barn, so the cows can be kept with their calves away from the rest of the herd, until we feel they're ready to go back.

"I just want to keep them separate, until I feel the rest of the herd will be good, with that cow bolting off yesterday, that behaviour is unusual for our girls and I just want to make sure there's no funny business."

I suddenly get the image of Carter, roping the cow, managing Max like he wasn't an arsehole that tries to kick everyone else who goes near his saddle, apart from me.

I bite my lip at the memory.

"Are we keeping the bull calf?" I ask.

Carter looks over at me, knowing that this is my least favourite part of being on a farm, knowing the bulls aren't needed and are often sold on for slaughter.

"Yes love," my dad answers with a smile, "We don't have a bull, so we are keeping this one."

I sigh and smile.

I look over at Carter, knowing full well why he's looking at me. I smile at him, and he smiles back.

"So, as I was saying, I want most of you working the barn, parlour and pens. Steve and Johnny, do you think we have enough logs for Sunday?"

"Yeah, I think so, we bagged up 60 nets, but we only loaded 25, don't think more than that will be sold at the market, so the rest are in the main barn."

"Great, thanks boys. There are a few fences I want building with the fence posts and wire that's in the main barn. Steve, remember me telling you about the land I wanted separating?"

Steve nods.

"Well, I want the fences putting round that land, it will probably be an all day job, do you think you and Johnny can do that, or do you need anyone else?"

"We will manage, but if we need anyone, we will come pull Jake."

My dad and Jake both nod.

"Sammie, what needs doing up at the stable?"

"Just the usual, but Carter fully blasted the whole place yesterday, while some of us were on a ride, even the tack room, so it won't take me long up there, I'll go up after breakfast though, it's too early."

My dad nods and Carter adds, "Y'all came back before I managed to wash the horse trailers down though." he's looking at me.

"Yeah, you really went to town up there, I'll do that before breakfast and go back up afterwards."

Louise comes downstairs,

"Morning," she says shyly with a little smile.

Sara beams at her best friend and Louise gives her a smile back. She heads over to Carter and he gets her a cup of coffee.

Sickening! Jake never gets me a drink.

"Is everyone good with that?"

We all nod at my dad and then I turn to Louise, "Do you want me to sort Flash out, or are you doing it?"

"Would you mind doing it? I need to get home."

"Sure," I nod.

"I spoke to Connie last night though, she said she was coming up to move Clover today, so you won't have to do anything with her."

"Move Clover? What do you mean move her?"

"She's not told you? Shit! Mollie told her what had happened, and she said that she was moving Clover to another stable, she's going to the same stable Zara has gone to."

I look at my dad, who looks furious.

She looks between us both, "I'm so sorry, I thought she would have rung you yesterday."

"Don't worry about it, it's no big deal."

I look back at my dad and he just stands up to walk into the lounge.

As he walks away and without looking at anyone, he says, "Have a good day everybody."

They all head out on their jobs, and I stand up to go in the lounge to talk to my dad.

"I'm not in the mood right now love," he says, before I even reach him.

My mum brings in a coffee and sits down next to him, rubbing his back in a soothing way.

"Dad—"

"No Sammie, I don't want to point any fingers, but if you had just bit your tongue, we wouldn't be down nearly £1,000 a month."

I sigh, "I know. I'm sorry, but you don't know what Mollie was like and I'm not about to tell everyone, but that had been a long time coming. I'll sort it."

"How are you going to sort it? Are you going to *force* people to keep their horses here? Do you know how hard it is for us to make money, consistently? We put a lot of money into what we do, the upkeep of everything, we speculate more than we accumulate sometimes, and we have staff to pay! We have bills to pay! I want my family to have a good, comfortable life. We are forever fighting against cuts and issues the government put on us, farming is far from a stress free, easy life, and only the other day, I was panicking, thinking I had blown £10,000!"

"But you found most of that didn't you?"

"That's not the point! The point is, a mistake was made, an easy mistake and this time it wasn't so bad, and we probably will make the money back up! Even though now, it's going to be more difficult! But what about when it's not a mistake? What about when we really can't manage? The World is getting harder and harder and farmers *used* to do well, we don't anymore, and I *don't* want that for my family!"

Chapter 21.
Sammie.

I start to tear up, as my dad carries on, making me feel shit.

"This farm, has been passed down to us, we've built and improved it over the years, and I want it to be yours and Carl's future, my grandkid's futures... until someone doesn't want it, not until they don't have a choice, but to *lose* it!"

I wipe my tears and glance out of the window, where Carter is stood at Louise's car with her, presumably saying goodbye, because they are now kissing and he's holding her body close to his.

My chest burns.

I clear my throat, and my mum and dad look back up at me.

"He will have some ideas on how to make some money!"

They both follow my gaze out the window and see Carter, now opening the door for Louise to get in.

"The ranch his grandad had, was worth millions. If he hadn't had been such a dick and got himself locked up, he would probably be running that ranch now, but his family have it and they have cut him off. He's never had much of a family, apart from his grandad, so he screwed everything up when he went to prison and he died. I know that we are never going to be millionaires and ranches are different to what we have, but I also know they have a lot of similarities too. They just have different practices and different priorities. But he knows what he's doing, he knows how to deal with the land, the livestock, the business. He has experience and will probably have ideas. We need to use him! He's here to work, he's here—"

I shake my head.

"He's here to be part of this, so ask his advice, I *know* he can help."

I start to walk away, then turn back round to my parents, "I really am sorry!"

When I go out, onto the farm, to head up to do the horse boxes, Carter comes walking round the corner to me and it's nice to just, see him alone for a minute and not wanting to put my walls up. I think realising my lack of feelings for Jake, last night, made me see this was all on me and I would feel this way, whether Carter was here or not.

"Hey," I offer.

He looks up from the floor, "Hey. You okay? You look like you've been crying."

"Oh yeah, I'm okay, I'm just feeling a bit guilty about a few things today. Plus, I'm tired," I glare at him.

He chuckles and I love the sound of the deep rumble.

"Yeah, sorry about that. I did keep telling her to be quiet," he smiles.

I smile back at him and even though, I probably always will be a little jealous, I am happy for him.

"Things seem to be going well between you guys! I thought you didn't spend the night with women, didn't you once tell me you were a fuck it and fuck off kind of guy? I'm sure they were your words."

He laughs and rubs the back of his neck, "Naw, that doesn't sound like something I would say."

I look at him under my lashes in a "*yeah whatever*" sort of way and he smiles.

"You heading up to the stables?"

"Yeah, going to finish what you couldn't finish yesterday," I smirk at him.

"What is this? Pick on Carter Day?" He asks.

"Well, you do bring it on yourself," I smile and start to walk away.

Just then, he grabs me by the arm and pulls me close to him, both of our chests are heaving, as I stare up at him. He leans down and whispers in my ear, as I close my eyes, "I always finish what I start."

With that, he turns around and walks towards the barn, to meet everyone else.

I still have goosebumps all over my body, even as I watch him reach the barn and go inside, out of sight.

I think it's my turn to get whiplash.

≈≈≈≈≈≈≈≈≈≈≈

We are all now having breakfast and the main farmhouse phone rings.

"Hello?" My dad answers.

After a few seconds he speaks again, "Oh yes, Louise told us today, you've left it until last minute, haven't you?"

I stand up and walk towards my dad, gesturing for him to give me the phone. He shakes his head, so I snatch it out of his hand and everyone looks at me.

I cover the mouthpiece with my hand when I say, "The damage is already done!"

Holding the phone up to my ear, I take over the conversation.

"Why are you moving Clover?"

Connie answers- "Well, I heard what happened between you and Mollie and I didn't want my horse at your stable."

"One thing, you heard *one* side of the story, and I bet it didn't, in any way, resemble the truth. You don't know Mollie as a person, I've known her for 15 years, she's a nasty piece of work and what *really* happened yesterday, was a long time coming, but I bet she embellished her own little version."

"Look, I don't care what happened between you, but whatever *did* happen, she has decided to move her horse, so that shows, you are not a professional or trustworthy livery."

"*Decided* to move her horse? No, she didn't, I *told* her to move her horse! It wasn't her choice, so that's your first lie- I bet there's many more!"

She's quiet on the line for a bit.

"We are not officially a livery no, we are a Dairy farm, with stable room to rent out. In order to do so, we follow all the correct laws and procedures, and we have full insurance! The horses are extremely happy and well looked after here and for the care Clover gets, you really should be paying twice as much as you do, because you're hardly ever here. Your horse knows me, more than she knows you. So go ahead and come pick her up, she will be ready at 11, but good luck getting the care for her that she got here, for the price you've been paying!! See you at 11!"

I put the phone down before she can answer and look around the room, to everyone watching me.

Carter starts the round of applause, and everyone joins in.

I blush again.

≈≈≈≈≈≈≈≈≈≈≈

I'm up at the stable and all the horses have been groomed, including Clover and are out enjoying the paddock, it's a nice sunny day again and getting really quite warm. I'm fully cleaning out all the stalls.

With us losing two horses, in the space of a couple of days, I thought it would be a good time to fully reset, I'm sweeping out every bit of bedding, so they're totally bare.

Going back and forth, in this heat, with wheelbarrows full of soiled and wet bedding is a killer, but we keep the used dirty bedding in a separate lockup a few yards away from the stable, for composting.

Once I've cleared all of that, I go onto removing the mattress matts and putting them in the yard for cleaning. I disinfectant the floors and walls of the stalls, as well as the matts and hose everything down, before letting it all dry out. While all that is drying, I wash all the tack and hang everything back up, in the nice clean tack room, courtesy of Carter.

As I am starting to pull the matts back inside the stable, to put them in the stalls, Carter appears.

"What you doing?" He shouts.

"Shit! You made me jump."

He laughs, "Sorry, it's nearly 11 o clock, so I thought you would want some moral support, when Clover gets picked up."

I smile and nod, "Thanks."

"Wow, you're really goin' to town."

"Well, I couldn't have you show me up could I? You set a good example yesterday, with the cleaning and organising of everything, plus, we've lost two horses, I may as well do a deep clean of all the stalls ready for, hopefully a new lodger," I smile.

Chapter 22.
Sammie.

"I take it you're only replenishing three of the stalls?"

"Yeah, no point doing the others, but I need to get the matts in and hose all the feed and water buckets. May as well do all 12 while I'm at it."

"I'll get the matts in, they're heavy and you've already got them out, you hose the buckets."

I nod and head into the stable, bringing all the buckets into the yard, for hosing, then look back at Carter, who actually lifts the matts, I didn't lift them, I dragged them, but I'm enjoying watching all his muscles flex when he is at work.

I bite my lip, and he looks up at me, from under the brim of his hat.

He stands up and slowly walks towards me, our gazes locked, there's no way I'm looking away, as *agonising* as this is.

His eyes fall down to my lip, still being bitten, then they lift back to my eyes.

He licks his lips, and my eyes track the movement, noticing the glisten left behind.

Carrying on walking towards me, painfully slowly, our chests are heaving again and just as he closes the gap, so there's only maybe, 6inches between us, we are dragged out of our trance by someone shouting.

"Hiiiiii! Sammie!! Over here!!!"

We both blink, as though we are just entering this world again and Carter looks at me with his brows furrowed, we look to the side, to where the shouting is coming from.

"It's Connie, she's here."

"Yeah…"

We step back, away from each other and Carter walks over, to open the yard gate for her.

I look at her car, there's no horse box.

Carter needs to get out of here, because I don't think it's good for us to be alone.

They both walk back towards me, and she looks around the yard at what we're doing.

I glance at Carter, "I'm good, you can go back to the guys now, I can manage."

He looks at me, knowing why I'm sending him away and I just give him a little pleading smile. Giving me a nod and a smile back, he turns and walks away.

Both Connie and I watch him leave, then she turns to face me, and I just cross my arms.

"Look, Sammie, I thought about what you said on the phone, I jumped to conclusions and acted impulsively, and I was wrong."

"Well, what you should have done, is call us and found out what happened, but you didn't and now, I'm not going to lie, you're going to have a much worse deal, than what you had here."

She looks down at her feet, over to Clover, who's running round the paddock, then back at me.

"You're right, Clover loves you and she loves it here, I was stupid, and I've come down here, without a horse box, in the hope that you'll forgive me and carry on keeping Clover here for me."

"Once upon a time, especially because I end up loving the horses here, I would have said not to worry about it, but I'm sick of being that Sammie, who never answers back, who always puts others first. The last few days, something has changed in me, and I thought I was being a bitch, and to a point, I probably was, but those actions have caused me to find my voice and not to put up with so much rubbish. You didn't care, if taking Clover out of the stable, with no real notice and without a real reason, would cause hardship to my family, so why should I just, sit down and let you mess us about, by not taking your horse now?"

"Because you love her."

"But I love my family and my family's reputation more, we are a business, we're not doormats, so I'm sorry Connie, but Clover is ready to go. You can take a horse box, and someone will come collect it tonight. She's all groomed, fed and watered. I'm sure you can manage to get her boxed up, I have a lot to do here."

I leave her to sort everything for Clover, while I get the last matt in the stalls.

I take a minute, inside the stables and try not to go back outside, to tell Connie that everything is fine and to leave Clover. I'll miss her, but I'm not backing down. We will sort the lost money.

After a while, as I put fresh bedding down in three of the stalls and even it all out, I hear the sound of a car engine starting and I slowly walk out to the yard, to see Connie driving away, with a full horse box.

I sit down and cry. Looking over at the hosed buckets, that I never got round to putting away, I think back to the moment between Carter and me.

I don't know how long I can fight how I feel for him and the lack of feelings for Jake, but I'm not the type to go behind anyone's back.

There wasn't just Jake now, after all, there was Louise and her and Carter seem happy. I couldn't hurt two people, and I had to try not to be alone with Carter anymore.

I'm not myself around him and I don't *trust* the person that I'm becoming.

I sigh and stand up, putting the 12 buckets, into the six stalls and refilling the feed and water in three lots of them, finishing off, by sweeping and hosing the main stable and yard floor.

Carter did it yesterday, but obviously, it needs doing again after all this. I lock up the yard, check the horses are safe and happy in the paddock and head back down to the farmhouse.

Walking towards the barns, I see most of the farmers standing closer to the pens, so I join them, to look at the babies.

I'm so happy we are keeping the bull calf, he is so cute, and I hate it when they get sold on. I've never become immune to it. It's one thing letting the cows go, when they're no longer of any use on a Dairy farm, but they've lived by then and we take good care of them. Sending the babies, is something I will never get used to.

I stand next to Carter and immediately regret it, the heat only makes his aftershave stronger, and he smells so good. I bet he showers every day!

He looks at me and smiles, "Cute huh?"

"Very, I'm glad we are keeping the boy."

My dad heads over to us, looking brighter than he was earlier.

"Right, everyone, I'm taking my wife out tonight!"

We all look at each other and look back at him.

"Yes, she deserves a date night, so I'm taking her. She's also having the morning off tomorrow, so there will be no breakfast. I know the family, including Carter, are off tomorrow anyway, with the rest of you having the day off on Sunday, so my wife is joining the family and having a lie in. So, guys, you'll need to have breakfast before you come to work, I will feed and water the cows before you get here, so just get here for about 6am."

Everyone nods at him.

"You're all obviously free to do what you want in the farmhouse, without breaking beds please," he looks at Carter, who coughs.

"But if you're drinking and staying up late, just remember, to be responsible if you're working tomorrow and my mum will be upstairs, so don't be too loud," he again, looks at Carter.

"What do you think I'm goin' to do?"

We all laugh.

"Just making sure you know!" My dad winks at him.

"By the way, the bed is sorted, you just popped a few screws."

We all laugh *again*.

"So, who's staying for a drink tonight?" Asks Carl.

"Oh no, I'm going home, you lot *drink* too much," says Miles.

"Yeah, I'm out too," adds Steve.

"Lightweights," says Johnny.

"Remember you and Jake are working tomorrow!" Miles replies to him.

He nods back and rolls his eyes, "Okay old man, we know. We can handle it!"

Steve and Miles say their goodbyes and head off home.

Sara comes outside, "Hey."

"Hey babe," Carl kisses her temple. "You all studied out?"

"Yeah, my brain is fried."

"Well, my mum and dad are going out tonight, gran is retiring upstairs early, so we are all going to have a drink and hang out, you staying?"

"Count me in, can we play truth or dare?!" She says, clapping her hands.

We all collectively groan at her, and she laughs.

Sat in the kitchen, we are busy deciding on what to eat tonight, when my mum and dad come down the stairs, all suited and booted.

Carter whistles, and my mum *actually* blushes a little, which I find funny.

"Oh, behave yourself," she says to Carter.

"Mum, you look *hot*!" I tell her.

"What about me?" My dad says, "Don't I look hot?"
"Well, you'll pass, but you're definitely punching," I reply and he laughs.
"That, I most definitely am," he kisses my mum, and she playfully taps him on the arm.
Carl and I look at each other and share the same proud smile, that says, we have parents, who are madly in love.
"Okay, get out of here, so we can get drunk and trash the place," Jake says.
"No red wine in the lounge," mum shouts over her shoulder, as Carl is ushering them both out the door.
"*Byeee,*" we all shout, as Carl shuts the door behind them.

Chapter 23.
Sammie.

Sara and I come downstairs after getting changed into something a bit more comfortable. She goes with one of Carl's shirts and a pair of sleep shorts and I go with the silk and lace short and tank top set I was eyeing up the other night.

I sneak a little look at Carter, to see if he notices and his eyes are nearly falling out of his head. I'm not confident in my body, but he makes me feel a little more daring. I smile to myself, and after he has gotten a bit of an eye full, I go to grab the hoodie, hanging by the back door, to cover my mid drift area.

"Why don't we just sit in the lounge until the food comes? It's more comfortable." I suggest.

"Mum will kill us if we spill anything in there," Carl answers me.

"We have white wine and beers, no food yet. We're not drunk, nothing is going to spill."

We all stand up and go to the lounge.

Jake randomly asks Carter, as we all sit down, "Do you call it a lounge?"

Carter looks at him and says, "No, we call it a den, or a family room."

"Strange how we all speak English, but then you lot try to change our language isn't it?"

I look over at Carter and smile, he throws a cushion at my head, and I laugh and snuggle the cushion for comfort, to hide parts of my body.

"Okay, I have to ask," Sara says to the room but the question is for Carter, "What's the deal with you and Louise? She's my best friend and I need to know your intentions."

Carter clears his throat in discomfort, but we all look at him and I brace myself to be upset and look down at the cushion I'm clutching.

"Well, honestly? She's great... but…"

I look up at him.

"It's not love or anything, it's just a bit of fun."

"Hhhmm… does she know that?"

"Well, we've not really talked about it but, it's been a few days, it's not really a conversation someone would just randomly have, is it?"

"Yeah," we all say back to him.

"What? You'd have the *"what are we"* conversation after a few days?"

Sara replies, "Well, yeah, no one needs to waste their time, or to develop feelings if they're not going to be reciprocated."

He swallows hard.

"I don't know what we are though, I like her, obviously, I just don't have a certain feeling for her that I'd usually have for someone I want to date."

"What feeling?" Jake asks.

"Well, erm. When I'm in a relationship, I'm..*intense?* Probably the lightest way to put it."

"You mean you're controlling?" Jake asks.

"Not controlling as such, no, but in certain situations, yes, I like to… be in control... but that's only the case

when I'm with a woman that I want, to be completely
and utterly mine."
"I need another drink," I say, standing up and going into
the kitchen.
Shit!! Why do I like that?? Why does that sound
interesting and intriguing and... sexy?!
Jake comes into the kitchen, "You okay?"
I spin round in surprise, "yeah I'm good, just needed a
top up, you want another Beer?"
"I still have this one thanks," he holds his bottle up.
Smiling, I follow him back into the lounge.
Carter looks up at me and holds my gaze, while I lower
myself back onto the sofa.
        He takes the heat off himself with a slight smile,
"What about you lot? Johnny and I are the only single
ones here, y'all are dating each other, what are your
little secrets?"
We all look at each other and look back at Carter.
"What do you mean?" I ask him.
He looks back at me as though he's looking into my
actual soul.
He does that deep rumbling chuckle again.
"Well, y'all know I like to control certain situations
with a woman. What are your little interests?.. do you
all actually have sex? Because I never hear anything!"
Our jaws drop at the directness of his questions.
"I'm not going to lie, I've had to gag Sara a couple of
times."
Sara blurts out a laugh and spits out her wine.
"Oh shit! I'm sorry, it's a good job it's not red," she
smacks Carl, "He's lying, take no notice."

He smirks at her, and Carter looks to me and Jake and I want to *actually* die on the spot.

"What about you two, no sex?"

"Yeah, we had sex last night."

I slap Jake, "Shut up, you don't have to answer him." Carter slightly lifts the corners of his fucking kissable lips into a small smile and I zero in on his mouth.

"No one has to make all that noise, we are *mindful* lovers, mindful of the other people in the house," Jake says.

Oh God, kill me now.

Carter looks back at Jake and replies, "That's the thing, if you're doing it right, she can't help but scream the place down, whether she wants to or not."

≈≈≈≈≈≈≈≈≈≈

After a while of eating pizza and shoving alcohol down our necks, not forgetting, listening to Carter and Sara talking, like two hormonal horny teenagers, the conversation starts to shift and becomes quite serious.

When we are in the middle of a game of truth or dare, to shut Sara up, one of the truths got us all thinking about missed opportunities, grief and fears. Carter had opened up to everyone about his grandad and I had started to talk about Hannah.

"How old was she?" Asks Carter.

"23," I reply, "It was awful, way too young to go."

"Yeah," he looks at me and I can feel the tears pricking. I don't know if it was because we had been talking in so much depth, or if it's the alcohol, but I don't want the tears to fall in front of anyone.

"Okay, I think we've all had enough," I look at Johnny, "You wanna stay?"

"Yeah, might as well, get me a sleeping bag."

I go to the cupboard and get him a sleeping bag and some pillows and throw them on the sofa for him.

"Night everyone," we all say, almost at the same time and everyone goes upstairs.

Jake puts his hand on my back to lead me to the steps, to follow Carter, Sara and Carl.

"I'll be up in a bit, you go to bed, I just need a bit of time to myself."

He nods and kisses me, heading upstairs with the rest of them.

≈≈≈≈≈≈≈≈≈≈≈

I've been sat out back on the decking for a while, when I hear the back door click behind me. I turn round to see Carter.

"Are you okay?" He asks.

He's in grey jogging bottoms and a plain white t-shirt.

Add grey jogging bottoms to the yes list- check!

"Yeah, it just got a bit heavy, didn't it?"

He sits down next to me and pushes his shoulder into mine with a little shove and I notice how clean and fresh he smells.

"Yeah, it did a little bit, when people have had a drink, it's when things come out though isn't it?"

I nod silently.

"Hey," he says and I look at him.

"Can I ask you something and you promise to answer me truthfully?"

Oh God! What's he going to say?

"Okay?.."

"What's the deal with you and Jake?"

"What do you mean?"

"Well, you've known each other a long time, dated a little while, you never told me about him, you don't seem very happy if I'm honest. Is he right for you? Are you in love?"

I just stare at him for a few seconds, trying to figure out what to say.

"Carter—"

"Just pretend we are still writing to each other, and you decide to tell me about him! How would you say it? How would you describe your relationship?"

I look down.

"I don't know," I answer honestly.

"What don't you know?" He presses.

I look at him, "I don't know how I feel about him. I don't know what we are, I don't know if things are just a bit stale at the minute and it's just a rough patch, or if things are over. All I know, is, I care about him, and I don't want to hurt him. So doesn't that mean I love him?"

He stays silent.

"I don't know if we got together because we were friends for so long and then one night, we kissed and it just seemed like the next step, to be a thing, or if we got together, because we fancied each other and wanted to be more than friends."

Chapter 24.
Sammie.

He looks at me, "I think if you question things and you question how you feel, you're actually answering a pretty big question in turn."
I stay silent for a bit, looking out over the fields.
He joins me in the silence, and we just sit there, together, for a while.
         "Why don't you want to be with Louise?" I suddenly ask, while still looking straight forward.
He sighs, "Well you know how you are with Jake, even though you don't know how you feel about him?"
I nod.
"Well, I'm not with Louise, because I feel the same. I don't want to be in a relationship with someone, because we had sex one night, then be left wondering, years from now, why we are together. I want to be in a relationship with someone, where I know why we started, where I know I am with her, not because of a circumstance, but because I don't want to live a day without her, where I want her to be mine, where every bit of her body and soul is mine."
I look at him, "But everything starts with something, everything starts with a circumstance."
"Yeah, but I don't want to feel like I'm *obligated* to be with someone because of a circumstance, so I don't want to feel like I should be with Louise because I fucked her, I want to be with her because I want to keep

fucking her and no one else. Do you see the difference?"

"Yeah, I think I understand. So, Jake and my circumstance was, we had too much to drink one night and kissed."

He nods.

"Do you miss home?"

"Wow, that's a change of subject," he laughs, "No, well, I miss some things, I miss the life I used to have, I miss the ranch, Pops. That's about it really."

"You don't miss your friends?"

"No, you know I hadn't been close to them in a while, so no. Besides, I like it here, I'm glad I came, so it would take a lot for me to miss something else."

I smile, "I was worried you wish you hadn't have bothered, especially after I was a bitch to you."

He laughs, "To be honest, I had my moments where I was swinging between, *"fuck this!"* And *"I love her attitude"*."

I laugh in reply.

"Tell me about Pops," I say, looking at him and turning my body slightly towards him.

"What you want to know?"

"Was he grumpy?"

He laughs, "Grumpy?"

"Yeah, I don't know why, but I imagine a grumpy man in a cowboy hat and a long grey beard."

He smiles, "Naw, he wasn't grumpy. He was a good man, hard when he had to be, but he was the one everyone turned to and he would always help, if he couldn't help, he found a way."

I smile at him and he carries on.

"He taught me everything, how to ride, rope, herd, how to look after and breed cattle, brand them, how to buy and sell- what to look for, how to train horses and break them in, how to build, fix and work the land. How to shoot, hunt, fight, stand up for myself and how to always treat a woman with respect."

"He sounds like a great guy. Was he handsome?" I smile.

He smiles back, "He was, got a bit grey and when he got ill, he obviously changed and lost a lot of weight, it was awful and upsetting to see the change in him, but I tell you something, he lived! He didn't miss out on anything, and I know he regretted nothing!"

"Imagine living like that! Experiencing everything you want to do and feeling everything, you want to feel," I smile at the thought.

"Yeah, he'd have a few things to say about how I've turned out."

"What do you mean? I think he'd be proud of you!"

"Pppffft! Naw, he was really angry when I got incarcerated, I really let him down. He used to be angry enough when I got into trouble in the past."

I grab his face and make him look at me, moving too quickly to second

d guess what I'm doing, "He *would* be proud of you! Yeah, you've made mistakes, a lot of people have, but not all of them people pull it back and you have! You used prison and got something positive out of it, you've not had a fight since, as far as I know, you know when to stop drinking! You have respect for other people and you're always wanting to help others.

You're a good guy Carter and he would be proud and so am I!!"

He swallows hard and my eyes shoot to his Adam's apple, what is it with that? Why do I find that attractive?

I let go of his face and look over to the side of the house, where I see headlights.

"Looks like my mum and dad are home."

He's still staring at me.

My parents make their way over, to where we are sat on the decking.

"What you still doing up? Is everyone up?" Dad asks, as they step into the garden lights.

"No, things got a bit emotional, and I came out for some air, Carter came out to see if I was okay and we have just been talking."

"Are you okay love?" My mum asks.

"Yeah, I am now. Everyone is in bed, Johnny is asleep on the sofa and I'm just about to go to bed too."

"Okay kids, goodnight."

"Night," we both say to my parents.

"Oh, Frank?" Carter calls, to my dad, as he's walking past us to get in the house.

"Yeah?" He calls back over his shoulder.

"That lipstick shade suits you!"

We all laugh.

Mum and dad have gone to bed when we come back in the house and I lock everything up, let out the dogs and turn off the lights.

Carter and I both head up the stairs together, I go first, and I suddenly feel self-conscious of my butt in shorts, but it's too late now.

We get to the foot of the second flight of stairs, that leads to his room and that is just outside my bedroom door, and he leans in to kiss me on the cheek. He stays there for a few seconds, and I close my eyes.

I'm so desperate to kiss him, but instead, we pull away from each other and say goodnight.

Then, I watch him walk up the last load of stairs, before going into my room and closing the door.

I look over at Jake in bed, snoring, and I sigh.

I need to end things soon!

Chapter 25.
Carter.

I'm laid in the fixed bed, with clean sheets (fuck- sorry Clara) goin' over all of the different things that have happened today.

We've met the calves, lost another horse, got drunk and had deep conversations. The thing that sticks out to me the most is, Sammie and I, have had a few encounters today. Times where it's just been us and there's been real intense moments and times when we've been with other people, and there's lots of little looks between us. Fixating looks at that. What's more, she's not really pulling away.

She seems to be opening up, allowing the interaction between us, rather than running away, like she was at the beginning. Her walls seem to be coming down and it feels good.

She even came downstairs in that little silky number! Yeah, I looked a little bit too hard, but fuck it, she looked good. I don't understand why she doesn't realize it though.

If I find out that Jake doesn't tell her constantly, how beautiful and sexy she is, I'm gunna have to put my fist through his face! Because she should be told *constantly* and she should be shown, even more often than that! My hands were jealous of the way the silk caressed her curves, her rounded smooth hips, the dip at her waist, her perky perfect tits, I was even treated to a little peek at some nipple, before she went and covered up with that fucking hoodie.

Didn't stop me looking at those long, shapely legs though, as she crossed one over the other on the sofa, the little line at the side of her thigh, defining her muscles. Those were some riding legs and I wanted her to ride my… *Okay that's enough of that, this sheet is goin' to end up looking like a tent, if I carry on thinking about her.*

One last thought- that fucking ass, walking up the stairs behind her, what a view.

Right Carter, stop it now, you need to go to sleep.

≈≈≈≈≈≈≈≈≈≈≈

It was nice to wake up, when I was ready to wake up, especially after a few late nights in a row. I didn't miss the sound of the alarm, I can tell you that.

I get a shave, brush my teeth and have a quick shower, before getting dressed into something a bit different to my usual wear.

Thinking I might even go for a run later, I go for a more sporty attire, with the same sweat pants I put on last night, seeing as though I only wore them to talk to Sammie, a white hoodie and sneakers. I think I will give my head a breather today, too and skip a hat.

Heading downstairs, to only Sara being there, in the kitchen. She's sat at the table, with a load of books and papers spread all around her.

"Morning," I call on my way down.

"Oh, morning, you sleep well?"

"Yeah, great, I needed it. Did you?"

"Yeah, no one keeping us awake last night," she looks up at me.

I pour her a coffee and put it down in front of her, "Funny," I reply.

"Oh, thanks!"

I start to head towards the den, when Sara calls me back, "Carter?"

Turning around back towards her, I reply, "Yeah?" and head back over to the table.

"Sit with me?"

I frown at her and sit down.

"What's up?" I ask.

"I was thinking about what you said last night, about you and Louise."

I nod.

"I know you can't help how you *feel* and if she's not the one, then she's not the one. But you won't hurt her, will you? You won't be mean to her?"

Sammie comes downstairs, but doesn't speak, she just goes to get a coffee and keeps her back to us.

Sara carries on, "You'll finish things with her before moving onto someone else, won't you?"

"Why would I move onto someone else?"

She just glances up at Sammie and I follow her gaze, she's still looking away from us, so I look back at Sara and she just raises her eyebrows at me.

Okay, so people have noticed then.

"I'd never hurt or disrespect her." I say, and she smiles.

"What are you studying?"

Carl comes downstairs and greets us all, "Good morning, everyone, god I love a lie in."
We all smile at him.
"Get me a coffee sis, while you're over there."
"I'm studying law," Sara answers me.
Sammie and Carl sit at the table with us, Sammie settling next to me and I find it so difficult, not to put my hand on her leg, glide it up and slip it under those little shorts of hers.
Stop it, Carter! Concentrate!
"Oh, that's good, do you enjoy it?" I ask, trying to ignore my cock straining, to find his way, to between Sammie's legs.
"Yeah, it can be mind boggling sometimes, but I do enjoy it."
"She's a brain box," says Carl, looking proud.
I smile at him.

Jake comes into the kitchen and sits at the other side of Sammie.
"I was thinking," he looks at Sammie and she turns to look at him.
"We should take a leaf out of your mum and dad's book and go on a date night tonight."
As I'm sat next to Sammie, I can feel her body deflating. Sara must also sense her reaction too and she jumps in with, "Why don't we double date? Carl and I will come with you!"
Jake's face falls a bit, and I feel bad for him, especially knowing that Sammie isn't sure how she feels about him.
Just then, Elsa and Frank come in the kitchen.

"Morning kids," Frank says.

We all look at them and smile.

"We are just planning a double date," Sara says to them.

"Is Louise not going? Then you can all triple date!" Elsa says.

I smile at her.

"Oh of course, I didn't know if you'd want to, shall I call her?" Sara looks at me.

"Oh no, don't worry. I'm not bothered about goin' out tonight," I reply.

"Oh tonight?" Asks Elsa.

"We were just actually going to tell you all about the place we went to last night, they're doing a Honky Tonk tonight, we thought we could all go and make Carter feel at home," Frank says, whilst looking around us all and settling on me.

"Yes!!!!!" Sara and Sammie both say at once.

"Yes, let's go there!!! Carter, do you have more cowboy hats people can wear?" Sara asks.

"Erm, no. Sorry but only one person wears a cowboy's hat. We don't share our hats."

I feel bad but rules are rules, and that's a big one.

The girls make plans to go shopping.

"Do you mind if we invite Louise?" Sara asks.

I don't answer, but Elsa says, "Why would you not? Of course, Louise should come, and you'll all have fun shopping, but you need to get out of my kitchen, all of you. Clara and I have things to make and bake for tomorrow."

All the girls are getting excited to go shopping, and head out to the farm, to ask the men what they need picking up.

"I might go out and see if anyone needs any help on the farm." I stand up to head out back.

"You're not working today!" Elsa replies.

"I know, but I don't have anything else to do, I may as well help out."

"Why don't you go shopping with them, you can advise on what to get for everyone."

"Go shopping with a load of women? Oh, hell naw! That's just asking for trouble," I smile.

Elsa laughs, "You know, sometimes your accent is *much* stronger than other times. I like that drawl you have."

"I'll spread it on like butter, so thick you can't miss it, at the Honky Tonk for y'all, *ma'am*," I say, with a wink. Elsa laughs again.

I walk over, to where they're all deciding what to get. Asking the men what they want them to grab, for them to wear.

"We don't know, just a hat, just get us all a hat each, that will be fine," Jake says.

Sammie looks at me, "Would a hat be enough? What do people wear to a Honky Tonk?"

"A cowboy hat or a ball cap- trucker hats are popular! A shirt, maybe a plaid shirt, jeans and cowboy boots, but their work boots will be fine, just wear what you're comfortable in," I reply.

I walk over to the pens, where Frank is stood and Sammie catches up with me.

"Hey! Is everything okay?"

"Yeah, why wouldn't it be?"

"I don't know, you seem a little off."

"Well, Louise has been invited, and I need to be breaking things off with her, not having her come on a night out with us all and likely coming back with us."

She bites her lip and looks as though she's thinking, and I really want to kiss her.

I lick my lips.

"I'll sort something, so that she doesn't ask to come back, besides, it's Market Day tomorrow, I don't think anyone will be coming back here."

I look up at the sky, "Okay."

"Are you wearing your full cowboy gear to the Honky Tonk? Hat and everything? Literally *everyone* else will be and if the only *real* cowboy in there doesn't, it will be str—"

"Sammie? Is that your way of telling me to wear the full gear?"

She bites her lip again and smiles.

Fuck! That mouth.

She turns and walks away, and I just know I am a fucking fool for her.

Chapter 26.
Carter.

"Need any help in here?" I ask Frank, who is just taking the moms and babies out of the pens and introducing them to the main cattle barn.

"No, it's your day off, go have fun! Why don't you and Carl do something, while the girls go ransack a western boutique?!"

I smile.

"I think he's gone to get new jeans," I say back, "Plus, I don't mind helping out really, I like to be kept busy, and shopping isn't goin' to cut it for me. Do you know if anything has been done at the stable? I Could go up there."

"I think Sammie, Sara and Louise are going for a ride later and they've already been watered and fed, so I wouldn't worry about it."

I nod.

"Okay. Well, if you think of anything, let me know, I'll be up in the guest room."

I turn and walk away.

"Hey Carter?"

"Yeah?" I turn back towards Frank.

"*First* thing, if you *really* want to help out, come help here, the new mums need moving with their babies to the main barn and the other cows want putting out in the field over there." He points.

"*Secondly*, it's *your* room!"

I smile and walk back towards him to help move the cows around.

"Hey Carter?" Frank asks.

"Yeah?"

"I was wondering, you know, I have some money to make up, from when we were doing the books and now, obviously, we've lost the money we got paid from keeping Zara and Clover?"

"*Yeah?*"

"Do you have any ideas, of what we can do to make some money, that we're not already doing?"

"If you didn't want to spend much more money, you could do *riding* lessons. Groups of three people, riding the horses already on the property- obviously you would have to speak to Louise for permission and get Max used to others riding him now and then. Charge them $50... sorry £50 a person per lesson. If they did that once a week, that would be 600 a month extra, on top of what you get from Louise to keep Flash... that's the minimum, they might even want *more* lessons per week, which would obviously mean more money and the only thing you would need to pay out, is the right insurance."

Frank looks at me and smiles.

"That's a *brilliant* idea!"

"That main barn over there, where you just store things... those things could be stored elsewhere, you have a lot of land... clear out the barn, clean it up, build a bar, put up some string lights and rent it out as a country music venue. I was told in the cab, on the way here last week, that country is *massive* in the UK at the moment, probably why we are goin' to a Honky Tonk tonight. You could do that here, but I can make it authentic."

Frank's jaw drops!

"You think we could do that?"

"Yeah, why not? You could even hire the space out for weddings et cetera, this is the perfect setting."

"Thanks son, *they* are some good ideas and definitely some things to look into."

I nod and smile back at him.

"Carter?"

"Hhhmmm?"

We are talking as we are working, and I'm concentrating on not letting the cows bolt off. Frank doesn't seem too bothered about it.

"Can I ask you an extremely personal question and it will not go any further than you and I?"

This sounds big, I look at Frank and nod.

"Are you in love with my daughter?"

I swallow hard and I think I feel my heartbeat in my ears. But I look him straight in the eyes and say, "Yes sir, I am."

He just puts his hand on my shoulder and nods once, then carries on leading the cows.

≈≈≈≈≈≈≈≈≈≈≈

The days' work is done, and the girls are still shopping, so we are helping, to box up everything Elsa and Clara have spent the day making, for the market tomorrow.

I don't know if they have over done it, or if this is normal, but I can't imagine how we are goin' to sell all this.

"We need to keep them in a cool, but dry place until tomorrow- the cream, butter and milk need to go in the fridges in the main barn, can you boys carefully carry it all over there please, but do not put any baked goods or jam in the fridges."

"Jam?.. what's a jam? I might put it in the fridge."

I'm kidding of course, I know jam is jelly.

Elsa looks at me, as though she isn't sure if I'm kidding or not, but also, like she's trying to quickly recall what we call jam.

"I'm messing," I reply back, and she shakes her head at me.

I smile.

"I might go for a run, if everything that's needed doing has been done," I say, when we all get back to the kitchen.

"Go for a run anyway, it's your day off," Frank replies.

"I feel like I've had no exercise."

They all look at me, like I'm from a different planet.

"*What?*" I look back at them all.

"You've been working a manual job all week," Elsa says.

"Don't forget all that sex!" Carl adds in for good measure, with a smirk.

I shoot him a warning look, and he laughs.

"But nothing *structured*, no actual planned exercise, I used to do it all the time. Obviously, when I was incarcerated, the only exercise we got was a walk around the yard and the gym, so I was in the gym all the time."

"That makes sense," Frank says, "You get yourself off for a run, before the girls get back and bombard us, with the stuff they bought for tonight, I dread to think what they've come up with."

I smile and head on out.

I've been running for about 40 minutes, around the land, and as I'm running back down the length of the drive, I hear an excessive honking noise behind me. I look back and stop in front of the vehicle, causing Louise to slam all on.

"You stupid idiot! Why did you stop? I could have run you over!"

I smile and walk to the driver door, pop my head in the window and playfully rub my sweaty hair over her chest.

She laughs.

"Urgh, you scruff!" She says, through giggles, while trying to push me away.

I lift my head and smile at Sara, who's sat in the passenger side, smiling back, probably happy that I'm still being friendly to Louise, after knowing I don't want to carry things on.

I think the best approach, is to let tonight be a good night and gently break it to her, another time. I want her to enjoy tonight, and I wouldn't want her to feel uncomfortable in front of others, I'll just try not to be too full on, so the *"breaking it off"*, doesn't come as a big shock. Somehow let her know, it's a bit of fun.

I then look back into the back seat at Sammie and give her a little wink, just a *friendly* one!

I go to open the back door, to get in with them and it's locked.

"Open up!"

"No, we don't let strange men into the car, plus you're sweaty."

"Don't let strange men into your car, but your *bed* is fine, yeah?"

Louise blushes, "Shut up Carter!"

"Open up!!!"

"No, I'm doing this for you, you need the exercise! Keep up!"

Then she drives off.

Maybe one last night of being together! She needs a spanking!

I run down after the car, keeping up pretty well, I may add, and stop, as they all get out.

"Help us with the bags, will you? You might as well make yourself useful!"

Sara pops the trunk of the car, and I've never seen so many bags of shit in my life.

"What the fuck have you been buying?"

"Well, there was everyone to buy for, apart from you obviously, you have everything you need, but we had to make do with the others. They have hats though, so that's good."

"You didn't buy me anything?" I say, as I grab all the bags.

Louise reaches over and grabs a bag from a place called *"Ann Summers"* and puts it on the back seat.

With that she says, "Well, maybe a *little* something," and winks at me.

I instantly look at Sammie, who gives us both a tight-lipped smile and walks into the house with Sara.

Louise and I walk into the house, after trying for a few minutes to have a look in the bag, that she put on the back seat.

Maybe it's best I *don't* look, because her actions and Sammie's *reaction*, makes me think that the thing in the bag, that she got for *"me"*, might be something for a boyfriend to enjoy and I'm not her boyfriend. I can't make her believe I'm her boyfriend either, she has to know it's a bit of fun, but I have to be gentle about it.

I look at the kitchen table, that is filled with plaid shirts, neckerchiefs, belts, cowboy hats, trucker hats, bolo ties and denim shorts.

"I don't have that much stuff in my closet! Where did you find all these?"

"They're selling them everywhere, it's really popular here at the moment! look what I got," Sammie holds up a pair of cowboy boots, "All us girls got a pair, I love them!"

I smile at her.

I want those boots in the air, while I've got her, on her back!

"Okay, they are doing food at the Honky Tonk, an American BBQ apparently, so if you want to grab something light before we go, help yourselves, I'm off cooking duty today," says Elsa.

Everyone heads off upstairs to get ready.

"All the girls are getting ready in my room," Sammie calls over her shoulder, "So Jake, you'll have to get ready with either Carter or Carl."

"Being thrown out? Great!"

"You're not, we are just making it a girly affair, you can still come in and out, but you can't stay. We are having drinks, doing each other's hair and makeup and listening to country music."

I smile and head off upstairs to get a shower- I stink!

Chapter 27.
Carter.

I had a shave this morning, so I don't bother with that, but I do re brush my teeth and wash my hair again, I had been running after all, so my hair was soaked and due to rubbing it all over Louise's chest, it was stuck up so much, it was almost leaving my head!
Why didn't anyone tell me I looked like the mad scientist?! And you should always go to a Honky Tonk with minty fresh breath.

I decide to go with all black tonight. Black Ariats, black Levi's, a black button-down shirt and my black buck skin. My black buck skin, actually belonged to Pops a long time ago, he first gave me it when it was too big for my head, I was just a kid.
Although it wasn't made for me, it fits well and it was my favorite hat, for obvious reasons.
I remember Sammie once saying in her letters, that *Boss*, was one of her favorite scents on a man, and I have that cologne, so I decide to go with that one.

Heading downstairs, I hear the music coming from Sammie's room and the door is ajar, so I knock, as I pop my head around the door and smile at them all.
The girls are singing away to *"Watermelon Moonshine."*
They look up at me and smile. They're more or less ready and they are looking great- all three of them.
"Y'all ready?"

They nod and stand, to walk out the room, Sammie bends over slightly, to look in the mirror, to put some shine on her lips and I don't know whether to look at her lips or her ass.

We all head downstairs, and I take in the look of everyone. I've not seen so many hats since I was back home, before jail and I get a bit of a warm feeling in my chest.

I think I'm going soft.

"Y'all look great," I say.

"Glad you approve," Frank tips his hat and that makes me really smile.

As great as everyone looks, I'm goin' to find it difficult, to keep my eyes off of Sammie all night. She's dressed in dark blue, frayed denim shorts, which are high waisted, showing off the perfect shape of her hips and waist. They come up nice and high on the leg too and I have visions of myself, running my tongue along the seam, high up on her thighs.

Her red and black, tight, plaid blouse is tucked into the shorts and finished off with a brown leather belt, which accentuates her curves even more and highlights her flat stomach.

I have no idea why she is always trying to hide that part of her, but I'm glad she's found a bit of confidence tonight. She's showing off a great bit of cleavage too. Her outfit is complete with chocolate brown, leather cowboy boots and a matching hat.

Her hair is curled, trailing down her back and the makeup she has on, is making her green eyes, too much to handle.

I'm sure she has glitter on her skin, and her lips look full, pouty and would look great wrapped around my…. I shake my head.

I have to control myself, she has a boyfriend. Whether she is happy or not, she's still with him and she isn't mine. The guy has feelings, I can't be a dick.

We took cabs to the bar and with 16 of us in total, it was a bit of a squeeze, but we are here, outside the bar, that has turned itself, into a one night Honky Tonk.

To the side of the entrance, in the parking lot, they have a BBQ, and I could see they had gone all out. Really trying to bring the southern States to the UK. I was impressed.

We head into the bar and are hit with a flood of cowboy hats and the sound of Shania singing, *"Man, I feel like a woman."*

The lights are down low, and they even have some neons going, the decor of the place, is perfect for the scene. All dark wood with red walls.

They have Stars and Stripes hung behind the stage, where the DJ is set up, also in a cowboy hat and there's a couple of mic stands and stools set out.

There are brown helium balloons dotted around, of cowboy boots, hats and horses heads and a large red, white and blue balloon arch at the door way.

All the staff have joined in, with the attire and they look great. They have done a good job!

The owner of the bar, they call them Landlords over here, comes over to talk to us, as we sit down.

"Howdy!" He greets us and I smile at his fake southern drawl.

"Hi John," Elsa looks up at him, "The place looks brilliant!"

"Oh, thank you, little lady," he carries on with the drawl and I laugh, everyone laughs after me.

"John, this is Carter, the cowboy working on the farm, the one we were telling you about last night," Frank gestures to me.

Suddenly, John looks embarrassed and straightens up, "I'm sorry young man," suddenly sounding English, "I hope I didn't offend, I'm just in character."

I laugh, "Not at all, that's how we talk."

He smiles.

"I better not let my daughters, or my wife, see you!" He says, I *think* absentmindedly, and I don't really know how to respond, so I just look around the table and land on Sammie. Who's trying not to laugh.

"Food will be ready soon, the DJ will let everyone know when you can all go fill your plates, I hope you all have a good night."

"John," I call and he looks back at me, I correct him, "Hope y'all have a good night."

He smiles back at me and nods his appreciation.

≈≈≈≈≈≈≈≈≈≈≈

When the DJ stops, halfway through a Leann Rimes song, to announce that the BBQ is ready and for us to go get what we want to eat in the car park, we all head out like a herd of cattle, it's almost hectic, but the food does smell amazing, so it's probably goin' to be worth the stress, plus, everyone has already had a few drinks, so they're wanting food to soak up any alcohol they've had, and will have in the near future.

We get to the front, and they have more or less, thought of everything, with every sauce and relish possible and known to man, on one end, and plates and cutlery on the other end, we are faced with more food than breakfast time at the farmhouse, in the middle. There are steaks, burgers, hot dogs, corn dogs, mac n cheese, sub meat, hog roast, ribs, surf and turf, sausages, brisket, the lot and it all looks and smells amazing.

I turn to Sammie, who's next to me and say, "This is pretty impressive, I don't even think there's anything missing."

She replies with, "What is a corn dog?"

I smile and tell her it's a hotdog wrapped in a cornmeal batter, that it has a sweet taste and feels a bit like a donut.

"I don't know if I want that."

I look at her and say, "They're nice, try one."

We all sit, and get stuck into the food, it tastes as good as it looks and smells, and the best thing about it is, Sammie is enjoying it too, she isn't hiding behind her food or picking at it, in little bits. She's fully enjoying it and I'm glad she looks more comfortable. After we have, more or less, cleared our plates, John comes back around and tells us that there will be a selection tray of desserts put on each table soon and that he hopes we enjoy them.

I don't know if he's trying extra hard with us, because he only seems to be coming to our table excessively, but he's nice enough.

It does make me uncomfortable when people try too hard though, I prefer people to just be themselves.

Post Malone and Morgan Wallen come on over the speakers, and a load of people get up to dance, including the girls and I love to see Sammie lose her inhibitions and let her hair down.

They all look great, and I have noticed Louise too, but while they're all together and I can get away with looking at Sammie, without anyone noticing I'm only looking at her, I'm goin' to make the most of it.

Chapter 28.
Carter.

The next hour, consists of everyone swinging between, being up and dancing, and sitting at their tables, singing along to the music.

I had been singing along absentmindedly to *"Worst Way"* by Riley Green, often looking at Sammie while I was singing the words, not realizing that people had noticed.

I caught a few glimpses from Elsa and Frank, so I had to try and stop myself from looking at her, especially whilst singing lyrics about, wanting someone so badly, you don't want to talk, but to just show them how badly you want them, but you'd better put away breakables before you get down to it.

After a few more songs, the dessert trays are brought out and everyone sits back down at their tables. The music is still playing, but they turn the volume down a little, so people can talk, while they're eating.

I'm not much of a dessert person, unless it's being licked off of someone, so I head over to the bar, for a load of whiskey and tequila shots.

I bring the shots back and put them in the middle of the table.

"What are those?" Sammie asks.

"Whiskey and Tequila," I answer, "We need to get a bit messed up. This night is good, but it's too clean cut for a Honky Tonk, we need y'all two steppin' on the table before we leave!"

"You know, every time you move, literally every fucking woman in here's eyes follow you! You're like a fucking babe magnet." Jake says randomly.

"A babe magnet? Great, I'm like a fucking *puppy!*"

They all laugh.

After dessert has been cleared and people are back up dancing, the DJ announces that the karaoke is open and if anyone wants to sing, they're welcome to. Surprisingly, Sammie asks if I will do a duet with her. I look at everyone else and they all look surprised.

"I think you're three sheets to the wind!" I tell her.

"No, come on, it will be fun, none of the other men know any country songs and I want to do a duet."

"What do you want to sing?"

"Either *"you look like you love me"* or, *"I'm gonna love you"*."

I look back at her surprised, "You gotta be kiddin'?"

"No!! Why would I be?"

She looks offended.

"They're *love* songs!"

"Yeah, and most duets are!!! Never mind if you don't want to, I just don't want to sing on my own and this isn't something I would usually do, but I'm feeling brave, and I heard you singing once in the shower and you have a good voice."

I look back at her, getting more shocked as time goes on, "How do you know I was in the shower?"

"Because I could hear *water* and it was echoey."

She's starting to get annoyed, and it looks like Jake is too.

She sits down in a huff and actually sulks.

"Bratty Sammie is back I see."

She scowls up at me and I laugh.

"Okay, fine, we will sing Cody and Carrie."

She jumps up and runs to the stage, I look around the table at everyone, and roll my eyes, they all laugh, apart from Jake and Louise.

≈≈≈≈≈≈≈≈≈≈≈

I love the way she sings, the way we look at each other, under a disguise, because we are singing a love song.

We sing a song, about, no matter what's goin' on in the world and how anything changes, these two people are gunna love each other, whatever.

We sing it, while looking into each other's eyes and at the end of the song, I feel I need to convince everyone, including myself, that it was nothing but a duet.

As we leave the stage, the DJ says, "All the cowboys, grab your girls for this next one."

On comes *"your man"* by Josh Turner, a song I would want to dance with Sammie to, it's a pretty sexy song, but it's not for two people that used to write to each other and are now colleagues and friends, it's for lovers, so of course, Jake grabs her hand and pulls her on to the dance floor.

Carl takes Sara's hand, and all the other couples get up on the floor, including Frank and Elsa.

Louise looks over at me and says, "Are you going to ask me to dance at all?"

I suddenly realize, I haven't really given her much attention, and I feel awful about it. I hold out my hand to her and we join the others on the dance floor.

They all dance, as though they're hugging, but I hold one of Louise's hands with mine and put my other hand at the middle of her back while she places hers on my shoulder.

I like to dance this way, so I can look at and talk to the woman I'm dancing with.

I look into her eyes and smile, "You look great tonight," I tell her.

She smiles back up at me and suddenly says, "Carter?"

"Hhhhm?"

"It's okay you know?!"

I look down at her, frowning.

"*What's* okay?"

"That you want to be with Sammie."

I feel a bit shit, well, no, I feel like the worst person in the world, because Louise is *everything* any man would want. She's beautiful, she's sexy, she's sweet, a real good person and yet, I can't deny that she's right.

I can't lie to her.

"I'm sorry, I've tried to fight it. She's with Jake though and you know, I wouldn't get in between them, but obviously, I wouldn't want to lead anyone on myself, either."

She smiles, "I appreciate that."

I pull her a bit closer into a one armed hug.

"She's not happy with him you know? I don't think it even has anything to do with you either really. I mean, I know she has feelings for you, I'm not blind, but I don't think she's ever been *truly* happy with Jake, not as a couple anyway."

"What makes you say that?"

"I'm not sure, there's just never been any PDA, apart from the odd little kiss here and there, they act like friends who sleep in the same bed. You know, don't tell her I told you this, she would *kill* me, but it's a big deal."

"What?"

God I'm such a fucking gossip!

"She's never had an orgasm."

"WHAT?!" I say a little too loudly, whilst pulling back to look at her again.

"Shhh! No, never. She thinks there's something wrong with her."

"Fuck! I'm actually surprised she's never told me that, she's told me a lot of things, but I suppose, she never told me she had a boyfriend so you wouldn't bring up the lack of orgasms, would you?"

She just shakes her head.

"Well, the ball is in her court, if she's not happy with Jake, she has to end it, I can make her happy, I know I can. But I can't do it behind anyone's back."

She smiles and says, "For an ex-con, you're a pretty decent guy," she smiles again and I kiss her on the cheek.

"Are you okay?" I ask her.

"Sure, it was fun, I'm not going to lie, but it wasn't love, was it?! I'll be fine. Just be happy and I'll be happy for you!"

"The guy who gets you, honestly, will be one lucky bastard."

She smiles, "Oh I know!"

And we both laugh.

≈≈≈≈≈≈≈≈≈≈≈≈

We have had the likes of Glenn Campbell, Dolly, Reba, Willie Nelson, Johnny Cash and the more up to date artists, such as Luke Combs, Tucker Wetmore, Ella Langley, Carrie Underwood and Morgan Wallen, to name a few and the night is almost over.

We are sat, finishing our last drinks, everyone is all sung and danced out, there's been drinking games, two stepping, line dancing, karaoke, the lot.

We even had the girls on the tables, and I've been teaching them all sayings that we use in the country and western world. Phrases like, *"a hog killing time", "lick and a promise", "pull in your horns", "wobblin' jaw"* and *"Ace-high."*

The DJ announces one last song, and it was another one for all the lovers out there. Since we sat back down from the slow dance to Josh Turner, Louise had been getting close to Johnny, who keeps looking over at me with a terrified look on his face.

I just smile and nod my approval at him, when she drags him up for the next dance.

Jake obviously takes Sammie up on the floor and Clara turns to Steve, "I know I'm an old woman, but I do want to have a little dance before we leave, would you feel dreadful dancing with someone old enough to be your grandma?"

He smiles at her and says, "Clara, there isn't *anyone* I would rather dance with."

I smile at them, and as *"Beautiful crazy"* plays over the speakers and everyone is coupled up, I stand and walk outside for some air.

Everybody is getting into cabs, to go home. They are all a little tipsy and saying goodbyes, with hugs and kisses, I'm hanging back, sat on a wall so I don't get pulled into it all. I'm not as drunk as they are. After they've crawled into their cabs and there's just Carl, Sammie, Elsa, Frank, Clara and myself, left outside the bar, they all come towards me where I'm sat.

"We will need to either get a minibus or two cars," says Frank.

"Sammie, Carter and I will get one car," replies Carl, "And you, mum and gran get another."

"Okay," Frank orders two cabs, and we just sit and wait.

Their car comes first and ours isn't too far behind. Carl gets in, next to the driver and Sammie and I sit in the back.

She's sat quietly, looking out of the window and Carl is talking away to the driver about football (soccer).

I look towards Sammie and watch her hair blowing in the warm Spring air, her hand is placed next to her on the seat, and I slowly reach over and stroke the side of her hand with my finger.

She jumps, and whips her head towards me, I don't stop, and she doesn't move her hand.

Finally, she smiles at me and carries on looking out the window, letting me stroke her hand.

I'm good with little things like this, until she finally ends the relationship she's not happy in, but when she finally plucks up that courage, I'm goin' in full force.

Chapter 29.
Carter, Farmer's Market.

We don't have to be up, until about 6am today, but I can hear noises outside, rustles, banging, whistling.

I look over at my phone, it's 4:30am. I walk over to the window to see Frank, messing around with buckets outside the cattle barn.

Not bothering with a shower yet, I brush my teeth, put on some jeans and a hoodie and go downstairs.

"Morning, why are you up?" Elsa asks.

"I heard Frank outside. I'll go see if he needs a hand."

"No, you won't! We have got up at this time, to make sure everything is done, before we need to pack up for the market. You go back to bed, no one else has to be up until six."

"Well, I'm awake now anyway, I may as well help."

"Carter! Bed!!"

I look at Elsa and each time I try to answer her back, she gives me a pointed look. She's actually quite scary. I'm a 30-year-old man, but I'm not about to argue with this woman! She's a *real* mom.

"Okay," I say, before goin' back upstairs.

I stop outside Sammie's room and think back to the cab ride last night, how it felt, for her to just allow me to run my finger up and down the outside of her hand, the electricity was immense. I also think back, to when the girls were getting ready in there yesterday and I stuck my head around the door.

It was the first time I had seen her room and in that split second, I took in everything about it.

The cream carpet, cream walls, light wood furniture, sage green and chocolate brown accents. It was so earthly and relaxing. It smelt amazing too, fresh and floral, just like her.

I've stopped near her door a few times since I got here, on my way to my own room, but I've never done anything about it, with the exception of yesterday, but the door was open then... when it's closed, I've always left her alone, but there is a stronger pull now, I can't help myself, I gently knock on the door and hope that she's awake.

Then, I shit myself and think of what the fuck I'm going to do or say if she is awake.

What the fuck is wrong with me?

I have never been like this before. I'm usually so sure of myself, I'm the one calling the shots, I'm confident and know what I want and how to get it. But now, I'm a fucking mess, I don't know what she has done to me, I need to sort my shit out and quick.

She's not answering. She must be asleep. Thank fuck for that.

I turn, and go up the second flight, to my room.

≈≈≈≈≈≈≈≈≈≈≈

The alarm sounds at 6am and I didn't really go back to sleep, I was just drifting.

I get up, jump in the shower and get dressed into my usual daily wear, minus the hat and boots and run downstairs to bump into Carl on the stairs, nearly knocking him over.

"Fuck! Carter what are you doing?"

Elsa, Frank, Clara and Sammie all look at me, in shock.

"Shit sorry, didn't know you would be on the stairs!"

"Why were you running? Is the house on fire or something?" Frank asks.

Nope, just my desire for your daughter, I think to myself.

With that, I look at Sammie, who is still looking at me with a shocked expression.

"No, I wanted to ask which boots I should wear? Is it muddy? And do I wear a cowboy hat?"

Sammie answers, "Yes! to the cowboy hat, you need to sell things for us and sex sells, we are *pimping* you out today! And no, it's not overly muddy so you won't need to use your work Ariats, but you can if you want."

I nod and go back upstairs.

"Don't fly down like a raging bull next time," calls Frank.

I come back down, and we all start packing up the trucks. The logs have already been packed for a couple of days. So, we need to get boxes and crates, to fill with all the baked goods, creams, jelly, milk, butter, cheeses, and chutneys that are in the main barn, keeping cool and fresh.

"Sammie, can you go help your gran to collect the fresh eggs and box them up please?" Says Elsa.

Sammie just nods and goes off to the coop to help Clara.

When they come out with boxes of eggs, piled high, I run over to help carry them to the truck bed.

We have two truck beds and one back seat, full of everything for the market.

Carl and I get in one truck and Frank, Sammie, Elsa and Clara get in the other. We drive the short distance to the village and I'm instantly missing being around Sammie.

"Sara said things between you and Louise are over," Carl says.

"Well, they never really started to be fair, it was just sex, but yeah, that's stopped now too."

"Why?"

I look at him.

"I mean, you're single, she's hot, What's the problem?"

I think for a bit before answering, "Everyone knows why, including Louise, the only person who doesn't have much of an idea is Sammie, but I've not made it a secret that I find her attractive."

"But she's with Jake, what if she *never* ends it with him?"

"Do you believe she is happy with him? Really happy?" I ask.

He sighs, "I think she could be, don't get me wrong, there's things missing from their relationship, but I don't think it's a them problem, I think it's a *her* problem."

That angers me, and I have to force myself to be quiet and not to punch him. So, I just sit in silence, looking straight ahead.

We roll up to the venue and the truck comes to a stop, I get out quickly to get away from Carl and try not to let anyone else see, that I want to hurt him.

I walk over, to where Elsa and Clara are trying to get the tables off the truck bed. I jump on, pick them both up with ease and jump down from the truck bed again and set them up, while Frank and Carl set up the marquee to put over the stalls.

"How do you want these placing?" I ask.

"In an L shape please love," says Elsa.

I look over at Clara, "Where's Sammie?"

"She's gone to register our plot, with the venue organizers."

We start to put things out on the table, in a way they would catch the eyes of buyers and putting up the signs and price lists, that Sammie did a great job of making.

I unload the logs, "Where do you want these?"

Frank looks over, "Oh, just put them at the edge of the table leg, just on the floor in a pile please, there should be a price sign for those too. Just stand that in front of the pile."

I nod.

We're all set up and Sammie comes over, with a tray of coffees and cookies, for us and puts them down on the truck bed closest to us all, then goes around to the back seat of the truck they were in.

"Okay Carl, you're up!" she gets out, a ridiculous cow costume and holds it in the air with a grin on her face. We all laugh.

"Oh no!!! I do it every time! It's your turn."

"It's *tradition!*" she throws it at him.

He huffs and puts it on, and we all laugh again.

I look around, there are so many different stalls, some selling similar things but not the same, some selling *completely* different stuff, some even selling livestock.

There are so many people, country people who live the same lifestyle and live in harmony with each other, all supporting each stall and who all seem to know each other. It's a happy occasion, that people seem to look forward to coming to and all joining together.

I don't see one person who isn't smiling, or one person who seems in competition with the next. They're a real community- friends.

I am just looking around at the people, all different ages and I see a familiar face, out of the corner of my eye.

Malcolm walks over to the stall with a woman and a young girl, probably about 14 years old.

"How's it going?" He asks and Frank answers,

"Oh, hey Malcolm."

We all smile at him.

"Carter, this is my wife, Jane and our daughter, Katie."

"Howdy. Nice to meet y'all." I say, to the two ladies.

"Nice to meet you Carter, we've heard a lot about you. Katie here, is into all the country and western stuff these days, so she got giddy when her dad said there was a cowboy on the farm."

I look at Katie and give her a little smile, she blushes, deeper than anyone I've ever seen blush before.

It's cute.

I hear Sammie giggle, next to me and I give her a warning look.

Malcolm looks at Carl and starts laughing, "Oh they've got you again."

"Every damn time!"

We all laugh.

Just then, there's a familiar voice, "Awwww my poor baby!! You look pretty."

We all laugh again, as Sara and Louise Walk towards us. Louise looks at me and I smile at her, leaning over the table to give her a friendly kiss on her cheek.

I can see out the corner of my eye, that Katie is staring *constantly* and I'm starting to get a little uncomfortable with it. There're also random women constantly coming up, to ask if they can touch my hat. I allow them to touch, because they ask permission, but I *do* warn them not to remove it.

Sammie pulls me aside and leans in close to whisper and I don't miss the look she gets from Louise, Katie and every other woman, that's been pestering me, since we got here.

I lean my head into her, "What?" I whisper.

She pulls back slightly to look at me and says, "Why are you whispering?"

I laugh and reply, "Well you pulled me aside and leaned in as though it was a secret."

She looks at me for a beat, then says, "The next time someone asks to touch your hat, you have to tell them to buy something first."

"No! I'm not doing that!!"

We both smile at each other, and just as we are moving back from our faces being centimeters away, Jake walks towards us, he doesn't look happy.

"I will then!" She says and I give her a pointed look.

She sticks her tongue out at me and smiles, as I think of all the ways I could put that tongue to work.

"Hey," Jake says and just like clockwork, someone asks if they can wear my hat.

Sammie jumps in, "You will nee—"

I cut her off, "Sorry, it's a big rule that no one wears a cowboy's hat, you can touch it though."

Sammie jumps in quickly again, "After you buy something, touching the hat, is for customers only."

I look at her and I hear Frank and Elsa laughing in the corner.

I glance at Jake, and he doesn't look impressed, by how comfortable his girlfriend is being, when it comes to me, today.

The woman picks up one of everything, apart from the logs and pays, before reaching over to stroke my hat.

She winks at me and walks away and everyone laughs. Apart from Jake.

"Awww maybe you are a puppy after all," Carl says and everyone laughs again.

Katie finds her voice and asks what the cowboy hat rule is.

Everyone looks at me and I look at Sammie, who is rolling her lips. I look back at Katie then to her mom and dad, "You're too young to know."

≈≈≈≈≈≈≈≈≈≈≈

I take a bit of time, walking around the other stalls and talking to the other farmers. I'm stroking one of the ponies someone is selling, when a man and woman come up to me.

"Hi," they say.

"Howdy," I reply back.

"You're that cowboy!" The woman says and I don't want to point out that she's stating the obvious, so I just smile and nod once.

"You're a bit of a celebrity 'round here you know," the man tells me.

I try not to laugh, "Is that right?"

"Oh yes! We heard about you, singing that love song with Sammie." the woman points at Sammie, "Is she no longer seeing that Jake?"

"Yeah, we are just friends!" I tell her.

"Well, I think she should be with you! She doesn't seem happy with him!" She smiles and they walk away.

"Yeah, you and me both lady."

I don't mean to say that out loud, and the farmer selling the pony looks at me. I pat the pony's neck, smile at him and walk back to the stall.

Sammie hands me a sandwich.

"What is it?"

"Sausage—"

I interrupt her, "Like a hotdog? For breakfast?"

I look at it, "That ain't no hotdog!"

"I never said it was a damn hotdog, you interrupted me! It's a sausage and egg sandwich, it's breakfast food!"

"Breakfast, in a sandwich?" I say back.

"Carter, shut up and eat it," she replies, with an eye roll. *I'd happily "eat it" baby, I think to myself.*

≈≈≈≈≈≈≈≈≈≈≈≈

It's time to pack up, and it's been a successful day.

We have sold out completely, apart from the logs, but we can sell them from the farm, Frank says, so he's not worried.

We've made a good few hundred bucks in profit and I have walked away with 20 different phone numbers. Sammie looks at me, as I'm looking at all the papers with the numbers on. I look down at her and she just laughs at me.

"Fuck off Sammie."

That makes her laugh even more.

Jake, Sara, Louise, Malcolm, Jane and Katie have all left now, the market is closed to customers, it's just the traders packing their vehicles up.

"Come on lover boy, help me get these on the trucks," Sammie giggles.

We pack everything up and I get into the truck with Carl and will him not to annoy me.

"Sorry about the journey up, what I was saying, I sense I annoyed you."

"It's not on her, she's not happy, she's with the wrong person."

Carl doesn't say anything in reply, we just drive back to the farm in silence.

When we get back to the farm, we unload any bits off the trucks, the logs, tables et cetera and put them in the main barn.

"Is there anything that needs doing at the stable?" I ask.

"Louise and Sara did it all today, before they came to the market, they're in the paddock, so I just need to run up and get them in the stable and everything is finished until tomorrow," replies Sammie.

"I'll come help," I say, and Carl looks at us both.

"It needs two of you to get them in?" He asks.

I give him a look, that says I want to kill him with my bare hands, but he doesn't look at me.

"No, I can manage," she smiles and heads up to the stables.

I'm finding it almost impossible, not to follow her, but it's been pointed out, so if I did, it would look as strange as it is. So, I just let her go.

≈≈≈≈≈≈≈≈≈≈≈

We've had a shower and changed into something more comfortable; the ladies are in pajamas and us men have gone for sweats and t-shirts.

We have decided, to have a movie night and a takeaway, that Elsa and Frank have insisted we eat in the den (they call it a lounge). So, as we wait for food and all sit watching some chick movie Sammie picked out, Frank turns to me and says,

"You've been here over a week now Carter and I just want to say thank you. You've been a big help on the farm, with the books, the ideas you've given, I've enjoyed seeing and hearing about your culture and it's been great getting to know you."

I smile, but reply with, "It sounds final, is the next line, *"but you can pack your bags now"?"*

"Oh no, not at all, we would love to have you here, indefinitely, you're part of the family now!"

I look at Sammie, who is sitting next to me, on one of the couches and we smile at each other.

"Thank you sir, that means a lot."

We all turn our attentions to the tv.

I notice, each time Sammie gets up, whether it's to get food, a drink or to go to the toilet, she gets closer to me, every time she sits back down again, until we have eventually all eaten, are all settled and she is so close, she's almost sat on me.

I love how comfortable she is, to be leaning against me. I am comfortable too, with her, with them and with this. I put my head back for a bit, to lean against the headrest and I feel myself drifting off.

Chapter 30.
Sammie, Farmer's Market.

I love the first full weekend of the month, because we get a lie in for two days in a row.
Day off on Saturday and a six o clock wake up on the Sunday.

I'm used to the early rises, and they don't bother me, usually, unless it sounds like someone's being *tortured* above me. But I feel extra refreshed today, when my alarm goes off and the sun is already properly up, shining through the window.
It's a great start to the day and I'm instantly in a good mood. I don't actually know, if it's because the sun's already shining, or because there was some soft, concealed contact between Carter and I in the back of the taxi last night.

It wasn't much, it wasn't like we were all over each other, it could even have just been seen as friendly and soothing, but I liked it, I know I shouldn't, but I did.
Jake hardly ever touches me, and I can't say it bothers me now, but at the beginning, I used to wonder why and it's probably part of the reason that I'm a little insecure in myself when it comes to... well, anything to do with sex, relationships and my own body, really.
We don't act like a couple and, even though we started dating when I was 23, he was my first actual boyfriend.
I was always too busy for boys growing up, I was either

in school and let's face it, Hannah and I were dorks, or I was on the farm.

I started working on the farm as a kid, we all did, it's not a job, it's a lifestyle and it's one that's been passed down through generations. So, because of all that, I'd never really had experience of boys or men, unless it was in a friends capacity and that's how Jake and I started.

I'm sure it was a similar situation for Jake too, he actually went to an all boys school and when he wasn't at school, he was here, with his dad, on the farm. So, he's not got much experience with dating either, although he does have more than me, because once he left school, him and Carl used to go out *"on the pull"* on their nights off. But that was in their late teens, and it was out of their system quickly.

Anyway, I'm losing the point! It was nice to feel a bit of a connection to a man, last night and the way I was feeling, with butterflies rolling around my stomach, I realised I wasn't broken after all and I *could* feel something, with the right person.

I brush my teeth, get a quick shower, do my skincare and get dressed. I go with my Morgan Wallen t-shirt, jeans and put my hair up in a messy bun.

We always wear Wellies to the farmer's market, it's not usually particularly muddy, especially when the weather is like this, but it seems to be a bit of a theme for us all at the market. Country folk and all that!

I head downstairs for a coffee, we don't usually have time for breakfast on market day, my mum and dad get up and sort everything that needs doing with the cows early, and then we get packed up and head off, so I will see what there is there.

My mum, dad, gran and I, are having coffee, and Carl is just heading down the stairs and all of a sudden, it sounds like a herd of elephants are stampeding towards us.
Carter comes flying down the stairs, nearly sending Carl arse over tit. It's a good job it wasn't my grandma. She definitely would have fallen.
Is he on bloody speed or something?
We all look at him, surprised, startled, shocked. There were some words exchanged between Carl and Carter, but I didn't take them in, something about the stairs, but I was just staring at him, partly because he came rushing down that quickly, colliding with my brother, that I wasn't sure whether or not he had actually fallen down the stairs, or if he had been running, and partly because, this man is *too* fucking good looking!
It's not on, I shouldn't be subjected to this, at this time of a morning. He looks amazing in his hats but his hair!! His hair, every time I see it, I want to run my fingers through it and even pull it a little.
I think I might start blushing again, if I don't clear my mind.

Just then, my ears prick, at the mention of *"cowboy hat"* and realise he had asked, if he should wear a hat and which boots to wear, asking how muddy it was likely to be. I told him, he had to wear the hat, because we were pimping him out. He just took that as normal, nodding and going back up the stairs.

"Don't fly down like a raging bull next time," my dad called up to him.

Once Carter comes back down, complete with boots and hat, looking like a sodding dream, we head outside, to get packed up.

The bagged up logs are already on the truck, so we fill boxes with all the baked goods, creams, jams, milk, butter and cheese that are in the barn.

"Sammie, can you go help your gran to collect the fresh eggs and box them up please?" Asks mum.

I nod and go to the coop.

"Carter is looking good as always," my gran wiggles her eyebrows at me.

"Gran!"

"Oh what? I'm not dead yet!" She says back and we both laugh.

I stop, "I'm not laughing about you being dead."

"You're not, you're laughing about me *not* being dead." I smile at her.

"I know he is," I finally say, whilst collecting the eggs.

"Are we taking chickens today too?"

"No love, no live animals, just the eggs."

I nod.

"Gran?"

"I know."

"You know what?"

"You're falling in love with Carter," she looks at me and I try not to cry, she comes over and hugs me, "I think he feels the same," she says, whilst boxing up eggs.

I've stopped boxing and I'm just stood watching her, as though I'm suddenly lost.

"You're supposed to be helping, come on, otherwise you'll be wearing the cow suit."

We both laugh and pick up all the boxed eggs we have.

When we head out, with boxes of eggs piled high, Carter runs over to help us carry them to the truck.

There are two trays and one back seat, full of everything we need.

Carl and Carter get in one truck and me, my mum, my dad and gran, ride in the other.

It's not a long drive to the market and I love gran dearly, but I'm not going to lie, I wish it was Carter sat next to me, stroking my hand, like he had the night before.

As soon as we get to the market, I go to the church hall to register our plot and get our tickets.

I then head to the little cafe they have at the side, to order us all some coffee and biscuits and a tea for gran.

"We will be doing sausage, bacon and egg later on love, if you're hungry. We know a lot of people don't have brekkie before coming up here," Mavis, the lady behind the counter tells me.

"Great, thanks Mavis, I'll nip in later, the biscuits will put them on for now."

"Who's the cowboy?" Mavis asks.

"An *actual* cowboy from Alabama, his name is Carter," I reply.

"He looks a bit yummy, doesn't he?" She giggles, like a schoolgirl.

I wink at her and take the drinks and snacks out, on a tray and put them down on the truck tray closest to where they've already set everything up, and I have to say, our signs stood out from way back at the church hall.

I then walk round, to the back seat of the truck I was in and grab the cow costume.

"Okay Carl, you're up," I shout, as I hold it up in the air and we all laugh.

"Oh no!!! I do it every time! It's your turn," he says.

"It's *tradition*," I reply, throwing it at him.

He huffs and puts it on, and we all laugh again.

I look around, at everyone set up for the day and it's nice to see the same people that do this every month, along with some different faces that aren't as familiar. I enjoy market day, it's a good day for everyone to come together, we all help each other too, if anyone needs any change, or their stalls watching while they go to the toilet et cetera, there's always someone willing to step up.

We all know how hard things can be and we have a mix of things to sell, so there's no competition.

Don't get me wrong, there are other baked goods, but mum and gran bake things like scones, buns, cakes and breads whilst others might bake pies and Cornish et cetera.

There're also fruit stalls, veg stalls, people selling livestock. There's sometimes a similar theme on some of the tables, but generally, we try to be different, not just for the traders, but for customers too, to give them a variety.

I start wondering if Sara and Louise are up at the stables yet. They said they would sort Max and Otis out for me, while Louise was seeing to Flash, and that they would clean out and replenish the three stalls and leave the horses in the field, for when we got home.

That was a big help, obviously Flash is Louise's responsibility anyway, but I was happy I could rely on them both, to help with the other two.
I then started to think about Louise and wondered how she felt about her and Carter, I should really talk to her and find out how she is. I felt guilty about the little interaction, between Carter and I, in the taxi last night, but it's not so bad really, is it? It was sort of, a comforting thing and friends comfort each other. Maybe not in secret, in the back of a dark taxi when there was no need to comfort anyone, but I'm sure it's no big deal. I don't still have the raging butterflies or anything.

I look back at Carter, who's stood having his coffee, looking around at the stalls and the people.
I wonder what he thinks of all this. *It's very Yorkshire.*
It gets busy, as soon as the gates open for customers and we have a steady stream of people coming to the stall. Mostly women, coming to get a closer glimpse at Carter. It's all good though, because we then have them here, and can start with sales talk… he's such good bait. *I smile to myself.*
I am selling some bread to a woman, who keeps eyeing Carter up, which makes me smile every time it happens. I'm not his girlfriend, but I'm his friend and I get this

weird, proud, smug feeling, when I know women are watching him.

Malcolm comes towards us, with his wife, Jane and their daughter Katie. I can almost see the look of *"schoolgirl crush"* on her face, as they approach and she glances at Carter.

"How's it going?" He asks and my dad answers,

"Oh, hey Malcolm."

We all smile at him.

"Carter, this is my wife, Jane and our daughter, Katie."

"Howdy, nice to meet y'all," he says.

Fucking hell, I think I'm drooling.

"Nice to meet you Carter, we've heard a lot about you. Katie here, is into all the country and western stuff these days, so she got giddy when her dad said there was a cowboy on the farm."

He looks at Katie and she blushes, the *deepest* shade of red ever, almost purple.

I giggle next to Carter, and he gives me a stern look- *God that's sexy!*

Malcolm looks at Carl and starts laughing, "Oh they've got you again," he says.

"Every damn time!"

And we all laugh.

"Awwww my poor baby!! You look pretty," we hear Sara say, as her and Louise Walk towards us.

There's a little smile, between Louise and Carter and it looks friendly, that's good. He leans over and kisses her on the cheek, and I think back to when he did the same to me, that night.

There's a constant stream of random women, coming up to ask if they can touch Carter's hat, I know some of the rules around a cowboy's hat, but I want to hear him say them, I will play dumb until he does.

He allows them to touch, probably because they ask permission, but he warns them every time, not to remove it.

I see a sales opportunity and drag him by the arm and lean in close, probably sparking annoyance, in all the women that keep drooling over him.

He leans his head in and whispers, "What?"

I pull back slightly to look at him and say, "Why are you whispering?"

He laughs, "Well, you pulled me aside and leaned, as though it was a secret."

I look in his eyes, for way too long and say, "The next time someone asks to touch your hat, you have to tell them to buy something first."

"No! I'm not doing that!!"

We both smile at each other, and just as we are moving back, from being really quite close, Jake walks towards us, he doesn't look happy.

"I will then!" I say and the only way I can react to the look he gives me, is to stick my tongue out at him like a cheeky child.

"Hey," Jake says and I give him a quick smile, but don't answer him, because someone is just asking if they can wear Carter's hat and I'm in sales mode.

I quickly jump in with, "You will nee—"

I'm cut off my Carter saying, "Sorry, it's a big rule, that no one wears a cowboy's hat, you can touch it though."

I quickly add, "After you buy something, touching the hat, is for customers only."

My mum and dad are laughing in the corner.

The woman picks up, one of everything, apart from the logs and pays, before reaching over to stroke his hat.

She winks at him and walks away and everyone laughs. Apart from Jake.

"Awww, maybe you are a puppy after all," Carl says, and everyone laughs again.

Katie suddenly speaks up and asks what the cowboy hat rule is. Carter and I look at each other and I roll my lips, trying not to smile or laugh.

Carter looks back at Katie, then to her mum and dad and says, "You're too young to know."

≈≈≈≈≈≈≈≈≈≈≈

After a while, it's time to pack up and it's been a successful day, we've had some breakfast- Carter had his first ever sausage and egg sandwich, he said they generally don't have breakfast sandwiches in America, the meat and eggs are usually on a plate.

We have sold out completely, apart from the logs and we've made a good few hundred quid in profit. Carter, also ended up with a handful of phone numbers too.

He's stood behind me, looking at all the papers with the numbers on. I look up at him and laugh.

"Fuck off Sammie," he says, which makes me laugh even harder.

Jake, Sara, Louise, Malcolm, Jane and Katie have all left now, the market is closed to customers, it's just stall holders packing their cars up.

"Come on lover boy, help me get these on the trucks," I say to Carter, whilst giggling.

We pack everything up and I get into the car with my mum, dad and gran, while Carter and Carl drive back together.

"That was a good day," says dad.

"Aye, it was, we made some money and there were a few laughs too," I reply.

"You seem more comfortable with Carter now," my mum says.

I think for a bit and look at gran, she smiles.

"Yeah, I didn't really ever think I would be *uncomfortable* with him, but things are different in person, aren't they? And I didn't tell him everything about my life at the beginning, so I think I pulled away from him then, to hide the fact I felt shit about it, but things are good now. We are friends."

I look at gran again and she pats my hand with hers.

≈≈≈≈≈≈≈≈≈≈≈

When we get back to the farm, we unload the remaining bits and put them in the barn.

"Is there anything that needs doing at the stable?" Carter asks.

"Louise and Sara did it all today, before they came to the market, they're in the paddock, so I just need to run up and get them in the stable and everything is finished until tomorrow," I reply.

"I'll come help," he says.

"It needs two of you to get them in?" Carl asks.

I want to shoot my brother, there and then, interfering prick!

I would have liked some alone time with Carter, just to talk! I also notice, Carter is looking over at him too.

"No, I can manage," I say, with a smile and head on up to the stables.

I don't turn back around to face the others at all, I just keep walking- hoping that Carter will follow me.

We've all had a shower, and Carter never *did* follow me to the stables.

My mum, gran and I, are all in comfy pyjamas and the men have gone for jogging bottoms and t-shirts. Carter in jogging bottoms... I don't know what it is, but they seem to highlight a certain part of his anatomy, and it's looking pretty damn good!

I need to stop looking at his crotch!

We have decided to have a movie night and a takeaway, so, as we wait for food, *Chinese!* We sit watching, *"What a girl wants,"*- I always get the movie choice, much to other's annoyance, but I don't care, I like a nice, easy watch.

My dad turns to Carter and says, "You've been here over a week now Carter and I just want to say thank you. You've been a big help on the farm, with the books, the ideas you've given, I've enjoyed seeing and hearing about your culture and it's been great getting to know you."

He smiles, but looks worried, "It sounds final, is the next line *"but you can pack your bags now"?*" He says in reply.

"Oh no, not at all, we would *love* to have you here indefinitely, you're part of the family now!"

Carter and I look at each other and smile, I know that will mean a lot to him, being part of a family. We are sat next to each other, on one of the sofas. Carter swallows and says, "Thank you sir, that means a lot."

We all turn to watch the tv.

Every time I get up for something, or to go somewhere, I *purposefully* sit closer to Carter each time I sit back down.

We have eventually eaten supper and by this time, I'm almost sat on him, just casually leaning into his hard, muscular, warm body.

I feel him relax next to me and before the movie has ended, I can hear a soft snoring sound.

I look up at him and he's fallen asleep with his head back against the sofa.

We all giggle softly.

≈≈≈≈≈≈≈≈≈≈≈

The movie is over, and Carter looks so peaceful, I don't want to wake him up.

I grab him a sleeping bag and pillow, we arrange the sofa to be comfortable, and my dad and Carl lay him down on it.

"Fucking hell, he's like a tonne of bricks, we are only fucking laying him down," says Carl.

"He's a big lad," my dad says, obviously talking about his height and muscles, but I look straight down at his crotch again. The jogging bottom material seemed revealing enough anyway, but now, gravity takes over and it's against his body.

Fuck!!!

"Hhhmmm," I say in agreement.

We all head off to bed, leaving Carter peacefully sleeping, on the sofa, and I find it so difficult, to *actually* leave him and climb the stairs.

"Night Carter," I whisper, as I'm going up and turning out the last light.

Chapter 31.
Carter.

I wake up, to the sound of things clattering and banging.

Opening my eyes, I wonder where the hell I am! Looking around, confused, I realize I am in the den. Oh shit, I fell asleep while we were watching the movie!

Sitting up, I look over at the clock on the fireplace. *4am.* It's time to get up anyway, it's darker in here. I walk through to the kitchen.

"Morning," voice sounding like I've swallowed a load of glass.

Elsa and Clara look up at me, "Nice hair!" Clara says and my hand goes up to smooth my hair down a bit.

"Sorry about last night," I say, "I'll go get a shower and that, see y'all soon."

They just carry on with what they're doing. I head upstairs, to hear Sammie, singing in her room, I smile and carry on up, to my own room.

I brush my teeth, get a shower, don't bother with a shave and get dressed.

Putting on my hat, I head downstairs, bumping into both Carl and Sammie on the way down.

"Morning," says Carl, as he carries on down the stairs.

I look at Sammie, "Morning," I say.

"Morning, did you stay on the sofa all night?"

"Yeah, didn't know where I was."

She smiles, "You looked so peaceful, we didn't want to wake you."

I smile back.

Even though, she's had a bit of an attitude since I arrived, seeing the Sammie, that I know I travelled here for now, feels just right.

I don't only think she's beautiful and sexy, I love her attitude, even though it stinks sometimes, but I also love, how deep down, she's vulnerable.

I love how I want to protect her and spank her skin right off her bones, all at once.

We head downstairs and by then, all the farmers are in the kitchen, as normal, having coffee.

"Morning," Frank says, and we all greet him back, with a united, "Good morning."

"Work today- before breakfast, if everyone could get the cows watered and fed, Sammie and Carl, can you stay in the house please."

Sammie and Carl look at each other, but Frank carries on talking to the rest of us.

"I need the mowers to be taken out of the back barn too, all of them please. The land needs cutting later on, so just leave them on the fields, one on each. No animals to be let out yet, obviously."

He looks around at everyone and takes a drink of his coffee, "And then, in for breakfast, no rush, finish your drinks."

Malcolm looks over at me, "You were popular yesterday! Think Katie has a little crush."

I half laugh, "Tell her to stay away from cowboys, the term *"cowboy reputation"* is a thing for a reason," I tell him, and he smiles back.

I look at Sammie and give her a smile, then I think about what Louise said to me about her and Jake, never really looking like a couple and I can count on one hand, how many times, since I got here, that they have looked more than friends- not even that, co-workers.

I watch him and he just walks out onto the farm, to do the pre breakfast work, doesn't even look concerned that Frank has asked her and Carl to stay back.

I hope everything is okay.

We head off out, apart from Sammie and Carl, and get to work, driving the riding mowers out, to each fenced in section, ready for groundwork later, and feeding and watering the cows, ready for milking.

"Do they only use this back barn for the mowers?" I ask Jake.

"Yeah, and those tools there," he points, "Sometimes things like wheelbarrows and hay, but they're usually up by the stables."

"But it's never full?" I ask.

"No, never, why?"

"Well, I suggested using the main barn, that only has a few bits laying around, as a way to make money, you know, rent it out or use it for parties et cetera. So, we could move the bits from the main barn, down to the back barn, so the main barn will be empty."

"Oh, I wouldn't, Frank can be funny about things, and he looks to be in a strange mood today, keeping Sammie and Carl in the house."

"Yeah, I wonder what that's all about," I answer.
"God knows," he says, with a shrug.
Fuck it, there's enough of them to do these jobs, I'm goin' to clear out the main barn.

I start, by organizing the back barn, putting up hooks to hang all the tools onto, along the back wall, and boxing up the things that won't hang.
I make room at one side, for the mowers and room on the opposite side for piles of hay. Then I bring in the refrigerator from the main barn and put it to the side, near the entrance and sweep it all out, so it looks clean. Everything is organized well and is all easy to get to.

I then go out to the main barn, which is now completely empty, and sweep and wash it all out.

≈≈≈≈≈≈≈≈≈≈≈

When we go for breakfast, I'm soaked, because the hose exploded on me.
"What the hell happened to you?" Carl asks, when I enter the kitchen, and Sammie's eyes rake over my soaked, see through t-shirt.
"I got attacked by a hose, I'll just go get changed."
I head upstairs, looking at Sammie as I go up the stairs, her eyes follow me all the way.

When I come back down, everyone has started breakfast and I go grab a plate and sit at the table, next to Sammie.
"Everything okay?" I ask her.
"Yeah, why would it not be?"
"Having to stay inside with Carl."

"Oh, yeah everything is fine, they just wanted to talk to us and then they wanted help with breakfast."

"Ah."

"Why did a hose explode on you?" Frank asks across the table.

Jake looks at me and I look at Jake, then back to Frank.

"Using my initiative," I reply.

Jake looks between Frank and I, and the expression on his face is, expectant.

I don't know what he's expecting to happen or to be said, but Frank just shrugs and carries on eating. It's good to be trusted here.

"Do you want to go for that ride later?" Sammie asks me.

"Ride?"

"Yeah, don't you remember? We said we were going to go for a ride sometime. I thought we could go later after work, if you want?"

"Oh sure, yeah, I remember. Yeah, that sounds good."

"Can anyone come on this ride?" Asks Jake.

"Well, no, seeing as though we only have two horses," Sammie replies.

"You have three," he says back.

"There's three *available*, but Flash belongs to Louise, we can't just take her horse for a ride, unless she's given permission. Besides, you don't *like* riding, it's not going to be a slow one," she replies back to him and then carries on eating her breakfast, as though to say, that's the end of it.

≈≈≈≈≈≈≈≈≈≈≈

I am just finishing up in the horse paddock and I look up, to see Sammie stood at the fence by the stable, just watching me cut the grass.

She looks beautiful, wearing her cowboy boots!

Once I finish up, I ride over to her.

"Howdy."

She smiles, *"Howdy!"*

I huff a laugh, "Rubbing off on you, am I?"

She blushes and I smile, knowing *exactly* what I said and why she's now, a lovely shade of pink.

"Nice boots!"

She smiles, "They're so comfortable!"

"Yep, the most comfortable you're goin' to wear, that's why we use them."

Her face drops a little and she suddenly looks…. sad.

"Are you okay? I don't think I've ever asked one single person if they're okay, as often as I've asked you," I smile.

"You do say it a lot! But I'm okay," she smiles back.

I just look at her for a couple of beats.

"I better get this back to the barn, you sure you're okay?"

"I'm good."

I nod and ride the mower back to the barn.

Once all the fields are cut, we bring the cows back from the parlor, to the paddocks, to roam for a bit. Frank comes outside and walks up to me, while I am just driving the last mower into the back barn, I wanted to put them all back so I could put them where I had envisioned them, for when Frank saw it for the first time. Even with all the mowers in and the hay on the other side, especially knowing most of the hay is up near the stable anyway, it still looks neat and organized, with plenty of floor space left.

"Hey," he says, "I've come to see what you've been using your initiative with."

I smile at him, "Sure."

I open the back barn up and show him the new place for everything. He raises his brows.

"I thought, because there's plenty of room in one barn for everything that was spread over two, that it would be better to organize it all into the back barn and then clean the main barn out, which is what I was doing when I got wet."

"You've cleaned out the main barn?" He asks.

"Yeah, it's totally empty and it's been swept out and washed down, ready for you to decide what you want to use it for, when it comes to making some more money. It's easier to have a vision when it's a blank canvas, plus, if you want it painting or anything, I can do that for you, or I'm sure Sammie would love something like that, to be let loose on."

"You know a lot about her," he replies.

"Not everything," I say back and smile.

"Thank you, Carter," he says, "This all looks great, good job son."

He puts his hand on my shoulder.

We turn around and see Sammie stood behind us.

"This all looks brilliant," she says, "And yeah, I would *love* to decorate the main barn, maybe we could do it together," she says to me.

I nod.

"Is everything done now?" she asks her dad.

"Yeah love, are you going up to the stables?"

"Yeah, I'm going to put them into the freshly cut paddock while I muck out, then go for a ride and groom them before they go back into the stalls for bed. I have some haystacks to move into the barn up there too, they brought a delivery at some point yesterday and they've just been left in the yard."

"Do you want me to come up now?" I ask her.

"Sure, you might as well, if you've finished down here?"

"Yeah, I'm done, but do you need to go see Jake first? Before he leaves?"

Her shoulders sag a little when she says, "Yeah, I'll see you up there."

Chapter 32.
Carter.

When Sammie gets up to the stable, I've already got the three horses into the paddock and started cleaning out the stalls.

It doesn't need a total strip down, just cleaning up, separating the dirty bedding from the clean bedding, composting all the dirty stuff and topping up the clean.

Sammie comes around the corner and I'm just about to top up the bedding.

"Sorry, he was pestering me to let him come for a ride, it's pointless though, he was a nightmare last time," she says, as she comes into the yard.

I smile at her and carry on, finishing up the bedding and replenishing the three feeding and watering buckets, for when they go back into the stalls, while she starts to get the tack ready for Max and Otis.

"Are we leaving Flash in the paddock while we ride, or is she goin' back in?" I ask her.

"We will leave her out, she might as well get some exercise and sun."

I nod, and move to tack up one of the horses, while she does the other.

"Who do you want to ride?" She asks.

"Either I don't mind."

"Do you want to ride Max? Seeing as though I know you can handle him?" She smiles over at me.

I huff a laugh, "Sure."

We finish tacking up, mount the horses and head off for a ride.

We work up, quickly, to a gallop around the higher land, and it feels good to be doing this again. I've only done it once in the last, nearly four years, and that was a very short ride.

I love seeing how confident Sammie is with the speed too, I can tell by everything about the way she looks, that this isn't just a hobby or even just a lifestyle, it's her, it's part of her soul, I know she wouldn't be able to live without it, just like I can't.

If I didn't truly love her before, I do now.

We slow down as we get to a gravel pathway and just walk around the path, side by side, talking about everything.

We talk about Hannah and Pops again, but the happy stories, the funny things they did and said.

We talk about growing up in the type of lives we have. About family or my lack of one, again, nothing sad though, just pure and utter truths.

"Did you ever keep any of our letters?" I ask her.

She smiles and says, "I love that you call them *ours.*"

"Well, they *are* ours," I reply back.

She smiles, and after a few seconds she says, "All of them, they're under my bed in a box."

I smile back at her, "Same," I reply and she snaps her head to me,

"What? Here?"

I nod.

Before we know it, we have done the entire round and are coming back up towards the stables. We put the horses back in the paddock, with Flash, while we go sort out the hay delivery.

"Where are these goin'?" I ask.

She points over to a large barn, "All the hay goes in there."

We get to moving the hay, well I say *we,* it's mostly me but I don't mind.

I tease her about it though, "If you're not goin' to help, why don't you untack those horses and get them all groomed?" I say to her, smiling.

"Bossy, aren't we?" She replies.

"Oh, you've no idea!" I say, without thinking.

She just looks at me, with a slightly shocked expression. Not overly shocked but, a little *surprised,* maybe.

I hold her gaze, until she turns around and walks over to get the horses.

I watch her ass walk away and it's getting more difficult, to stop myself with her now.

I need her to really know how I feel.

She comes back, with the horses and we remove the tack. There's a few more bales left to move, but I help her with the horses for now, instead.

We untack Max and Otis and secure all three horses, before goin' on to groom them.

As we groom, we talk some more about our letters.

"Why didn't you tell me about Jake?" I ask her straight out.

She looks over Otis' back at me and sighs.

"I don't know, I didn't lie to you, I just didn't tell you about the whole thing, I didn't tell you the whole story."

"But you told me lots of really deep stuff, so it's not like you didn't want me to know everything about you or anything, do you not even know the reasoning behind it?"

"What do you mean the reasoning?"

"I don't know, did you think that it would be hurtful or something? Or I'd be angry? What was it that stopped you?"

"Do you want the truth?"

"Yeah, that's why I'm asking."

She looks at me for a beat, as though she's studying me. "As much as I told you about myself and I told you the truth, it was because what I told you, I was *happy* about, they were things I *wanted* to talk about, I didn't want to tell you about my relationship with Jake. In the world of our letters, I could forget about it."

I stare at her.

"Why are you with him if you're that unhappy? That unhappy that, not only did you hide him, but the reason you hid him, was because it was worse to talk about it, than it was to forget him."

She doesn't reply, she just finishes up with Otis, I finish with Max, and we are both onto Flash now.

She is doing the soft brushing on her legs and face and I'm brushing her body.

I look over Flash's back, into her eyes.

"You deserve better," I tell her.

"He's a good guy," she says back, almost defensively.

"I'm not saying he isn't, but being a good guy isn't enough. You should be with the person that you're meant to be with. The person who gives you goosebumps and makes you blush, just by looking at you. The person who touches you and sends electric bolts through your body. Someone who can kiss you and make you feel it in *every* bit of your being. Someone who is affectionate in public and who sends you *wild* in private."

She breaks my gaze, but doesn't speak, she just puts the horses into the stalls, locking them up and sweeping the main floor.

She obviously doesn't want to talk anymore.

I help to tidy things away silently, and we walk out of the main stable and lock it all up.

"I'll finish moving the last of the hay into the barn," I say, while walking over to it.

"No, it's fine, it can be finished tomorrow, it's getting late now."

I ignore her and carry on, she just sits down on a bench and watches me.

I am just loading the last bale into the barn, and she is sweeping the bits up from the yard floor.

I stand in the barn, looking around at all the hay, and she comes in behind me.

"Look, I want you to know that Jake and I might not have a conventional relationship and I know what you're saying, but I'm fine you know, I'm gener—"

I stop her from speaking, by quickly turning, walking the couple of steps towards her and crashing my lips to hers.

She stumbles backwards with the force of the kiss, but I've got her!

My hands are on her waist, and I walk us both towards the door and push her back against it, sliding one of my hands, down to her hip and digging my fingers into her flesh, enough to mark her.

She gasps.

I slip my tongue into her mouth and caress hers as she melts into the kiss.

My other hand comes up, to the back of her head and tangles into her hair, grabbing a fist full and pulling her head backwards... another gasp! I then dip my head and trace my lips along her jaw line, chasing the trail of goosebumps with my tongue, before sliding my mouth down to the column of her throat.

Kissing my way down to her collar bone, I suddenly sink my teeth into her flesh, as I pull her body closer to mine, rolling my hips into her.

Her chest is heaving, and her breaths are heavy and short. She runs her hands through my hair and then pulls my face towards hers, kissing my lips as though she can't get enough.

"Sammie.... Carter?"

We hear a man's voice and briskly pull away from one another.

I stare at her face, she looks fucking beautiful, doe eyes, swollen lips, from the kiss, hair a mess.

I'm insanely turned on right now.

Frank comes into the barn, "There you both are."
We look at him and his eyes dart between us, his
expression suddenly changing.
"Everything okay?" He asks.
Never fucking better!

Chapter 33.
Sammie.

Laid in bed, I can't stop thinking about the kiss. I can't even explain how good it was. His tongue was warm, and he moved it with skill.

I've only kissed, using tongues once before and it was dreadful, nearly choked me! But not Carter. It was perfect!

Thank God my dad came into the barn, because I have no idea where that was going and if I'm honest, I'm not sure I could have stopped it if I tried!

I do have a boyfriend, although, it's safe to say, I can't keep fighting the inevitable, I have to end things with Jake. Today!

I've never felt that passion before, the pushing, the gripping of my hips. I'm sure I have bruises! The way his lips felt, soft lips but a firm kiss, the contrast between those two things was too much to handle, the way he swept his tongue against my bottom lip and my own tongue. I can still taste the mint, that man must brush his teeth constantly.

He always smells of mint, aftershave and fresh air.

I love the way his strong, muscular body felt against me, the grinding of his hips drove my mind wild and my body into some sort of weak arsed submission. Not forgetting the feel of his stubble, scratching against my skin, the man is just pure man, he's the *epitome* of masculine.

I wonder if the hair grabbing is something he does often, or if that was just a spur of the moment thing, but I had to find out.

I was going to end things with Jake, and I would then be whatever the hell Carter wanted me to be.

I had no choice in the matter after all.

As well as the kiss, there was also the ride and the time I got to spend with him yesterday afternoon, alone.

The deep and happy conversations, the riding, the laughing, just spending time together. I know he's a confident person, I know he could also be dangerous and that he likes a fight, but he also has another side to him.

He's hard working, he's helpful, he's thoughtful and the Carter I have experienced over the last 10 days, wasn't what I had been expecting, with his past of being a bit of a bad boy, who am I kidding? He had been a *hell* of a bad boy and last night, I felt a bit of that, a different side to what he has been portraying around everyone else.

I had experienced a little bit of his darker side, and it was intriguing to me. Maybe this is what I've been missing?

I can't lay here, in my head all day, I need to get ready and get to work.

Oh shit! I need to face Carter too.

I suddenly feel intense nerves. This is worse than the first time we met!

When I come downstairs, ready to start the day and trying my best not to show how stupidly nervous I am, everyone is already having coffee and talking about the jobs that need doing.

I look over at Carter, who is stood watching me, whilst drinking his coffee. He has a light in his eyes, a cheeky light…or is it a hot heavy darkness?

I'm not quite sure, but it's making it equally difficult to look at him and look away from him.

How is that even possible?

I clear my throat, trying, just to stabilise my thoughts, but I end up drawing attention to myself.

"Morning," my dad says.

I cough again, "Morning," I reply.

I look over at Carter again, who is still watching me like a fucking cat watches a mouse.

Is he even blinking?!

Here we go again, I'm blushing, why do I keep doing this? I'm a grown woman for crying out loud!

Jake comes over to me with a coffee, wow, there's a first time for everything, I guess. He gives me a kiss, and I glance over at Carter, he looks like he's about to commit murder.

Gone from a cat wanting to play with a mouse, to a lion wanting to rip an antelope to pieces.

I give Jake a weak smile.

"Are you okay? You're quiet this morning," he says.

"Yeah, I'm fine, just didn't sleep much last night, lot on my mind," I reply.

"Didn't sleep? I can stay tonight if you want? Rock you to sleep," he winks.

Carter clears his throat very loudly and I want to keel over and die.

I look over at him and he raises an eyebrow at me.

I've never wanted to get out of my own house so much, or so quickly in my life.

"Dad, I'm not feeling very well today, do you think you can all manage without me?" I ask.

"Of course, love, there's plenty of us, I'm sure Carter will go see to the horses, are you okay?" He replies.

"I will be, are you going out onto the farm today, or do you have paperwork to do?" I ask, aware that it's a very strange question, this being confirmed by the look my mum and dad are giving me, but I'm their daughter and they know what I want them to say.

"I'll be in the lounge with your mum this morning if you need anything," he says, with a smile and both my mum and dad look at me with concern on their faces.

I nod in reply.

All the farmers go out onto the farm to start work, and I watch Carter, walk out the back door, he looks back at me with a small smile.

I smile back and just give him one nod, in acknowledgment, and to let him know I'm okay.

I walk into the lounge, with my coffee, where my mum and dad are sat on the sofa, drinking theirs.

"What's going on kid?" My dad asks.

I sit down on the other sofa and face them both, then before I know it, the tears are streaming down my face.

My mum and dad look at each other and my mum rushes over to sit next to me, putting her arm over my shoulder, as my dad leans forward on the sofa, he's on. I can see their worried expressions through my tears.

"Are you pregnant?" My mum asks.

I whip my head to face her, "What? No, I'm not pregnant, thank god!" I sigh, "Carter and I, we kissed," I finally say.

They both look at each other…. and *laugh*.

I look at them, confused.

"What are you laughing at?" I say, pretty annoyed at their reaction.

"Is that all?" My dad says, "I thought it was something serious!"

"It *is* serious! I have a boyfriend, who works on the farm, is my brother's best friend, who's dad also works on the farm and who is my dad's best friend! Not to mention, the guy I kissed, *also* works on the farm and is an ex-con, who, I know, has a slightly dangerous streak and I can't stop thinking about him. I want to be with him and I'm pretty sure, even though he has no idea of this, that I, quite possibly am in love with him."

I look at my parents and they stare back at me.

"I'm sorry, that's a *lot* of information, but I want to be with Carter, I've actually never wanted anything *more*, but it's going to cause a lot of issues on the farm, possibly for the family and I need to break up with Jake, today! I don't know if I'm crazy. What if I don't know Carter the way I th—"

"Sammie," my mum says, as she puts her hand over mine, "It's not news to us that Carter has been locked up before, for fighting and issues with substances. Is it ideal? No, but we do believe he is a good lad. I don't doubt he has another side to him, but as long as he treats you well, the way you *deserve* to be treated, only ever protects and supports you and never hurts you, then I'm not worried."

My dad adds, "And if he *does* hurt you, I have a gun!"

I smile at him and huff a little laugh.

"You won't hate me for breaking up with Jake and possibly causing some issues?"

"We've known Jake all of his life and yes, we love him, but we are not blind, we know he isn't the one for you. He's a good guy and he treats you well, but you're no more than friends really and we all know, us women, need a bit of excitement in our lives," my mum winks at me.

"Mum!" I blush slightly.

"Don't be daft, I know you have a sex life, but I wasn't born yesterday. I'm a married woman and I know a good sex life, is important in a relationship and I am very aware that Jake does not do that for you."

"Mum! Stop!"

I look over at my dad, mortified that he is in the room. My mum replies with, "You do know how you got here right? Me and him made love!" She says, while having a little laugh at my expense.

"Okay, I'm going now!"

I stand up and walk out of the lounge, leaving my parents, who are *complete* couple goals, by the way, laughing like two kids.

As soon as I walk outside, Carter comes straight over to me and puts his hands on my waist.
I quickly get hold of his arms and gently move them off of me. I don't want him to feel rejected, because it's far from that, I just need him to cool down a bit.
He looks at me, like he doesn't understand why I'm stopping him from touching me.
"I'm sorry," I say, looking up into his eyes, "I'm not pushing you away, I just think I should speak to Jake first."
He nods.
"Did you talk to your parents? Do they know?" He asks.
I nod at him, "Yeah."
"I really want to kiss you," he says.
"I want that too, but I need to break it off with Jake first."
He nods in agreement.
"I'm going to go up to the stables and get started there," I say to Carter.
"I'll come with you!" He says.
"No, you won't! You need to stay away from me, until I have spoken to Jake," I smile and walk away.
"Hey, I was told by the boss man that I was working in the stable today!" He shouts over at me.
"I am the boss!" I call back at him, over my shoulder, giving him a little smile as I carry on walking, trying to get my heart to stop beating out of my chest.

Up at the stables, I get on with the normal jobs that need doing, letting the horses out into the field and getting the stalls cleaned out.

I keep glancing over at the hay barn, thinking about the last time I was in there.

I am starting to go lightheaded, wondering what I am going to say to Jake.

There was no going back on it now, I know one thing for sure, There was no way I could live the rest of my days out, without tasting Carter's lips, so I either break things off and be a bitch to Jake, or I cheat on him, go against everything I believe and hurt all three of us.

Chapter 34.
Sammie.

I have been at it for a while now, doing things that don't need doing, just to put off, having to deal with the mess I'm in at the moment.

I've never broken up with anyone before and this is going to be extra shit, because he is so heavily involved in my family's life and business and I am really shitting myself.

I am just finishing up all the cleaning, when I glance up at the hay barn again.

Putting down the yard brush, I walk towards the barn, stepping inside and feeling as though it is a crime scene, and it's not a place that *belongs* to me, that I go in and out of, on a daily basis.

I push out a shaky breath and look over at the hay that Carter had brought in yesterday. My mind goes back to the way his corded arms flexed, as he lifted the bales, the way his tanned biceps popped, and the material of his t-shirt stretched across his strong back muscles.

What the hell does he see in me?

He actually *could* have any woman he wanted, he's perfect from head to toe, everything any woman would want, they're fucking *falling* over themselves to get near him and he looks at me, like I'm a work of art, rather than the big old mess I am!

I've never been confident in the way I look, it doesn't help that I always have horse muck under my nails, my hair resembles the haystacks that he moved last night, and I don't have a good body.

I've fought with an eating disorder most of my life and I don't understand why he would want someone like me.

Just then, whilst I was away with my thoughts and self-bashing, I hear a crunching noise behind me and spin around.

Before I know what's going on, I am pushed back, into the high pile of hay and I have soft, warm lips on mine, there's that minty taste again!

My hands run up, over his back and when they get to his broad, strong shoulders, he grabs my wrists and pushes them to the side of my head into the hay, his hands feel like a vice.

I gasp, and he bites my bottom lip, so hard, he draws blood and pulls his head back slightly so he can look into my eyes.

I see something *different* in his gaze, I've seen a twinkle before, I've seen sarcasm, softness, fun, but this look is *dark*… I was confused in the kitchen, that look definitely wasn't dark, this is!

It's dark and it's heated, but I'm not afraid.

My cheeks flush, as he lets go of one of my wrists, never taking his deep, sapphire eyes off of mine and strokes the blood off my lip, so softly and delicately, with his rough finger, and pops it in his mouth.

My jaw drops in shock of what he's doing, he's tasting my blood!

His eyes close, as I watch him savour every bit. Then his eyes pop back open, staying hooded, as he leans and whispers in my ear, almost growling out the words, "I'm the fucking boss *and you belong to me!*"

How the hell am I supposed to be in a room with another man, thinking of the feral fucking creature that is running through my mind right now.

"You belong to me." I recall.

I think I'm still burning up and I've walked all the way back from the stable to the farmhouse.

I take a deep breath, as I walk towards Jake, who's helping Carl with some barbed wire that has broken.

"We need to talk!" I blurt out and both him and Carl look at me. I look at Carl, and notice, that he looks like he knows *exactly* what is going on, he looks worried and sad, all at once and I just give him a tight-lipped smile.

"Sure, what's up?" Jake asks, not getting the seriousness of what it is I need to say, typical!

He's always so unaware of everything. He needs to open his eyes to what is *actually* going on around him, he needs to be aware of the fact I'm miserable in our relationship.

"Not here!" I reply and start walking towards the house. I look at my mum and dad on the way in and they just give me a reassuring smile.

We get into the house and I look around, to make sure no one is here, I don't know where my gran is, but she's not in, and we are alone.

I sit down and motion for him to do the same, he does.

"Is everything okay? Gotta say, you're making me nervous," he looks at me and I stare back at him, trying to find the words, I don't know how to start.

I take a deep breath.

"Something has happened," I say.

"Okay? ... well, whatever it is, it's okay, we can deal with it together."

Sure, choose now to be thoughtful.

"I've been trying to figure out how to tell you this and there is no way really, only to be totally honest with you and even if it's hurtful or brutal, it's better than lying to you and to myself."

He reaches his hand across the table and finds mine, which until this point, I wasn't even aware was on the table, and as I look down at our hands, I realise I am shaking and he's trying to stop it.

I feel like shit, like a total bitch, in fact no, I'm a monster!

I look back up from our hands and into his eyes and by now, I'm crying again!

"Sam, what is it?" He asks.

People only ever call me Sam, when they're concerned and are trying to have a soft approach.

I finally open my mouth, "I'm sorry, I don't want to hurt you, I really don't, and I have *tried* not to, I've tried to fight it. I can't hide from it anymore."

He gently lets go of my hand and says, "What's happened?"

I toy with the idea of not actually telling him the whole story, not telling him about the kiss, but just telling him that I have feelings for Carter and that I think we should break up.

No, I can't do that, I didn't tell everyone the whole story at the beginning of all this, I need to say it all now.

I close my eyes and brace myself.

"Carter and I,"

His eyes widen...

"We kissed," I finally say.

He stands up from the table, suddenly and loudly, and it makes me jump.

I look up at him, he looks furious, looking at me with pure venom in his eyes.

"WHEN?!" He shouts.

I jump again, but I don't answer straight away.

"WHEN SAMMIE??!" He repeats, this time bending down, to shout in my face.

I am shocked, he's never talked to me this way, he's never talked to *anyone* like this.

Then again, I've never kissed anyone else before.

I can feel the blush creep up, over my face, but this time it's a guilt blush, it's not a cute blush.

"Last night," I reply quietly.

For a minute, I think he's calmed down with my tone, and he sits back down and puts his head in his hands.

"Last night?" He repeats. "Why?" He then asks.

Don't say you don't know, Sammie, that will annoy him further. You're hurting someone and you can't even be bothered, to think of a reason behind it.

So, I am honest with him, because at least, hurting him with the truth, makes the pain worthwhile and mean something.

"Because I can't fight it any longer," I say, honestly.

He slowly pulls his fingers away from his eyes, so I can see the hatred in them again.

Okay, maybe he hasn't calmed down.

Suddenly, he's back on his feet and this time taking the whole table with him, flipping it on its side towards me, so I have to quickly, stand up and move to the other side of the room.

His face is red with anger, and he proceeds to pick up the kitchen chair he was sat on and hurls it across the kitchen, towards me, screaming the words, *"You fucking slag! You couldn't fucking wait, could you? You're nothing but a cheap whore, I can't believe I wasted time loving you."*

The time between him throwing the table and the chair, that made a massive crashing noise which, I imagine everyone outside will have heard, and him calling me all the names he could think of, must have been the time, that people ran towards the farmhouse, to see what all the noise was about.

The back door flies open and my dad and Carl dart towards Jake, trying to restrain him, while my mum and Sara, who I didn't realise was here, run towards me, to check on me.

I can barely breathe, and I can still see Jake heading towards me, shouting.

There's lots of noise around me and I can't take it all in, all I hear is Carl saying, *"fuck he's strong!"*

Him and my dad seem to be struggling to hold him in place, although they are managing to slow him down.

I can hear my mum, shouting for Jake to stop, and I can see and hear Miles panicking, trying to get his son's attention.

Johnny is quickly heading towards us now and I suddenly scream over everyone, to Johnny, just two words, *"GET CARTER!"*

Before he has even got back, out the door, Carter comes running in, eyes wide open.

He looks at me and what's going on around us, and instantly flies to the front of Jake, pushing my dad and Carl off of him, before putting his hand around his neck, lifting him clean off the floor and throwing him like a piece of rag, against the kitchen wall.

He lands in a heap, next to the chair and table he threw, and Miles runs towards him, to check he's okay.

They both look up at Carter, we are all looking at Carter, but he's only looking down at Jake.

I can't see his face, but I hear the anger in his voice, he's *growling* when he shouts, loudly but very clearly, whilst pointing at Jake, with all his muscles flexed, from throwing a grown man across the room, with such ease,

"IF YOU HAVE ANY ISSUES WITH MY GIRLFRIEND, YOU COME TO ME, YOU DON'T TAKE IT OUT ON HER. NOW GET THE FUCK OUT OF HERE, BEFORE THEY HAVE TO CARRY YOU OUT IN A BODY BAG!!!"

He then, turns towards me, his face soft, walks up to me and holds out his hand.
Pulling me towards him, in a crushing hug, before cupping my face and kissing me, softly, with his whole heart.

Chapter 35.
Carter.

It was great, to wake up with my girl this morning, I open my eyes before the alarm sounds and watch her sleep.

Yesterday ended up being a stressful day for her, Jake was a real aggressive asshole, but if he thought he was goin' to get away with that, he had another thing coming.

No one scares the woman I love without consequences. Despite the day she had yesterday, she's looking very peaceful now.

Nothing sexual happened between us last night, she even requested we sleep fully clothed, which I'm not used to but I did it anyway, I would do anything she wants and needs me to do. She just needed comfort last night and I had no expectations of her, it was enough just to hold her close.

Not something I usually do with women, but, I had never been in love before now.

It was always just sex, even in previous relationships, it was very sexual and without that, I've never had much of anything else with anyone.

Things were different with Sammie though.

She stirs, and makes a little moaning noise, which goes straight to my cock.

What can I say, it is morning after all.

"Morning," she says, "Oh! It feels like someone has died!"

And yeah, that will do it, bang, soldier down!

"It's a big change for you, but it's goin' to be fine, this is what you wanted. Not to be with him anymore."

"I know, but not like it happened, I wasn't expecting that. That rage!"

"Well, it shows him up for what he is, doesn't it? No man should ever act that way towards a woman."

She cuddles into me and puts her head on my chest.

I wrap my arms tightly around her and kiss her forehead.

The alarm sounds and it's time for another day.

≈≈≈≈≈≈≈≈≈≈≈

We get downstairs, the mood is sombre there too, why is everyone sad for Jake? The guy is a fucking idiot, who didn't know how to treat Sammie like the queen that she is!

"Miles and Jake won't be in work today, probably not for a while actually," Frank says.

"Probably not for a while?" I ask, "You mean, they're still *employed?*"

I don't hide my annoyance.

"Carter," Sammie says, as she glares up at me.

"What?" I reply, "He threw a fucking table and chair at you! The guy is lucky I've not killed him! I still haven't decided whether or not I *might* yet, the last thing he needs to be doing, is coming back here!"

I glare around at everyone in the room, to make them *very* aware that Jake had better not come anywhere near me or Sammie.

Clara comes into the den, where we are all sat talking.

"Seeing as though the kitchen table and one chair are broken, breakfast will be, to go today. Sandwiches only, I'm afraid. I have left a pen and paper on the kitchen unit, so if you can all write your name down and what you want in your sandwich, and I will bring it out to you when it's time."

We all look at her, nod and smile as she walks out, into the kitchen.

"I can't understand why everyone is so upset that Jake and maybe Miles, may not be coming back, you shouldn't *want* them to!" I say, my annoyance growing at their depressed state.

"Carter, they have been a part of things round here for a long while, we are angry at how Jake acted, but if we can make things right and Sammie gets a heartfelt apology, we would rather go back to having the full workforce, with them two on it!" Says Elsa.

"This is the most ridiculous thing I've ever heard," I snap, in reply.

Sammie looks deflated next to me and I'm losing patience with everyone.

She looks up me, "We would rather things were friendly and professional between everyone. It's something that's happened and it was awful, but we have to move on from it."

I stand up and walk away from them all before I say something I will regret, walking into the kitchen where Clara is.

"What do you feel about Jake?" I ask her.

She looks over to me from the stove, "Well, I'm disappointed in him. I do understand the dull feeling and atmosphere here, because him and Miles are a big part of the way things are made up around here, but the biggest thing that people will be upset over, including Sammie, is the way he changed. It won't necessarily be sadness, but more disappointment."

I think about what she just said, the wise words of a grandmother.

"Yeah, I guess that makes sense," I reply, "It is frustrating though, what he did, he could have hurt Sammie, and everyone seems more upset over him not being here, than what he actually did."

"I don't think that's what it is, I think they're upset over *all* of it, as a full picture," she says.

"But why is Sammie upset? Shouldn't she just be happy that it's over and we can be together? Because if feels like she's pulling away now."

She blinks at me.

"Sorry Clara, I shouldn't be bothering you with this, I'm just thinking, if *that* had been me, which it never would be, not towards a woman anyway. The cops would have been called, immediately and it doesn't seem to have entered their heads, to do it now."

"No one knows how anybody would react to anyone else doing that, but things were very heated yesterday and it was *extremely* out of character for Jake. So maybe Frank and Elsa want to talk things through and handle it their own way. This is no longer my farm, I have passed it down to my son and I live here, it's down to him and his wife, how everything around here is done now," she says.

Just then, everyone else comes out of the den, into the kitchen, to write their names and sandwich orders down, before heading out onto the farm.

≈≈≈≈≈≈≈≈≈≈≈≈

Breakfast was good, although it isn't gunna keep everyone goin' like the usual feast we have on a morning, but we will have to see how we get on. Frank comes up to me, as I am underneath one of the tractors, that's decided to stop working.
"Carter?" He says and I slide out, probably looking like a grease monkey, I know for a fact my hair isn't blonde anymore.
"Oh, if the women could see you now," he says.
I just smile back, not really in the mood for jokes.
"What's up?" I ask, as I wipe my hands on my t-shirt because I don't have anything else. *Fucking hell.*

"I just want to let you know, because I don't think you realize it, that I am *extremely* angry at Jake and I haven't decided what I'm going to do about him and his job prospects on the farm yet. But I've known him all his life and I have been good friends with his dad for a very long time. I feel like I should talk to him before I make any decisions and Sammie is in agreement."

"I just don't understand why you don't have the urge to kill him," I reply.

He huffs a little laugh, "The dad in me does, the employer in me wants to get rid of him off the workforce, but the friend in me, when it comes to his dad and knowing he acted out of upset, wants to hear him out a little."

"Well, it's up to you how you run things, but with all due respect, I think you're crazy."

I just carry on with fixing the tractor.

Frank stands for a little, but I ignore the fact he's there, so he eventually walks away.

≈≈≈≈≈≈≈≈≈≈≈

The tractor is fixed and most of the other jobs on the farm are complete, so we all head back into the house for some lunch.

I've not seen Sammie for most of the day, I have stayed out of her way, so when I walk into the kitchen and see her stood there, looking a bit lost, I give her a little smile.

"I'm just goin' to change my t-shirt, oil leaked all over this one." I go upstairs and Sammie follows me.

We slept in her room last night, sleeping in the same bed for the first time, but I go straight past her room, to my own, at the top of both flights of stairs.

"Why are you going up there?" She asks, as though the action is a let-down to her.

I turn to look at her, with no emotion.

"It's where my clothes are."

"Maybe we should bring your stuff down here?" She says, treading carefully.

"I think it's best we keep our own space," I say, then walk the rest of the way up and close the door behind me.

Chapter 36.
Carter.

Later that evening, I walk over to the stables, where Sammie has been spending most of the day.

I saw her heading into the hay barn, but I'm not goin' to make this a thing with us. I follow her in, but keep my distance, staying back away from her.

"Hey," I say from behind her.

"What is it with you and hay stores?" She replies.

"I have just come, to talk to you."

I don't know if that's a bit of disappointment I see on her face, but I walk over to the haystack and sit down, on one of the bales.

"I'll start," she says and I look at her, in surprise.

"I've noticed something about you today," she carries on.

Before I can answer, she keeps goin', "If something happens that you don't agree with, or if people *aren't* agreeing with you, then you sulk."

She looks at me pointedly, as if I don't have the right, to be in a bad mood.

"Damn fucking right I'm sulking and it's not in the way you are making out, as though I'm a child who hasn't got his own way over something. I'm angry because of the way you and your family are goin' about this whole situation!"

"Jake isn't—"

"I ain't finished," I interrupt her, and she looks back at me, with annoyance.

"I get he has been a big part of the farm, spending more or less, his whole life here, I know that he is involved in a lot of ways, not just, your now ex. But he threw a fucking table and chair at you, he *purposefully* threw a chair, across a room, at you! And y'all are going around as though it's a massive shame he isn't here. I don't fucking understand it, what is wrong with y'all?"

She suddenly looks angry, "Nothing is wrong with us! We just know that it was very much out of character, and I hurt him, this is my fault."

"You have the right to break up with someone. Are you supposed to just stay in a loveless relationship and be unhappy forever, in order not to hurt someone else?"

She sighs and her eyes begin to fill.

I fucking hate it when she cries.

"Look," I say, as I slowly walk over to her, "I do understand, and I know I have no right to tell y'all how to feel and how you should act and if you weren't acting inappropriately, then I wouldn't. But y'all are acting inappropriately. Like Jake is a victim and y'all miss him being around."

"He is a victim," she answers.

"Hell naw! He isn't, you are!"

I'm not getting anywhere here, I'm never goin' to agree with the flippant way they're all handling this, or with the fact that Jake will more than likely come back to the farm at some point.

My job isn't to upset Sammie, my job is to protect her and that's what I will do, if he ever shows his face again.

Until then, I'm gunna have to respect the family's decision on how they run their business and their lives, but I don't have to and never *will* agree with this.

≈≈≈≈≈≈≈≈≈≈≈≈

We are laid in Sammie's bed, again, fully clothed. *What the fuck is with that?*

"Are you angry with me?" She asks.

"No, of course not, I'm angry with the *situation* and how people have reacted, or their *lack* of reaction to be more specific. I'm not goin' to lie, I'm angry at your family, they should be wanting to kill him for what he did to you. That chair could have hit you! I get that the table was a reaction, he tipped it, but he chose to pick up the chair and launch it at you. Are you telling me that if someone did that to anyone else in the family, you wouldn't be wanting to beat the shit out of them?"

"I don't think I've ever beat the shit out of anyone."

"You almost beat the shit out of *Mollie*," I point out.

She rolls her eyes but stays silent for a few minutes, thinking.

"You're right, I know you're right about the seeming lack of reaction, but they are angry. My dad isn't sure what the outcome is going to be, he won't know until he sees him, but he's a very calm person. He has to be. Whatever he decides to do, I know it will be the best decision all round and I will respect it," she says.

"Okay, I'll try do the same, if that's what y'all want... but I'm not saying I like it, or that I agree with it."

"You're so stubborn!" She says.

"Naw, not stubborn, protective," I reply.

After a good half an hour of silence, thinking she has gone to sleep, she asks,

"Carter? Are you awake?"

"Yeah."

She turns around to face me, "What is with the whole blood thing?"

I give her a little laugh, "It's where the moment took me," I smirk at her, "Plus, you keep biting that fucking lip and I was getting jealous. It was my turn."

"It was shocking, but very hot," she replies in her timid voice, which says to me that she knows what she wants, but is too afraid to ask for it.

"Well, hopefully soon, when we get the chance to lose all these fucking clothes, that are making me feel suffocated by the way. We will see what else you find *"hot"*."

"I don't know what I find hot."

"You don't have any fantasies?"

This is getting interesting.

"I don't think so, I've never thought about it."

"Well baby girl, that's what I am here for, to help you explore all that, I am more than willing to be used for that, helping you find out, what turns you on. We can do whatever you want, find your limits."

"What are *your* limits?" She asks.

I think for a minute, "Apart from doing anything sexual with a man, or sharing you in any way, I don't have limits."

"Good night, Carter" she says.

Is this woman for fucking real?!

Chapter 37.
Sammie.

It's been just over two weeks since the whole thing with Jake.

You know, since he went wild and sent the kitchen furniture hauling towards me, breaking it in the process.

We'd had that kitchen set for years, it served us well, for our big breakfasts with the whole workforce on a morning, the time we spent reflecting, planning and having a bit of banter, but we had to buy another. Safe to say, dad took it out of Jake's wages, rightly so.

He's actually back on the farm, things are bearable, but I'm not sure they're ever going to be good again.

He came back after a couple of days and, well, he grovelled. To me and to my family.

He apologised *profusely* and said he had no idea what he was doing at the time. I always thought, men (and women) who said that, were just using it as an excuse for their appalling behaviour, but knowing Jake, I believe it.

He said it was like he was someone else- he's never had a violent outburst before.

He is thoughtless and says stupid things sometimes and those things can be hurtful, but he's not malicious and he's not violent. So, I do believe him, and I accepted his apology, we all did, apart from Carter that is.

When Jake came back to apologise and beg for his job, my dad had made it clear that he was on a strict warning and that, if anything, whether personal or professional, got out of line, he would be out without question.

My mum had let him know, she was extremely disappointed in him, and he had a lot to do, to build up our trust.

Carl had threatened to kick his arse, if he ever stepped out of line again, especially with his sister.

My gran just keeps shooting him daggers, whenever he looks in her direction. I think that's going to be an ongoing thing. She might even spit in his food.

Carter, well, he was never going to be as calm as anyone else. He walked up to him, gave him one extremely hard thump, knocking him to the floor and told him, to stay the fuck out of his way and to stay away from me.

I actually thought, we might have needed to take him to hospital, he must have seen stars. I think we all felt it.

I'm not going to lie, even though everyone was on my side and they all gave him a piece of their minds, I'm happy that Carter gave him a piece of his fist instead. That's how they handle things in his world, and I felt really protected.

One thing was for sure, I knew he wouldn't *ever* let anyone hurt me.

The men are going to an auction today, to buy another cow. Not sure why we need another one, but maybe my dad has other thoughts behind it.

The jobs on the farm, had all been done before they left and mum and gran were doing some home baking. Maybe it was a really boring version of boy's time.

Sara and Louise were up at the stables with me, and we were all dealing with one horse and one stall each but taking our time and having *less* boring girly time.

"You girls got time for a ride?" I ask.

"Sure, always have time to ride a big powerful man," Sara says, while heading over to Otis.

"Why are you with my brother then?" I reply.

Louise laughs and Sara gives me an *"unimpressed"* look.

We tack up the horses and set off on a slow walk.

"How's things with Carter?" Asks Louise.

I look over at her, "You know, I never really asked how you were, when things ended with you two, or how you felt when him and I got together. I'm so sorry, I'm such a shit friend!"

She laughs, "Oh yeah, you're the worst! I can't rely on you for *nothing*, imagine having to rely on you all the time to take care of my very demanding horse? I'm so glad I can always manage to get to her myself."

Sara and I laugh.

"I'm serious, I should have checked in."

"Don't be daft, it's fine, I spoke to Carter about it all, we were and are still fine. It was just physical."

She looks a bit embarrassed about saying that, to his now girlfriend, then quickly recovers, realising it's me and we are friends before anything else.

"You know what it's like with him, sex is good, it's fun but that's all it was with us."

I halt Max and the others stop too, looking at me.

"What's wrong?" Sara asks.

"Well, I don't know what it's like…with him…. sex."

"You've not had sex?" Sara replies, eyes almost spilling out of their sockets and falling to the floor.

"No, well. The first night we slept in the same bed, was the night everything kicked off with Jake and I felt like shit, so we just had a little cuddle, a little kiss- which was great but that's as far as it went. We even stayed clothed, we do every night actually."

I look at both of them and try not to laugh, at their expressions, before carrying on, "Then things got awkward very quickly, he was always in a mood at the thought of Jake, possibly coming back to the farm, he didn't agree with how anyone handled it, said it wasn't enough. We even sleep in separate beds sometimes, he still uses his room now and again. I've told him I want him to move his stuff into my room, but he says it's best we have our own space sometimes."

"You've not seen him naked?" Asks Sara.

Sure, that's what she got from that!

"He still uses his room?" Adds Louise.

I don't necessarily answer their questions, I don't need to, I've already done so.

"I worry that, now we are actually together, the excitement might have worn off for him and he's not interested."

I look between them both.

"Why would the excitement wear off? This is when it can get very exciting and should do!" Says Sara.

"Well, I'm not someone else's girlfriend now, am I? The chase is over, the thrill is over. What if that's all it was?"

"No!" Louise shakes her head, "Has he not told you how he feels about you? Do you not know how he feels? That guy is in love with you."

"Is he bollocks!" I reply.

"He is!" They both say, "I don't know how you can't see that!" Concludes Sara.

We ride in silence for a few minutes, while I think about what they have just said.

Does he? Nah! He can't possibly.

The silence is suddenly broken by Sara saying, "Right, you have a task!"

"Oh no!" I say, horror sinks in, this girl is a pain in the arse.

"Shut up!" She says, "When you get back to the farmhouse, you have to make a move on him!"

"No! I never make the first move!"

"Well, you are this time lady, you don't have a choice, if you don't make a move, I am going to tell everyone at the farmhouse, what is in your top drawer."

Louise whips her head towards me, "What's in your top drawer Samantha?"

"Nothing, she's being a dick, ignore her," I reply, while giving Sara the stare.

We drop back into silence for a bit.

I could make a move, it doesn't have to be sex, I've never kissed him first, that could be a move.

Chapter 38.
Sammie.

We head back to the stables to groom the horses.

Securing the horses, I go to grab all the brushes we need and we get currying and brushing.

I even braid Max's tail.

"If he was a human, he would be fucking furious at you for that!" Says Louise.

"He looks pretty," I reply and we both laugh.

We look over at Sara, who just gives us a little subtle smile.

"Everything okay?" I ask Sara, as Louise puts the three horses in their freshly clean and replenished stalls, they get straight into eating, greedy shits!

"I have a little issue of my own ladies," she replies.

We all sit down on the bench in the yard.

"What's wrong?" Asks Louise.

"Well, I don't know if anything is wrong really, it's just, a feeling at the moment."

Louise and I look at each other and look back at Sara.

"Oh, for fuck's sake," she says, "I think I might be pregnant!"

Our jaws drop, simultaneously, and we just stare at her.

"You think you might be pregnant, why don't you know?" I ask.

"Well, I'm late, I've not taken a test, but I have a test and I'm too scared to take it. What if I am? I've worked so hard at uni, I can't just give all that up now!"

"But isn't uni nearly over? If you are pregnant, you'd only be early stages when uni finishes," I reply.

"I know, but then what? I train for the last five years to be a solicitor and then I can't actually do it, because I'm bare foot and pregnant, tied to a sink."

I let out a snort, "Don't be stupid! Women have babies and careers all the time."

She puts her head in her hands and sighs.

"Okay look, don't stress, nothing is certain, we don't know what the crack is right now. Where is the test?"

"At home, I wanted to be at home to take it, incase I had a mental breakdown."

I give her a look, that says she's a drama queen.

"Well, that's understandable, that you would want to do it at home, but you don't have to do it alone! Either one of us would come over, or both! And I know Carl would be there if you wanted that."

"No! Carl can't know anything! Not yet," she says.

We all sit, looking at each other in shock.

We are shocked and nothing is even definite yet!

"It's going to be okay," I say.

She nods, "Anyway enough about me!"

She claps her hands together, with a change in personality.

"You need to go ride that cowboy! It's time to save a horse Sammie!"

They both laugh, and I roll my eyes.

When I get back to the house, my dad is home, the farmers have left, and my family are in the lounge.

"Hey," I greet them, "How did the auction go?"

"Fine, bought a cow."

"We have such weird conversations to the outside world!" I reply, and my dad smirks.

"How did it go with Carter and Jake being in close proximity?"

"Well, Jake is alive," Carl says.

"Where is Carter?" I ask.

"Think he's in his room," my mum replies.

I feel a bit of pain, at the fact he wants to keep that room, but I have to respect his boundaries.

I smile at them all and head off upstairs.

Getting to the top of the stairs, I approach Carter's door, and it dawns on me, that I haven't been in that room since he has been staying here.

I wonder if he's messy. I turn the doorknob and step inside.

It smells like him, like boss aftershave, soap, mint and fresh air.

The soap could be, because he's in the shower, the En-suite door is open and I can see and feel, the steam from the bathroom, seeping into the bedroom.

I listen to the water and imagine it pounding off of his body. The body I still haven't seen in total flesh.

Yeah, I saw it through a wet t-shirt, and I can imagine what he looks like under his clothes, but I've never seen his body, with nothing on. Just his skin.

I've not seen how high up his tattoos go, or if he has anymore elsewhere. I don't know if he's hairy or smooth.

As I am wondering all these different things, to myself, I hear the shower water cut off and the door slide open.

Shit, I need to get out, what if he doesn't want me in here?

I head towards the door, quickly, but not quick enough. "Howdy," he sounds, in a bit of a better mood, than he has been over the last couple of weeks.

I slowly turn around, to face him and I can't help it, my jaw drops at the sight.

He looks taller when he's not dressed, I don't know how that works but he does, maybe because I feel so damn small and insignificant right now.

I look up at him, with a smirk on his sexy kissable lips, his face is a little rosy, probably from the heat of the shower, but it just gives a glow against his tanned skin, how does he not have tan lines?

His blonde hair looks mousy brown because it's dripping wet, hung over his forehead, he looks like a super masculine boy bander or Hollywood actor, with an edge. His blue eyes are caught by the rays and are shining right at me.

His stubble is highlighted in the sunlight, that is still coming through the window, it's that golden sun that you get, as it's starting to go down in the sky. It looks good against his features.

My eyes drop down to his thick strong neck and I notice his Adam's apple, bobbing as he swallows. His broad shoulders and chest, the defined muscles in the tops of his arms and his pecs.

By the way, the tattoo from one arm, trails all the way up over one shoulder and onto one pec muscle, it's a

black tribal pattern. The tattoos on the other arm stop at the shoulder. On that side, he has a horse, with mountains and wildflowers on the bicep, flames going down his forearm and a rose on the top of his hand.
All in black.
He has a smooth dusting of fair hair on his chest, nice and neat, that's good!
My eyes rake down over his stomach, *oh God!* His ab muscles are so defined, I remember having this thought to myself when I first saw him, but he really must have been created by Greek gods.

There's a grey and black stars and stripes flag on one side of his ribs and I just get the urge to scratch my nails all down the front of his body.
I'm suddenly very aware that I'm staring and have been for a while.
Looking up at him, I see his reaction, the smirk that was on his face when he first saw me in here, was still present.
I lick my lips and look back down to where my eyes got to, a few seconds ago. A neat line of hair, trails from below his bellybutton to the waistband of the crisp white towel, he has wrapped around his bottom half.
I quickly look down to his legs, that are also muscular, he looks like an athlete.
A boy bander, Hollywood actor and athlete, of a cowboy. God damn you!
Big feet! Just thought I would finish the visual off!

I roll my lips and look into his eyes.
"You finished looking?" He asks.
"I wasn't looking!" I push back.

He chuckles that dark, gravelly sound again and walks over to me, then, as quick as a flash, his strong calloused hands and fingers are wrapped around my neck, as he forces my eyes to look up at him.

My breath catches in my throat and when I swallow, under the pressure of his hand, he gives me a menacing, but insanely sexy smile.

"Next time you either, lick, bite or roll those fucking lips of yours, I'm goin' to force them around my cock, do you understand?"

My chest is heaving, and my entire body is tingling, I don't even know if it's my body or just my skin, but it's on fire!

I compose myself and try get a grip of my own mind, before looking straight into his face, and with a smile, *I bite my lip.*

Chapter 39.
Carter.

I watch her teeth sink into her soft, plump bottom lip. "Get down on your fucking knees," I growl.

The corner of her perfect mouth tips up slightly and she slowly lowers herself onto her knees, in front of me.

I put my hand under her chin and tip her face up to look at me.

"Tongue out!" I demand.

She follows my instruction immediately, sticking her tongue out for me.

I remove the towel, releasing my cock, giving it a little pump before slapping it a few times onto her flattened tongue.

I then reach around to her hair, wrapping it right into my grip and holding her head backwards a little, away from me.

I stare down at her, while her tongue shoots out again, to lick the bead of pre cum and she swirls it all around the head of my dick. I suck in, through my teeth, at the sensation.

Fuck, she is a goddess.

I can't take it anymore, I grab her towards me, forcing myself into her mouth. Her lips feel how I imagined they would, soft, wet, warm, plump.

I'm filling her pretty little mouth perfectly, she was fucking made for me.

"If it gets too much baby, push on my thighs," I say to her.

She bobs her head slightly in a nod, so I ram my cock, further into her mouth.

The feel of her smooth tongue on the underside of my shaft, has me spiraling and the moan she gives me, causing vibrations to rock through the blowjob, sends me out of my fucking mind.

My sight is starting to darken around the edges, I'm almost seeing another damn fucking world!

I hang my head back, still gripping her hair, and push my cock to the back of her throat. The feeling is intense, I can feel her throat close around me, as she swallows me down.

Looking down at her face, I see her tears forming, falling down the side of her cheeks and she looks like a fucking dream!

"You're so good at taking my cock, in that filthy little whore mouth of yours," I say.

Her eyes widen even more, as I continue pushing into the back of her throat. Gripping her hair tightly.

"Remember baby, if it gets too much, you need to let me know."

She moans around me, and runs her tongue up and down my length, while holding me deep.

My head falls back again, breathing getting heavier and shallower.

"You're such a good girl, you look amazing on your knees for me," I breathe out, while thrusting in and out of her throat.

"I wonder if your pussy will feel this fucking good!
"You're driving me wild," I say, while pumping in and out of her mouth, still going as deep as she is allowing me to go.

She brings her hands up as far as she can reach and drags her nails down my chest and stomach.
I look down at her, to make sure she's okay and feel her smile, slightly, around me.
One of her hands land on my hip, to steady herself, while the other cups and massages my balls, it's almost too much to take, I can barely see now.
Everything feels mind blowing, I've never had it this good before.

My breathing speeds up even more and I can feel the pressure brewing.
"I'm close baby, where do you want me to come?"
She puts both of her hands around the bottom of my back, and pulls me further down her throat, choking around me.
I take it, she wants to fucking milk me dry.
My thrusts get more hectic, and the rhythm is out.
I'm about to explode in her mouth and I'm seeing stars.
"FUUUUUUUUUUUUCCCCKKKKK!!!" I growl out, as she drains me, sucking the fucking life out of me and swallowing, everything I have to offer, down.

I let go of her hair, slowly, because my muscles aren't working, they're not connecting to my brain.
She pops her lips off my cock, which is insanely sensitive right now, so the sensation of the pop, sends me feral.

My baby, then looks up at me with a smile, while licking every trace of me from her lips.

I collapse onto the bed, it's a good job we were so close to it because there was no way my legs were gunna keep me upright.

She crawls onto the bed next to me and I feel like fucking Jello.

"What the fuck are you doing to me?" I say, to the most beautiful woman I have ever seen, in my entire life, the one who is all mine.

≈≈≈≈≈≈≈≈≈≈≈

We lay there on the bed for a while, her head on my chest, my arms wrapped tightly around her.

"Are we okay?" She asks.

"Are we okay?" I say back, "Why wouldn't we be?"

"It's been awkward for the past two week, surely it's not just me who's felt it," she says.

"Baby, it's not been awkward. I just don't like people hurting you or any sort of threat of that happening. You're the only thing that matters in my life. As your boyfriend, I was angry that people weren't as infuriated as I was, but let's just move on from that now."

She looks up at me, from my chest and I look down, into her beautiful green eyes and smile.

"That blowjob was fucking amazing," I say.

"It was the first time," she answers me.

I sit up, knocking her off my chest.

"Carter!" She squeals.

"Sorry!" I say, looking at her in shock… "What?" I mean, I'm pretty glad to hear she hasn't had another man's dick in her mouth but I'm very surprised, with the skill she has and just the cultures of the modern day. *People have oral sex, it's a normal part of a sex life.*

Although, I don't always receive, I prefer to give, but the thing she just did to me, was fucking incredible!

"There's no way you haven't done that before!" I say to her.

She smiles, seemingly proud of herself.

"There's only ever been Jake and we never had oral sex, it wasn't a thing we ever wanted."

"He never went down on you?" I ask.

"No, but it's fine, I wasn't ever into all that. I didn't know how I felt about it."

I'm silent for a bit, thinking to myself.

She's going to find out how she feels about it, that's for sure.

≈≈≈≈≈≈≈≈≈≈≈

We are all sat on the couches in the den, watching something on tv.

It's some television program about buying and selling, not my kind of thing, but I'm not really thinking about what's on the tv.

Sammie is sat in my lap, curled into me with her head on my shoulder and my hand is trailing up and down the outside of her thigh, counting down the moments, until I can have my head, buried between them.

Chapter 40.
Sammie.

I don't know what got into me, I never would have thought I would have had the confidence, to act the way I did with Carter.

To follow his instruction without shying away, to have his knob in my mouth whilst looking into his eyes. Where has this Sammie come from? Don't get me wrong, I've not turned into a sexual mastermind or anything.

In fact, when we went to bed last night, I was incredibly nervous and dreading anything else happening between us.

I loved giving him a blowjob, I loved the way his body looked, perfection from head to toe. I didn't think I would be able to handle the size of his dick though. It was *colossal!* No wonder he is so confident and I'm not going to lie, when we do eventually have sex, I'm a little worried about how it's going to fit! I loved the way his dick felt, the way he tasted, and I would have done that over and over all night, but the idea of anything else happening between us, especially anything, where I would have to be naked and vulnerable, terrifies me.

Growing up, I was overweight and it's one of the things Mollie used to bring up in school, all the time.

I did lose weight, and I know I did, but I still think of myself, as I was before.

My mum says that she thinks I have body dysmorphia, I'm not too sure, I just don't see what others seem to want me to believe.

I know I don't have a flat stomach, I know parts of me jiggle when I move. I have fat thighs,

I'm not blind, I can see all these things and although Jake used to like having sex and he used to say he fancied me, he never seemed to reassure me when I was having a bad day.

If I said I felt fat, he would say things like *"well just eat an apple."* and if I was enjoying my food, he would point out the fact that I have a healthy appetite. I don't think he meant it to come across the way it did to me, I think he was saying it in a positive way, like *"who wants a stick for a girlfriend?!"*. But sometimes a woman just wants to hear *"you look good"*.

If I had a new dress and I asked if he liked it, he would be too honest! He would say things like *"hmm, it's not the best."*

Friends were there to give you honest opinions and advice, boyfriends are supposed to say something like *"would look better on the bedroom floor"*.

So yeah, I was very self-conscious about the way I looked, especially naked and I was scared, of the chance of Carter wanting anything last night, which would mean I would have to be in that situation with him.

He is so much more experienced, he knows what he likes and what he's doing. He's forceful and confident and he looks so fucking good naked!
My sexual experiences involved, laying down and praying it was over soon.

Being in bed with him last night, I reverted back into my shell.
He was very touchy feely, requesting that we didn't wear all the clothes we had been.
He was naked, which was great, why would you not be, when you looked that good?! But I couldn't get past a t-shirt, so I went with knickers and a t-shirt. That was naked enough!
We were kissing a lot, and he was pulling me close to him, with my legs wrapped around his waist, which felt great, it really did, but once I could feel that he was rock hard and notching against my centre, I froze.
I froze like an idiot!
"I can't," I remember saying to him, and although he respected my choice and moved away to give me my space, I could see the disappointment on his face.

I go downstairs and help my mum and gran, with some housework, I'm only needed at the stable today but I'm going to go over later.
All the men are working on the farm and there's enough of them to do what's needed, without me really.
I sit down on the sofa in the middle of dusting and my mind drifts to thoughts of yesterday. I can't think of anything else, I just can't get over how perfect he looked, how perfect he felt, how perfect he is!

I *know* deep down that he's going to end up leaving me.
Even if he never sees that I'm not even in the same
league as him, he's going to get fed up of my
insecurities, scaring me away from giving him what
men need.

I don't want to lose him, but it's only a matter of time.

My mum comes in, "Have you done in here?"
She asks.

"Oh, erm, yeah."

I haven't but it looks clean.

I don't feel like cleaning.

I should feel great about yesterday, for that time,
making him feel the way he did, I felt powerful. But I'm
terrified. I am terrified of what happens next, whichever
way it goes.

"Hey!" Sara calls out, sounding quite chipper!

"I'm in the room," I shout back.

Her and Louise come through and sit down opposite
me.

"So?" Sara says, "How did it go? Did you jump his
bones? Or at least, one bone?!" She wiggles her
eyebrows.

I roll my eyes and they both giggle.

"No, not exactly," I tell them.

"Sammie!" Sara replies, "Why?!!!"

"I'm not saying nothing happened, but we didn't have
sex."

"Oh?" Asks Louise, prompting me to spill.

"Mouth work, to put it politely," I say.

"Oooooh, he's good with his tongue, isn't he?" Louise
says, then immediately apologises, realising, how

strange it is that my friend and my boyfriend, have been together in that way.

I feel a bit sick now, if I'm honest.

"I wouldn't know, I was the one using the tongue."

Again, another awkward statement, but a bit better than the last, "He didn't let me suck him off," she says.

Fucking hell.

"But he didn't return the favour?" Sara says, "What a selfish twat!"

I laugh, "No, I didn't let anything else happen."

"Let it!" They both say at the same time.

"Definitely!" Says Louise, "Let him, you'll see that you are in fact, *not* broken and that you can have an orgasm!"

"Anyway, enough about all that, what's going on with you?" I ask Sara, "What's happening with the p—"

I am cut off by Carl and Carter coming into the room. Carter comes over to us.

"Hi ladies," he says, then grabs me around the waist and kisses me.

Carl sits down next to Sara and puts his hand on her knee.

"Hi," we all reply.

"Carter, can I have a word? Upstairs? I need to talk to you."

He looks at me with concern, "Sure."

He smiles at everyone, before standing up and following me upstairs.

We get up to my bedroom and Carter sits on the bed while I shut the door behind us.

"What's wrong?" He asks.

I sit down next to him.

"I just feel like I need to talk to you, about yesterday and last night, the way that a sexy afternoon changed into a bland night. I feel I ruined the mood in the end."

"You didn't ruin anything, that was an *amazing* blowjob and if you didn't feel comfortable goin' any further, then that's okay. I'm not gunna lie, I wish you *had* let things go further, but we have forever."

My eyes snap to his, "Forever?"

"Well, yeah, I hope so," he smiles.

"What is it that stops you though? Why do you shy away?" He asks.

"I don't think it's any secret that I don't have a lot of confidence in the way I look. I don't like my body, I'm not as slim as the likes of Louise and probably every other woman you have been with."

He's frowning at me.

"Why are you looking at me like that?" I ask.

"Just wondering where you buy your mirrors, because there's something not quite right about them," he replies.

I huff out a laugh. "Idiot."

"Look, I'm not going to push you, to do something you're not comfortable with, but I do want to push you into finding your boundaries and what you're into and not into. So instead of getting stuck inside of your head and pulling yourself apart, tell me what you are interested in trying."

"I don't know, I've never really thought about it before," I reply honestly.

"Well, what we did yesterday, the way I acted, the way I spoke to you, was you into that?"

I nod.

"I thought that was sexy, I liked everything about it, but then when I think of us building on that, branching out, doing other stuff, you know. I panic."

He looks at me as though he's trying to think of what to say.

"I'm not used to reassurance, I'm not used to feeling sexy or even sexual, I'm not used to being told things like that, or being made to feel good about myself, or anything I'm doing."

I look down.

Carter puts his finger under my chin and lifts my face gently, looking into my eyes.

"No one comes close to you, you are beautiful inside and out, there's not one thing about you I would change, and I am the *luckiest* man alive to be able to call you mine," he says, before kissing me, slowly and softly.

≈≈≈≈≈≈≈≈≈≈≈

It's late evening now and I've been up at the stable, grooming, watering and feeding the horses for hours. Louise was up here with me earlier, so she sorted Flash out before she left, giving Sara a lift home on her way.

I've mucked out all the stalls and all three horses are back in for the night.

Just as I am sweeping the last bits up and getting rid of the rubbish, I spin around, after sensing that I was being watched.

I put my hand on my chest and breathe heavily, I can feel my heart jumping out of my body.

"Why do you keep creeping up on me?" I say, as Carter walks slowly towards the entrance of the main stable.

I swallow and watch his movement, slow and purposeful. He's staring into my eyes.

I swallow again.

He stops, just inside the main doors and says, "I was thinking about what you said, how you feel about yourself, how you don't know what you're into. How no one has ever made you feel the way, I believe you should have been made to feel, every single day. We have to rectify that."

I watch him, as his lips tip into a dark smirk, before he turns around and slides the stable doors closed, with a very audible *click*.

Chapter 41.
Carter.

I slide the stable doors closed, with an audible *click* and slowly turn to face Sammie.

She's looking at me, doe eyed and her pretty lips are parted slightly.

I stalk towards her, she's frozen in place, just staring at me.

Not moving, not speaking, not even blinking.

With every slow step I take towards her, I make sure to tell her something that should make her ooze confidence,

"1- your smile lights up any room,

2-your eyes are incredible,

3-you're beautiful inside and out,

4-you're sexy as fuck,

5 -your tits are amazing,

6- you're smart, funny, and loving... I'm goin' to run out of steps,"

I smile.

"7- you've got a fuckable ass,

8-I love the way your figure curves into a *perfect* hourglass, women *pay* for that!"

I've run out of steps but I'm nowhere near finished with the compliments.

I reach her and put my hand out to the side of us, pulling the light switch, turning on the light.

"What do you need the light for?" She finally speaks.

"So I can see your impeccable body, so I can see all your reactions," I answer.

I take a hold of her hand and slowly spin her, like in a dance.

When she is back facing me, she gives me a confused look.

I gently pull her towards me, with the hand I spun her with and put my other hand on her cheek, lifting her face to mine.

I kiss her, slowly, softly and passionately, finishing the kiss with a little soft nip of her bottom lip. *No blood this time.*

When I pull back, to look her in the eyes, I tell her, "By the time we leave this stable, you're not going to doubt anything about yourself. You will know only the truth. Truths like…"

I kiss the side of her neck, just under her ear, "How milky and clear your skin is,"

I lower the kiss to the curve of her neck, where it meets her shoulder, "How soft and delicate it feels under my hands and lips."

Moving my lips across to her collar bone, I whisper, "How every time I think about you, it drives me *wild.*"

I slide my fingers firmly, over all the areas I have just kissed, letting them trail further down, to the side of her breasts, down her waist and to the hem of her t-shirt.

I take a grip of her top and she freezes.

Whispering in her ear, I continue, "How I've not been able to shake you from my mind, since your very first letter, the letter where I was only a number to you and you had no idea, what my name even was."
I gently slide her t-shirt up her torso and surprisingly, she lifts her arms for me.

When I get to removing the t-shirt, completely, and it slides off her hands, I keep her arms held up above her head, while I scatter soft kisses, the whole length of her arms, gliding my fingers to follow my lips.

"Imagine that! You didn't even know my name and you had already *branded* yourself into my entire *soul!*"
Her breath hitches.
I glide my hands around the back of her, stroking her shoulder blades and over the top of her back, unclasping her bra.
Her amazing tits spring free and I smile, like a hormonal teenager, who has just discovered a way to get free porn.
She bites her lip.
"Told you your tits are amazing," I stroke my hands over her generous, smooth breasts, giving them a gentle squeeze, her eyes flutter closed, so I give her nipples a twang.
She gasps and her eyes fly open.
"You like that?" I smile at her.

She doesn't reply, she just watches me, listens to me, takes everything in.
"You have an incredible, beautiful, sexy body, Sammie. I need you to believe that." I grab her chin, roughly and

hold it tight, "If I could look at one thing, for the rest of my life, it would be you, like this," I say, as I start to unbutton her jeans and drag them down over her curvaceous, but firm hips.

I bend down to remove them completely, her hands on my shoulders as she steps out of them, trailing my fingers up her long, shapely legs, on my way back to standing upright.

She keeps her hands on my shoulders the whole time.

I step back and look at her.

"Fucking perfection," I whisper.

She starts to squirm, away from my gaze.

"Don't shy away baby, the only way I want you wiggling and writhing, is due to the *intense* orgasm that's goin' to burst out of you."

She's stood with nothing but a black, lacy thong and she looks like all my Christmases have come at once.

I walk over to the hooks at the side of the stalls, where there is a long rope hanging.

Unhooking the rope, I head back towards Sammie.

"Hold out your hands," I tell her.

"What are you doing with that?" She asks, eyes wide.

"I'd *never* hurt you, I have a few more things to tell you before we leave, but I need to know you trust me first."

I look her in the eyes, "do you trust me?"

She nods, so I take her hands and hold them both together, out, between us both.

She keeps them there, while she watches me put a Honda knot into the end of the rope, before looping it over her wrists.

Pulling it tight, the loop restrains her wrists, holding both hands firmly together.

Her eyes snap up to mine and I smile.

I then throw the other end of the rope, up over one of the ceiling beams and she watches, as though she has only just realized, the beams are there.

She swallows hard.

Then, I pull the rope, towards one of the posts on a stall, forcing her arms *up high*, above her head, and when I'm satisfied, that she is on her tip toes enough, I tie the end around the post, to secure it.

"Carter?!"

She seems unsure.

"Shhh baby, everything is going to be okay, like I said, I have a few more things I need to tell you."

She swallows and nods, but she looks a little wary.

I walk up behind her and wrap my fist in her hair, pulling her head back and to the side slightly, so I can suck and bite her neck, "Your hair is so soft, it smells amazing too and I want to see it, cascading over your bare skin, as you save a horse," I smirk and she rolls her lips.

I bite down on her neck, another gasp.

Soothing the bite, with soft, slow licks, I continue... "I love the way your lips look around my cock, seeing you choking on it sends me feral," I say as I let my hands wander, slowly, all over her very exposed body.

I can see and appreciate every inch of her when she is restrained like this.

I push my groin against her sweet, firm ass, "I want you to know that there isn't a grain of your skin that I don't

want to taste, there isn't an entrance I don't want to stuff. I want to *own* every part of you, your body and soul! You're mine baby girl, but don't be mistaken,"
I walk around the front of her body,
"That doesn't mean that I won't get down on my knees for you."

I do just that, I lower to my knees in front of her, sliding my palms down the length of her smooth skin, looking up at her face the whole time.
When I am on my knees, I put my hands around her ass and lift her legs up, to slip over my shoulders.
She's now suspended in the air by her hands, while her sexy, smooth, fucking legs are hooked over my shoulder muscles.
"Put your weight onto my shoulders, otherwise your arms are gunna hurt," I say.
"No, I'm not putting my weight on you, I'm heavy," she replies, breathing quickly.
I look up at her, "Put your fucking weight on me," I snarl, while I tear her panties in half, to get a look at everything she has to offer.
Fuck yes! She's already glistening.

I look up at her face again, she's flushed and unsure.
"Just relax and enjoy it baby, but don't you dare close your fucking eyes!"
I glide my tongue all through her slit, from her center to the little sensitive bud of nerves.
I groan.
I'm watching her the entire time, her head falls back as she moans.

"Eyes on me at all times baby girl," I say.

She snaps her eyes back to me and watches me, as I run my tongue, again, along her entrance, this time sucking her clit into my mouth.

"Oh god, Carter," she screams as her head falls back again.

"As much as I am fucking loving tasting your, sweet, tight little pussy and hearing you scream my name like that, if you keep breaking my gaze, I'm going to have to stop!" I smirk.

She looks back at me, "Please, no Carter, please," she says, and I swirl my tongue all along her cunt again, this time quickly flicking her clit with the tip.

"Oh god yes!" She moans.

Reading her body's reaction, I concentrate on her bud some more, alternating between sucking on it, flicking with the tip of my tongue and roughly licking with my tongue flattened.

While using my mouth, to stimulate her clit, I push two fingers inside her pussy.

"Fuck, you're so tight!" I grit out, before returning to swirling my tongue around her and she starts to buck her hips into my face.

I growl into her and push my fingers upwards, to hit her g spot, while simultaneously, licking and sucking on her mound.

Her hips are gyrating, and I can feel she's close, she's trying, frantically to chase her orgasm.

I've never heard anyone scream my name, as well as she does. If I was to go deaf tomorrow, it would be fine, because I've now heard everything I need and want to hear.

I keep goin', each time she screams or moans, it spurs me to go further.

I let my tongue join my fingers now, pushing deep into her. She tastes so fucking sweet.

She's panting, moaning, screaming, grinding and shaking and I can feel her muscles contracting around my fingers.

I pull my tongue back, to roll around her clit, while I pump my fingers in and out of her, hard and quickly.

Suddenly, she screams my name so loud, everyone in the village must hear and I'm soaked!

"Stop stop stop!" She shouts. "Fuck! I'm s-sorry," she stutters, panicked, "I don't know what happened," she says, mortified.

"I do," I reply, smiling like the Cheshire Cat, "You squirted and there is *nothing* to be sorry for! That's hot as *fuck*!" I tell her.

I smile and gently shoot my tongue over her pussy, just to check if she's had enough, or if she could take more.

She jumps and makes a noise, that sounds somewhere, between a laugh and a cry.

I chuckle darkly.

Standing up, I untie her, and she stumbles against me. I catch her and smile.

"Do you think you will be able to use your legs?" I ask.

"I think I'm ruined," she replies, with a soft smile.

"I didn't know things could feel that good," she says, as I help her get dressed.

I smile at her.

"The things you said?" She adds, sort of half a question.

"I meant *every* single word," I reply.

Chapter 42.
Sammie, 4 Months Later.

Quite a bit has happened, over the last 4 months. I'm sitting in the kitchen, with a coffee. Just thinking back, over what's gone on, how certain things have changed and how I have changed.

Business is good, the farm is thriving, and we managed to pull back the bit of money we needed, back when Carter and my dad went over the books.
It's a good job, it was nowhere near 10k in the end, because that would have been a problem, but as it stands, we managed, and we are now in front. Working in profit.
Most of it was due to having a few more markets and using Carter as bait. I actually loved seeing women flirting with him and then knowing he was going to be sleeping with me later that night, I found it a bit of an aphrodisiac.

The biggest change in our little family is that Sara's pregnancy test, came back positive. She finally plucked up the courage to take it and her and Carl did it alone, just a moment for the two of them.
She was three weeks gone and obviously, it was a shock, to everyone, especially them two. They quickly came round to the idea though, her biggest fear, was finishing University and working, with a baby.
But she went on to graduate with honours and is now officially in charge of all our business and legal

responsibilities, being the highest paid member of the team.

My dad thought it was the best option, with her being pregnant with his grandchild, for her to move in and work on the farm as our solicitor. She's now nearly five months pregnant and is blossoming.

I'm going to be an auntie!

She is booked in for a scan next week and they have decided to find out the sex of the baby, so that's exciting.

Her and Carl have moved into the attic room, which is the biggest room of the house, so that makes sense, with them expecting a newborn. It also has an en-suite, so it's easier for them to have their own little set up, privately.

Carl's old room is now Sara's office and Carter and I are in my room, permanently.

Speaking of Carter and I, he's incredible! Things are going really well, and the sex is insane. He has an *extremely* high sex drive and it's a lot to keep up to, honestly, but I'm determined to, because I'm enjoying it.

He has this way about him, the way he speaks, the way he looks at me, just the feel of his hands. He oozes sex appeal and confidence. It's even rubbing off on me.

Every time we have sex, he always makes sure there is something different thrown in, just a little detail that I'm not expecting, to throw me off edge and it's so exciting.

I never thought it would be possible to enjoy sex and to actually feel *good* about myself, whilst having it.

It's just difficult, when he sneaks in halfway through the working day and pulls me into the pantry, where we have to be both, quick and quiet.

Or when he drags me into the chicken coop and we cause the chickens, to lay more eggs at the sounds of our moans and screams.

He doesn't let up, and I then have to try and get on with work, whilst not being able to walk or think straight. The guy drives me insane and he's one kinky son of a bitch!

Him and Jake, are also, now getting along better.

I convinced him, with, not going to lie, *sexual blackmail*, to speak to Jake and sort things out.

It was uncomfortable and even though I understood, why Carter didn't like Jake, it still stemmed back to me, and I didn't want to be the core of any discomfort, awkwardness or an unprofessional vibe on the farm. There were a lot of people to consider, and a lot was going on in the family and business, that were good changes, and a line had to be drawn under all the bad vibes.

So eventually, after nagging him constantly, Carter approached Jake and told him that it was time to start a fresh, they shook on it and have been fine ever since. They've even been on a few boys' nights.

Things are fine between Jake and I, too and everyone else is getting on well, as a unit.

Building things up nicely, we have a few ideas in the pipeline for the near future.

One of those ideas, is setting up a riding school at the stables. Louise couldn't keep Flash anymore, due to other commitments, so she gifted her to bubba. Said he or she, will need to learn to ride when they're old enough and Flash would be an ideal Mare, so it was her early baby gift and we are obviously going to keep her as a family, and use her as part of the school.

We have also been looking at *another* horse to add to the family, but Carter said he wants to go meet him first, as he is a Stallion.

We don't have experience with Stallions, whereas he does and he said that we've to be careful, if we are going to use him in a riding school. He says they can be aggressive and unpredictable. I trust his judgement.

Sara is currently looking into the legalities, around running a riding school, and building up a business plan.

There is also talk of Carter offering training packages. That's only an idea at the moment, but we are always thinking up ways to build up and expand the family business.

Anytime anyone talks about it, there's a lot of excitement and buzz, I actually think people just want to watch my boyfriend do cowboy shit in a cowboy hat. I can't blame them, I want that too.

God he is gorgeous, he has really improved my self-confidence and, with four months, of *never* being allowed to put myself down, every day starting the day telling me that I'm beautiful and sexy and he *"can't wait to eat"* me, I no longer have the self-doubt, I have had, my whole life.

He even makes me believe I'm sexy sometimes and it's a nice change. I wouldn't have ever thought, of buying lingerie before. But now, I make sure, every Saturday on my day off, I go shopping and look for a sexy something, to wear, that's going to make me feel good.

In fact, that's what I did earlier today. I'm sat, reflecting with you all, over a steaming cup, with my Ann Summers bag, sat proudly on the table.

It's not something I hide anymore, I don't care if people see my lingerie bag… No toys allowed in the kitchen, obviously, I don't want my family to know about the little bullets Carter has placed inside different parts of my body, but there is no use in trying to hide everything.

May as well be open with it, seeing as though I can't stop the *murderous (yes, I said what I said)* sounds, he drags out of me on a nightly basis.

Chapter 43.
Sammie.

I still remember the first time, *"I'm clean and on birth control,"* I told him.

He relished in the thought of owning me in every way and said to feel me bare, was a primal need of his.

His interest in restraints didn't just start and end in the stable either.

It had been kinky, electrifying, hot, steamy, rough, passionate and everything I didn't know, I needed.

I thought his tongue was going to end me, but feeling him buried deep inside me, being so rough, I didn't think I would be able to walk for days, was *staggering*.

I never thought anything could get any better, but every single time, surprisingly, it does!

"What do we have here?"

Here he is, my sexy arse cowboy. I am sat with Sara, my mum and gran at the table. We've been laughing at how men react to something as simple as a suspender belt, as I was showing them, what I had bought.

Carter never knew, before recently, what Ann Summers was, but now I think it's his favourite shop.

I look up at him and blow on my coffee, he looks at my lips and smirks, then his eyes dart to the bag.

He reaches in and pulls out a barely there, very flimsy, black lace body suit, with green (his favourite colour) silk accents and a matching suspender belt.

Just as he holds it all up, admiring, blowing out, in a whistle, everyone else walks into the kitchen and I could quite happily die of embarrassment.

My mum, gran and Sara laugh, and my dad looks mortified.

Unfazed, Carter says, "Dayum! Hell yeah! I am goin' to tear *that* fucker off, with my teeth later."

I blush and everybody laughs.

"What are you up to today? Aren't you on a day off?" I ask Carter.

"Yeah, but I thought I would paint the main barn. Make a start on doing that up. The stage we ordered is coming in two weeks," he says, "Are you coming to help me?"

"If I must," I reply with a huff, looking down at my nails, that I really want to get done, and treat myself.

He puts his hand under my chin, lifting my face to look at him, saying, "You must!" With a suggestive smirk.

"Fine, I will just finish my drink and come help," I reply.

He heads outside, to the barn and everyone else goes back to work.

My dad looks at me and then to the lingerie that Carter just left on the table.

"Put that away will you?" He asks.

I huff out a small laugh, "Sorry dad."

I kiss him on the cheek and go upstairs with my shopping bags.

Putting on some leggings, an oversized t-shirt and some wellies, I head into the main barn.

Carter looks at me and smiles, "I've never wanted you more!" He says.

"Fuck off arsehole!" I throw back, and he walks towards me, darting his hands out, to nip at my sides. I laugh and squirm away from him, trying to stop him from tickling me.

Stupidly, I back myself into a dark corner of the barn.

"Uh oh!" He says, glaring at me and I roll my lips tight. "That wasn't very smart, was it?"

His eyes turn dark and he holds me against the wall, with my hands out to the side.

I bite my lip, looking into his eyes, "What are you going to do?" I ask, challenging.

"Watch your tone with me baby girl, otherwise I'm goin' to have to add more marks to the collection."

"You can't," I say. "It's coming up to Summer, what if we go swimming? People will see them."

He leans in towards me, pushing his whole body into mine, I can feel his erection against my stomach. He whispers, "Do you think I care about people seeing? I *want* people to see, I want them to see every bite, bruise, handprint…the proof of me, the mark of my ownership. My territory!"

Every time we have sex, which has been a *lot* over the past month, he marks my body.

Either with an actual bite mark, bruises from his fingers digging into me, or a love bite. He also likes to put handprints on my arse and see how long they last.

Told you-kinky!

I smirk up at him, challenging him again, I like to push my luck.

"You don't own me!" I say, knowing full well he does. I'm his, to do with whatever he wants, whenever he wants.

He growls at me, "You own my heart, soul, my very being baby girl, you always will. But I fucking own this body," he whispers, as he rakes his eyes over my entire form, before fisting my hair and dragging my lips to his.

He pulls both my legs, up around his waist and slams us both against the wall.

Between kissing and biting my neck, he pulls back and says, "I hope you're not particularly fond of these leggings."

"Well, I do need-"

He rips them straight off, pulling them apart like they're a sheet of tissue paper.

"Carter!"

He laughs.

"That's not funny, I need those, what am I going to--"

He rips my t-shirt in half too, clean off my body.

"*Carter!!!!*"

"Yeah baby, keep screaming my name!" He laughs.

I stare at him, in disbelief and he kisses me.

"By the way," he says, "Thank you for the lack of underwear, you've made my job a lot easier." He smirks and I push my fingers into his hair, kissing him deeply.

He uses one hand to hold me up, in place, while the other slides down between our bodies, so he can unfasten his jeans.

Then, in one quick movement, he is inside me.

I will never get used to his size, the way I feel the stretch, as he fills me to the hilt.

I scream out in response, as he pumps in and out of me, hard.

"Shhhh," he says, as he pounds in and out of me, like he's not the size of an elephant's foot.

I look at him, "A minute ago, you told me to scream!" I moan.

He chuckles, "We have to be quick and fairly quiet. It's a fantasy of mine to be watched, but I don't think you will want anyone here, walking in on us."

I look at him, "To be watched?" I say, and he laughs.

"You're a fucking pervert!" I tell him, as he keeps ramming into me, while squeezing my hips.

≈≈≈≈≈≈≈≈≈≈≈

We are sweaty, panting, our chests are heaving and I'm not sure if there is a part of me that isn't sore.

I'm not stood up, but I know, from the sheer volume of orgasms I have had, that my legs are going to be no good, whatsoever.

I'm breathless now, wrapping my arms around Carter's shoulders and pushing our foreheads together.

Our hair is stuck to our faces and our skin is glistening.

His thrusts lose their rhythm a little and I manage two more orgasms, before he buries deep inside me one last time, stilling, with a low moaning growl in my ear.

Panting, he pulls back and kisses me slowly, gently lowering me to my feet.

"Wow," is all I manage.

He nods, staring at my naked body.

I look up at him, "I'm going to need some clothes!"

Chapter 44.
Sammie.

I shout up the stairs to Carl and Sara, "Hurry up! You're going to be late!"

Honest to God, these people are going to be responsible for a *person* soon and they are useless at organising anything!

"Okay, I'm coming!" Says Sara, "Don't rush someone, who is the size of an elephant, down the stairs!"

"Size of an elephant," I roll my eyes, "You talk crap."

Carl comes down, "Right come on, we have to go," he says, as though Carter and I haven't been waiting half an hour for them, to get a move on.

I look at Carter and he rolls his eyes, as he grabs the keys to one of the trucks.

"I'll drive," Carl says, holding out his hand to Carter, for the keys.

"No, you won't," Carter says with a frown.

I roll my eyes and smile to myself, this man and his need to be in control.

"How you feeling?" Carter says, while looking in the rear view mirror at the parents to be.

I look back over my shoulder at them. Carl just nods, think he's nervous.

Sara answers, "Yeah, excited, but I'm thinking of keeping the sex a secret."

"Fuck off!" I say to her, "No way, are you making us all wait until it is born!"

"Babe, it's not your decision," Carter says.

I look at him, "I'm not organising a baby shower in yellow, brown or grey!"

He looks back at Sara in the mirror again.

I think I'm more nervous than they are, well not Carl obviously, he looks like he's going to be sick.

"Speaking of the baby shower," Carl says, "Why do men have to attend? Isn't it usually just women?"

"Men are attending because, just like when the baby comes, it's not all down to the woman. So just like the scans, the showers, the birth…men have a part to play too, plus, you should help out!" I glare at him.

"Sorry I asked," he replies.

≈≈≈≈≈≈≈≈≈≈≈

We arrive at the hospital.

"Are you sure you don't want us to come in?" I look round to the backseat at them.

"Absolutely fucking not!" Carl says, and Carter laughs.

We watch them get out the car and walk hand in hand to the hospital.

I look at Carter, "What do you think he meant by that?" I ask.

He looks back at me, out the corner of his eye, "I think he means, no thank you," he smiles.

"Thought so," I smile back.

He takes a drink of his water, and I choose that moment to say, "When do you think we will have babies?"

He spits out his water, coughing, spluttering and choking all over. I frown at him, while he tries to breathe.

"God, what an overreaction," I tut.

"Sorry, I wasn't expecting that. Slow down baby! Let's enjoy being together for a bit first yeah?" He replies.

"How long do you think they will be in there?" He asks.

I shrug, "Maybe an hour all in all?" I reply.

He turns the engine on and starts to back out of the parking spot.

"What are you doing? We can't leave them," I say, looking around us, trying to figure out where he's going.

"I'm not leaving them, I'm just moving up to the top of the parking lot, I will come back down for them when they come out, we will still be able to see them."

"Why are you going up there?" I ask.

"Why do you think? It's a little bit more private," he smirks.

"Are you serious?" I say, as he pulls into another spot and unclips his seatbelt.

"Carter, we can't. It's a public place!"

"Yeah, I told you, I want to be watched," he replies.

I stare at him in shock, "It's illegal!"

"No, it's not, not unless anyone *actually* sees any nudity, they won't see anything, but they will know what we are doing, that's allowed and it's the best of both worlds," he says, while unbuttoning his jeans and pushing back the driver's seat slightly.

"Carter we can't have sex here, what if someone actually sees something?"

He's not listening, I look down at his crotch and his dick bobs free.

"Climb on, you dirty little slut!" He says with a smile.

I look around in a panic.

"Don't make me say it again baby, fucking lower that tight little pussy onto my cock, now!"

I bite my lip and take off my panties, he holds out his hand to take them from me and I straddle him, lowering myself slowly, bracing myself for his size.

"Fuck, you take my cock so well!" He groans.

He leans over to the glove compartment, and I watch him, wondering what the hell he could be looking for.

He pulls out some rope and I look down at it, in his hands.

"Put your hands behind your back," he demands.

I look at him, unsure.

"Is that a good idea? What if someone comes and we have to move quickly?"

"Oh, there will be people coming baby, I'm counting on it, but those people are already in the truck, so stop panicking and just do as I say."

I put my hands behind my back, knocking into the steering wheel and sounding the horn. I jump.

"Fuck! That's loud!"

"Horny baby?" Carter laughs, as he ties my hands behind my back.

He reaches up to me and kisses my neck, then he pulls his mouth away from me.

"Ride me cowgirl!" He says, before grabbing the panties I handed him and putting them in his mouth, rolling his eyes back in his head.

He's a fucking animal and at the moment, his strong, powerful body is underneath me, his dick totally filling me.

I look into his face, seeing his eyes burning while he has my underwear in his mouth.

He wants me to control the pressure, the tempo, the penetration. He wants me to ride him, and I've never taken charge, of how things go down before.

He usually takes complete control, and it always runs so smoothly, because he knows, what is going to feel good and it's always so seamless.

But here I am, straddling his body, needing to ride him and take some control…with my hands tied tightly behind my back, it's quite a contrast!

I look at him, suddenly losing confidence, needing reassurance, needing guidance.

I thought he wanted to own me, I thought he wanted to control everything, he's not doing that right now, and I don't know what the hell to do about it.

I'm lost and uncomfortable.

He looks back at me, straight into my eyes, as though he is reading how I'm feeling and what I'm thinking. He simply nods and winks, holding my hips and gently moves my body, so I'm gliding up and down on him, rolling my hips.

He takes my panties out of his mouth, he seems to know I need something softer right now, and that I'm feeling unsure about things.

Still looking up at me, he keeps his hands on my hips, guiding me.

"That's good baby, you feel so good," he says, softly.

I look down into his eyes, he smiles at me.

"You're doing amazing, you know what you're doing, that's it, you're in control right now, use me for your pleasure," he says quietly.

"I'm sorry," I say, "I wasn't sure what to do, I was confused. You always take control, I thought that's what you preferred, this is a shift, and I wasn't sure what to do with it."

"I control the pleasure, my aim *isn't* to control you. My *want*, is to own you, but in the best of ways."

"So, this isn't some BDSM stuff?" I ask, shyly.

He chuckles.

"Even if it was, you would still *always* be in control," he says, rolling into me, causing my head to fall backwards.

"I love to control the situation, I love to control what we do, but you have to remember, even in the heat of all that. When I'm fisting your hair, spanking you, tying you up, marking you, forcing my cock, into all your holes as hard or as fast as I feel like goin', It is *only* ever goin' to happen if you want it, nothing you don't enjoy and nothing you don't want, would ever go ahead, and you can stop it at any point. You may submit yourself to me, but I would only ever want you to do that willingly, so with that being said, whatever I'm saying to you and whatever I'm doing to you, there isn't a second, where you're *not* the one in control," he says.

He then sits up, still inside me, rocking my hips on him and kisses me deeply, sliding his tongue into my mouth and swirling it with mine.

I find my confidence, with that amazing speech, but still wanting to keep it slow and steady, knowing I'm in control to do that, I carry on, rocking and gliding up and down on his dick, enjoying the sensations of the different angle.

My orgasms rip through me, several times and the windows have all steamed up.

As Carter said, no one can see anything but with the rocking of the truck and the steam, people are likely to know what's going on and there's nothing that can be done about it. That makes things even more thrilling.

As I chase a strong orgasm, that is creeping up on me, I pick up the speed as I feel the pressure in the base of my spine building.

"That's it baby, keep goin', I can feel you're close and I won't be far behind you," Carter says, and knowing he is close to his orgasm is enough for me to catch my final one, riding it out.

His breaths get heavier. Jerking inside of me, he holds my hips still, as he empties himself and I fall forward, putting my forehead on his chest.

He reaches round and unties me and as he places a soft kiss on the top of my head, he whispers, for the first time, "I love you baby."

We are back in our own seats and the windows have been down for a few minutes, clearing all the steam and any trace of that famous sex scent.

My hair is a mess, I try and smooth it down but there's not much hope, Carter can get away with it because he has his hat on.

It's Summer, I'll use that as a reason!

We drive back down, to where we had dropped them off, we are in the same area but not the same spot, so hopefully, they will be too full of baby goo, that they won't realise.

I look at carter, who's just casually tapping his hand on the steering wheel, while quietly singing to himself.

My mind is going back to him saying those words. He said he loves me. Was it just a heat of the moment thing?

We've had sex loads of times, and he's never said it before now. I love him too, obviously, but I froze and missed the moment to say it back. I'm so stupid. It doesn't seem like it's bothered him, me not saying it back, maybe he just knows already, somehow.

Just then, the back doors open up and there's an excitement in the truck.

Both Carter and I look back at them, expectantly and I love that Carter seems as excited, as the rest of us.

"Well?.... you better not say it's a yellow!" I say to them.

They both look at each other and smile, then together, they say, "*PINK!*"

Chapter 45.
Carter.

I'm stood outside the main barn, looking out at everyone, working on the farm.

I've taken it upon myself to control what happens in the barn, making it suitable for country music events and weddings.

It's a good job Frank is so laid back about things. He just leaves me to make decisions, as though I really am part of the family, I feel like I am.

The painting inside and out, has been completed. Sammie and I finished it last week.

We went for an off white, almost a very light grey, on the inside, and it's somewhere between a light brown and a mushroom grey on the outside, it probably has a name, but that's not information I tend to want to find out.

At the moment, there're some guys here, installing an extremely large crystal chandelier, in the center of the ceiling.

It's a large space, so we went for grand lighting. It will look good for any weddings et cetera.

It's a warm day today, Summer has arrived.

"Carter", Elsa calls across the pasture.

I look over at her.

"Someone is on the main telephone for you, something about a horse," she shouts.

I back into the barn and check the guys are okay on their own for a bit.

"Sure thing, it's going to take a while yet," one of them says.

I head over to the farmhouse and step into the kitchen, where they keep the telephone.

"Yeah?" I say into the phone.

I look over at Sammie, who is sat at the table with her mom and grandmother. She rolls her eyes at me and they all smile. I frown back at them.

The guy is calling, for me to go over and see a Stallion he has for sale.

"Did you say he's fairly young?" I ask.

"Yeah, he's not been ridden a lot, I haven't had time to get him trained because we got him, and then my wife fell ill, so I've been busy. I'm not going to lie, he needs a lot of work," he replies.

I sigh... "Has he been put to stud?" I ask.

"Well, no, but that makes no difference to his behavior," the man lies.

"Yes, it does, if he's been bred, he could actually be *more* aggressive and have the tendency to dominate or nip, so I'm glad he hasn't been a stud, *however*, we are needing a horse for riding lessons, so a Stallion isn't ideal anyway," I say back.

"You knew he was a Stallion, before contacting me, so why did you contact me, if you knew you preferred a Mare or Gelding?" The man asks, with more attitude than I appreciate.

I take a breath so I don't get angry, and answer, "I am experienced with Stallions, particularly wild Mustangs, so I believe I can handle him, but I wanted to meet him, to make sure. We could always castrate him, but at the same time, we have a Mare here, he could come in useful."

"You've bred horses before?" He asks.

"I've been involved in *every* aspect of a horse's life cycle," I reply.

"Well, we are home all day, so you're welcome to come meet him if that's what you want to do?" He asks.

"Yes, that's what I want to do, I will be there at around three o clock if that's good for you."

"Yes, that's great, see you then!"

"See you then."

As soon as I put the phone down, Elsa, Sammie and Clara look up at me and Sammie says, "You answer the phone with *"yeah"?"* Shaking her head.

"What's wrong with that?"

"It's rude!" She scolds, and I laugh.

"No, it's not, answering it with *"what?!"* Is rude!" I say, while walking out the door.

Back at the barn, the chandelier is still being installed, it takes a few of them because it's so large. I am just watching, and thinking of how good it looks, when I hear a vehicle approaching.

I head back outside, to a cargo van, must be the furniture arriving, or maybe the stage.

I walk towards the van, and the driver gets out.

"Frank?" He says.

"Oh, no, I'm…he's my boss, he owns the place but I'm taking the deliveries for the barn, is it a stage or furniture?" I ask.

"It's more than that, we have tables, chairs, a stage and some instruments for you," he replies.

"Oh! I didn't know one person was bringing them all. Great."

Where the fuck am I going to put everything.

We start unloading the van.

"Where do you want them?" He asks.

"Just to the side there, on the grass. They can't go in yet," I reply.

I check everything I ordered, has arrived, at least now, I can get it finished today.

The guy takes off in his van and I go down to the farmhouse.

I can't do much else at the minute, so I might as well get a coffee.

Entering the house, all the Farmers, Sara, Elsa, Clara and Sammie are in the kitchen.

"Full house here!" I remark, "What's happening?"

"Just talking about you and how it feels like you've been here forever," Frank says.

"Really? that bad huh?" I smile, as I pour a coffee.

Frank suddenly looks horrified, "Oh no! I mean, it feels like you've always been a part of things, a part of us," he says.

I smile at him.

"How's it going up at the barn?" Elsa asks.

"Yeah, good, I just can't do much at the moment, because the chandelier is still getting installed. I think they're struggling with the weight of it. The other things have been delivered though, it all came together. So at least I can finish it all tonight. It will be a late finish, but I'd rather get it done and then Sara can sort the paperwork for the insurance, licenses et cetera. Hopefully I can get started on building the bar tomorrow."

"Sounds good," replies Elsa, "Can't wait to see what you've done with it, when it's all finished."

I smile at her and drink my coffee.

I look over at Sammie, who's sat opposite me at the table, staring at me.

"You been up to the stables yet?" I ask her.

"Hmmm? Oh, no, I am going up later. Carl let them out earlier on, so I need to go muck out and groom them. Why you ask?" She says.

"I've got this Stallion to go see later, I need a horse trailer, just in case he comes back with me," I reply.

Frank looks at me, "Do you think he will be okay?"

"Well, there will be different levels of riding experience at the school, plus, a Stallion is useful if you want to mate Flash. She's still young and it's an idea to have a Stallion here too."

"Is it safe? To keep a Stallion with other horses?" Sammie asks.

"Usually yeah, but obviously each horse is different, so we would have to see how they get on. I will suggest a trial period. It's Summer, which means Flash is likely in season. So, we may have to separate them at first. We could either keep the Stallion separate, or Flash away from the others, unless secured in their pens. However, the Stallion would have to get used to being around the other horses, so I would maybe put him with Otis, then put Max and Flash together. Max is a Gelding, but he's a feisty fucker, so it's probably best to put Otis in with the Stallion, balance them out a bit," I answer.

"I'll come with you," says Frank, "I've never really been involved in the horse side of things and I want to see what it is you look for."

I nod, "Okay, I'll just go see how things are goin' at the barn, and I'll get ready to set off. I'd rather get it sorted soon, so I can finish things over there."

Frank nods and I head outside.

I turn around to close the door and catch Sammie checking out my ass.

I smirk and raise my eyebrows at her and she winks and smiles back.

As I head into the barn, the guys are climbing down their ladders.

"Oh, have you finished?" I ask.

"Yeah, all done, what do you think?"

We all look up at the light.

"Looks great!" I say, "Good job boys. Just send me the bill through and I'll get our lawyer to sort out the payment for you. She handles all the finances."

They nod and we all say our goodbyes.

Frank and I head out to see the new Stallion, all loaded up with tack and a horse trailer.

"Everything goin' well on the farm all round?" I ask Frank.

"Yeah, we are doing well. Sara takes a chunk of finances," he laughs, "But she does a lot for it and as a solicitor, she has the earning power, I don't want her working with us for less than she would get elsewhere, I want to make it worth it for her, especially with the little one coming and she is already going to miss out on full maternity pay."

"Maternity pay?" I ask.

"Yeah, over here, an employer or the state, may pay mothers to be off work to have and look after babies for up to a year. Do you not have that in America?"

"No, I don't think so. I've never had a baby obviously, so I'm not sure, but I can't imagine it. I think over in the States, we probably just keep their job available to come back to, if that," I say.

"Well, if she was working at a company, or for herself, she would likely be entitled to some financial help. I can't cover that, so while she is off work, with the baby, she will be relying on what I pay Carl. However, we will all be around, as a family, to help with the baby and she will always be around, obviously."

"Yeah. How are you feeling about being a grandfather?" I ask.

"It was a shock at first, I don't know why it was a shock for everyone, they have sex, it happens. But I just never thought they would even *want* a child. I thought Sammie would be the first to give me a grandchild," he looks at me.

I look back at him.

"That's not an invite!" He says, "I need the manpower," he smiles.

"There's no plan for that in the near future," I reply, "I wouldn't make a good father."

"What makes you say that?" Frank asks.

"Well, I don't have a great one of my own. If it wasn't for my grandfather, I would probably have been put into foster care. My family are big Christians, but they're hypocrites, because they're not a very good family, and I know for a *fact,* they're all over there now, running my grandfather's ranch into the ground and there's nothing I can do about it," I say.

"Can't you fight it somehow? Can't Sara help?" He asks.

"I doubt it, law is obviously different over there. Besides, I've come to terms, with the fact it's probably too late and it's best to just cut it all out, move on and get on with my life. Getting involved, would mean being involved with my family again and I'd rather not," I reply.

After a few moments of silence, Frank says, "Hey Carter, I reckon, your grandfather would be proud of you. Everything you've overcome and, in my opinion, I think you'd make a great dad! You're hard working, stubborn, you have good morals, fight for what you believe, you'd do anything to help anyone and you're protective of those you love. That's all you need to be." I smile in reply, and we ride the rest of the way in a comfortable silence.

Chapter 46.
Carter.

We head to the stables first, to take the Stallion to the yard, Sammie is up there with Elsa, Sara and Clara.

"Wonder why they're all up here," Frank says, just as we are getting out of the truck.

"Howdy y'all," I call over to them and they walk over to us, Sammie coming up to kiss me.

"Hey," she says back.

"What's going on?" Frank asks.

"We just thought we would come see what Sammie was doing with the horses, rather than sitting in the kitchen, plus we knew you might be coming back with a horse, so we have come to nosey."

Just then, there's some whinny noises and stomps coming from the horse trailer.

"Is he kicking the shit out of my horse box?" Sammie says, slightly annoyed.

I walk over to the trailer and open it up, the women and Frank watching me.

"He's a beauty," Frank says, "But he's a fucker! Going to need training, he didn't like Carter being on him."

"Would do if it was a Mare!" Sammie says and everyone laughs, while Frank rolls his eyes.

I lead the Stallion out, he's a chestnut with black tail and mane.

"He's handsome," Sammie says.

"He is, but his attitude stinks," I reply, "I don't want you dealing with him until he's trained baby, I'll do everything that's needed with him."
She nods.
"Are the others in their stalls?" I ask.
"Yeah, just finished now," Sammie answers.
"I'll groom him tomorrow, he needs to settle in first, can you set up another stall and I'll secure him?" I ask her.
She nods and goes off to put bedding down in an empty stall and fill a water and food bucket for him.

Once it's ready, I put him inside, with a bit of a fight, the little fucker! And lock his pen.
We secure the main stable and walk back towards the house.
I head in the direction of the barn, and they all go to the farmhouse.
It's Early evening now and Sammie says to me, as we are parting ways, "I'll come over in a bit and give you some help, just going to do dinner prep."
I nod and walk to the main barn, to finish setting up the place.

≈≈≈≈≈≈≈≈≈≈≈≈

By the time Sammie comes to "help", I have almost finished.

The stage is set, the string lights are up, all around the barn and the arch is done, I've put that where the bar will be built, for now.

The tables and chairs are all set out, around the room, ready for an event to take place.

She walks in, just as I'm setting up the instruments on the stage.

Sitting down on one of the chairs, she looks around.

"Wow! This looks amazing! How the hell have you done it all? It looks like it was made to be this way, I'm so impressed!"

"Oh yeah?" I answer, "How impressed?" I smirk.

"Compliment seeking, eh?" She smiles.

"Why the fuck not?"

"Well, it's deserved, this is incredible," she replies.

I had put up the keyboard stand, put the keyboard on top and set the mic stand up in front of a stool, while she was talking to me.

I'm just putting the guitar, on its stand, then I sit down on the stage to set up the drum kit. She watches me closely.

"What?" I ask.

"How do you know what you're doing with the drum kit? I get the keyboard and guitar, they're pretty standard, right? But how do you know where to put each drum?" She asks, as she's walking towards me.

"I play," I reply.

She rolls her lips, those fucking lips do something to me.

"You play the drums?" She asks, stepping onto the stage, as I finish connecting them.

I'm sat on the stage floor as she comes around, in front of me, to sit on the drum seat.

"I've always had a thing for drummers," she says, before biting her lip.

I kneel up, in front of her, sliding my hands up and down her legs.

"Sit on that bass drum!" I tell her.

She smiles, stands up and doesn't take her eyes off mine, until she reaches around the other side of the kit and sits on the bass drum.

I love how confident she is getting.

I stand up and follow her around.

Standing in front of her, I ask, "What took you so long to get down here? You were only prepping food, weren't you?"

She looks up at me and says, "I lied, I wasn't helping with the food. They've not started that yet. I was getting changed. Do you like my new dress?"

She looks down at her own dress and back up at me.

"Yes," I answer.

"How do you know? You've not taken your eyes off mine," she says.

"I can see *all* of you," I reply.

"Hhmmm, all of me? Really?" She says, in a cheeky tone, "I don't think so, not yet anyway."

"Do you think the length of the dress is appropriate, for the baby shower?" She asks.

I look down her body and my eyes stop at her waist area, as she slowly opens her legs, exposing that she is wearing no underwear.

Holy fuck!

I glance back up at her face and she licks her lips.

"Thought we could work up an appetite before dinner," she smiles.

I get down on my knees in front of her, "Appetizer time!" I smile back.

Diving my head in between her fucking sexy thighs, I put my hands underneath her ass and pull her hips towards my face, sliding my tongue deep into her hot, tight pussy, wanting to taste every bit of her.

I completely and utterly *devour* her.

Her screams and hip grinding, send me over the edge, I can't cope with how fucking sexy she is, how sweet she tastes, how heavenly her moans and screams sound, my name echoing, throughout the barn.

She does something to me, that no one has ever done before. She's like a magnet for me and I can't get enough of her.

I slide my fingers into her, while I keep licking, flattening my tongue and rubbing it, roughly over her clit, making her grind harder into my face and closing her legs around my head.

I can feel her tightening and getting ready to break loose, then suddenly she shatters on my tongue, pulling at my hair to move me away, but there was no way I was moving my tongue off of her delicious cunt.

I wanted every last bit of her.

"Stop, I can't take anymore," she whispers, panting.

I keep my tongue, firmly on her, forcing her through the ride, lapping it over her sweet little clit and then forcing it inside her, until she begins to shake uncontrollably.

I'm soaked, and she is shaking above me.

"Carter, seriously, I'm going to pass out," she almost screams.

I move away from her, looking up at her hooded eyes. She's panting, her skin flushed.

She smiles down at me.

"My turn," she says, "I want to see, how deep I can swallow you."

I smile, "You dirty fucking whore!" I say, as she smiles back at me.

She stands up and holds onto my bicep, "Oh! I'm wobbly," she says.

We both laugh.

I get down, off the stage, it's only fairly low, so I kneel on the barn floor, in front of it.

"Lay down on your back, on the stage, let your head hang off the edge in front of me," I say.

She does as I tell her and as her head drops backwards in front of me, I unzip my jeans and let my cock, that's been straining painfully against my zipper, spring free, giving it a few strokes.

"Open up baby girl," I say.

She opens her mouth, and I force my dick past her plump, soft lips, pushing deep, into the back of her throat.

Having her head, hang off the edge of the stage, is allowing for some great access and my cock is loving the way it feels.

Sliding in and out of her, I'm trying not to be too rough. Her moans and groans, make me wild for her and I can't believe how fucking good she is at taking my cock, in whatever hole I want to shove it into.

I watch the column of her neck as she's swallowing me whole, *it's too hot, I'm not goin' to be able to last much longer, if she keeps doing this.*

I slide my dick out of her mouth, get up and step back.

She sits up, turns around and looks up at me.

"Is something wrong?" She asks.

I don't say anything, I just walk back towards her, lift her up, wrapping her legs around my waist, and walk us over to one of the tables.

Laying her down and pulling her hips towards me, I ram my cock high up, into her tight pussy, feeling her warmth stretch, to accommodate me perfectly.

"I need to come inside your perfect cunt," I whisper, in her ear.

Driving in and out of her, I know I'm almost ready to spill everything I have into her.

She's made moves that she never usually would, her confidence has grown, it's a massive turn on and the reminder of everything she has done and suggested here, now, is causing the pressure to build in my balls.

I'm so fucking glad that she has come already because I am just about to fucking explode.

A few more pumps into her and I can't take anymore. Her tight little cunt, milking me dry.

I collapse my head, into her neck, kissing up from her collar bone to her jaw.

She tips her head down towards me, so I can kiss her lips, then I kiss the tip of her nose, finishing the trail of kisses on her forehead.

Both of us out of breath, and dripping with sweat, I say, "I love you so fucking much."
Looking into each other's eyes, she replies, "I love you more!"

Chapter 47.
Sammie, 4 weeks later.

It's baby shower day and although, traditionally, it is celebrated by women, I had requested that *everyone* join in!
Women, Men, kids, dogs, the lot!

The invitations stated that people were to wear pink, or at least, a small bit of pink, to recognise, that the baby is a girl.
I've gone for, a white milk maid dress with tiny pink flowers and white cowboy boots.
The mum to be, has gone all out in literally, a pink ball gown! Complete with a pretty good sized bump!
Everyone has been invited!

Obviously, the parents to be's families were all present, their friends, all the farmers from our farm and surrounding farms and *their* families, the entire village really. John and his family, from the pub too. *Everyone!*
Not only was everybody invited, but they also all turned up, to help celebrate.
I look around the barn house, which my amazing boyfriend, had done a fabulous job sprucing up, not only with his decorating, building and planning skills, but he had also helped me set it up for today.
We did it all, early this morning, while everyone else was doing what needed to be done on the farm.
Louise even came over early, to help with the horses, so that we could set up here.

The main barn had started off being a dirty, dark, wooden, smelly barn, with nothing but a sawdust floor, a few stacks of hay, some fridges and tools.

Carter had moved everything that was here, and organised them into the back barn, with the mowers and the hay, so it was all in one place and that even looked good too!

In doing that, he *completely* emptied the main barn, which is a really large, generous space with lots of potential- potential we never really saw, until he made us see it, with one of his many great ideas.

Now, the barn is clean and white, with a large crystal chandelier in the centre of the ceiling and warm, twinkling, white fairy lights are draped all down the walls.

An arch he built, to add decoration, whether with flowers, balloons or more fairly lights, today, is filled with baby pink balloons of different sizes.

There are white circular tables dotted around the room, with white wooden chairs surrounding them.

The tables are dressed, in white tablecloths, pink confetti and each have a vase of pink and white roses in the centre, with each chair, being draped in baby pink bows.

On the very end of the barn, the closed end, there is a stage set up with instruments, a stool and a mic, but today, we are just playing some soft music, out of the speakers that are mounted high around the walls, out of sight really, unless you're looking for them. They're pretty neatly tucked, out of the way.

In front of the stage, is a wooden dance floor installed, and in the middle of the dance floor, we have one of those "BABY" cube piles, filled with more baby pink balloons, matching the arch.

Next to the stage, for today, over to one side of the room, stands a white sweet cart, holding pink and white sweets and pink and white cupcakes.

Then carrying on down that wall, we have a long table of finger foods.

On the opposite side of the room, on *that* side wall, there is the bar. Carter built it and its stunning!

Amazing wood craftsmanship, it's curved, with a white, grey base to match the colour of the paintwork inside the barn, and a light oak top, which matches the original ceiling beams.

Spirits are lining the back wall behind the bar, with fridges for wines, beers, cordials et cetera.

A fully stocked bar for any occasion, but for this occasion, we have two cocktail trays set out on the top, filled with orange juice and *"nosecco"* for the mum to be, any non-drinkers and any kids.

At the back of the room, to the side of the entrance, is where we will be keeping the gifts and cards that people want to bring for the baby.

We also have a white bouncy castle outside, on the freshly mowed land, for the kids to enjoy.

It's all come together really well, and it looks pretty damn good, if I do say so myself.

I've also never *seen* such a sea of pink!

From the barn decor, although that's mostly white, to be fair and it looks so pretty, but also from the amount of people, that are wearing either, full pink outfits or pink accents.

Most of the men went for a pink tie.

I've never seen Carter in anything but farm work gear, complete with cowboy hat and boots of course, or jogging bottoms and either a hoodie or t- shirt, both of which, he looks fucking yummy in, but I was looking forward to seeing him in something dressy.

I wonder if he will have followed my request for everyone to wear pink. If he hasn't, he will be the only one.

I can hear the horses in the background, I look over towards the stable and although, I can't see them from here, I get to thinking about them.

We ended up keeping the Stallion, who Carter called Buck, because he took ages to allow anyone to sit on him.

Eventually, we took him to a lake, which was the perfect way, to get him used to being mounted. Carter said it's a popular way to train a horse where he comes from, because they can't really try to throw you off in water, by rearing et cetera.

Flash is no longer in season, so they can be kept in closer proximity, without being watched all the time, plus, they've all grown accustomed to each other. I think we are going to mate them though, someday.

The riding school hasn't picked up properly yet, but we do have a bit of interest, so we are keeping our fingers crossed.

"This is amazing Sammie!" Sara says, interrupting my thoughts, while hugging me.

"Oh, I'm glad you like it, only the best for my sister in law and little niece," I reply.

Carter walks over to us, he's wearing jeans *(at least they're clean!)*, a white shirt and black cowboy boots. No hat today and no pink in sight.

Sara and I look at each other and look at him.

"Where's the pink?" I say, with my hands on my hips.

He looks back at me, "Well, if you carry on with that attitude, you're goin' to need shutting up! So, it looks like, the pink I will be wearing, is that pretty little shade of lipstick you have on, around my fucking dick!", He replies.

My jaw drops, we have company!

He looks at my mouth and says, "Hhhmm already getting ready for me, I see?!"

Sara chuckles and says, "Well, I'm going to go say hello to some people, before you two, cause me to go into early labour."

Carter winks at me.

Carl walks over to us, handing Carter, a very faint pink tie.

"You're bigger than me, you're stronger than me, but if you don't wear this fucking tie for my daughter's shower, I'm going to kick your arse," he says.

Carter and I look at each other and laugh, while he takes the tie and puts it on.

Chapter 48.
Sammie.

We walk into the barn and the buzz of people enjoying themselves, is electrifying, everyone is here.
Full families, the whole village, they've all shown up for my brother and his girlfriend, to help them celebrate their little girl.

I look over at our farmers and their families and smile, all of them sat together, laughing and talking.
I glance at Jake, who is talking to Louise at the bar and Miles who is stood with my mum and dad. Everyone is back to normal, everyone is getting along, other farmers are here, and no one is in competition, everybody has just come together, having a good time, lots of cheer and laughter.
The kids are ransacking the sweet cart and then going to bounce around on the bouncy castle, I hope they're not sick!

Carter, who is still stood next to me, puts his arm round my waist.
When I look up at him, he's smiling down at me.
"What you smiling about?" I say.
"You've done an amazing job organising all of this," he looks around.
"I didn't do it all, you helped set an awful lot of it up and you made the barn look this way, it's a remarkable change, I can't believe it's the same place." I turn towards him and slide my hands up onto his large,

broad shoulders. I push up onto my toes as he leans forward, and we press our lips together.

Before we have separated, I can feel the burn of stares, from all the females in the room.

I love that they want him, I smile to myself, as I straighten his tie out.

"Looks good," I say, before kissing him again, and enjoying being the envy of the village.

The gift table is filling up, everyone is enjoying the food and drink, the kids are all running round spiked by sugar and there's a steady stream of conversation rocking through the room.

Carter and I are sat with the family, the employees and their families, although, by this point, the chairs have been moved around and people are all cramming in to speak to each other, at a few tables.

Carter is running his hand up and down my thigh with quite a lot of pressure, which usually means he's horny. Who am I kidding? The guy *breathing* usually means he's horny.

I look at him and he leans in, to quietly tell me he likes my lipstick.

I think back to what he said, knowing what he's getting at, and I blush.

I haven't blushed in a while really, because I was starting to get used to it, but sometimes, when things aren't expected, I do catch myself going a bit pink, at least now, I match the theme of the room.

Sara sees he has leaned in, and I had reacted by blushing, so she brings attention to us, causing quite a few people, including my parents and grandmother to

look at us and says, "What are you two whispering
about and why are you blushing Sammie?"
That makes me blush more, bitch!
Carter answers, "Oh, I was just suggesting that her li--"
I slap my hand over his mouth.
Everyone laughs and I give Carter a warning look, as he
smirks under my palm.

≈≈≈≈≈≈≈≈≈≈≈

Carter gets up on the stage and grabs the mic.
He taps it and everyone looks up at him. He doesn't
look in the slightest bit nervous and I'm envious, that
he can be so confident, in everything he does.
    "Howdy, do y'all have a drink?"
People hold their bottles and glasses up.
"Good," he says… "Hey kids! Shush will you,
otherwise I'm gunna feed you to the pigs!"
There's no pigs.
The kids snap their mouths shut and the parents
involuntarily laugh, in reaction.
Not what you expect someone to say, but people either
laughed, or tried *not* to laugh, so him threatening their
kids, went down just fine.
"The parents to be, want to say a few words to y'all, so
please give them a cheer, after all, they have made one
of those little monsters!"
He points to the kids, who are all sat at the back of the
barn, laughing and drinking pop.
    Everyone laughs and we all clap for Sara and
Carl, as Carter sits back down next to me.

I whisper, "You can't say you'll feed kids to pigs!"
"Sure I can, I just did," he says, with a wink.
Carl and Sara thank everyone for coming, thanking them for their gifts and cards, saying how generous they all are and how they appreciate having an amazing bunch of family and friends, before finishing with,
"So please raise your drinks and join us, in toasting the upcoming arrival, of our little princess, Victoria."
"To Victoria!" We all say back, in unison.
This was the first time anyone was hearing the name they had chosen and so, it was an emotional time for all.

≈≈≈≈≈≈≈≈≈≈≈≈

Everyone is in deep conversation, as Carter whispers in my ear, "You know that tree out the back of the barn?"
I look at him.
"I have been thinking all day, about fucking you against it."
"Stop! We are at a baby shower, people are around, kids are around, we could get caught!" I whisper back.
"We won't get caught, it's around the back. But there's the small chance that we will, and that is making my cock, painfully hard for you right now. Please tell me you're not wearing any panties under that dress, like the last time you had it on."

My eyes shoot over to the drum, the stage and down at the table.

"Yeah baby, imagine if it was *this* table, that we ended up fucking on that time, the one that's now being sat around, by so many people you know," he whispers.

I look at the people sat around the tables, knowing we had sex on one of them, I especially think about all the women here, who are undressing my boyfriend with their eyes, at any opportunity they get.

He reaches for my hand and places it on his dick, which is in fact, hard and I squeeze my thighs together, heat rushing to my core.

"You can't walk out there like that!" I say.

"I'll walk directly behind you, come on," he drags me up and holds me close, so my back is pressed against his front.

"That fucking ass of yours is not helping my situation," he whispers in my ear on the way out the barn, as he places a trail of kisses down the side of my neck.

"Carter! Wait, we haven't left the room yet," I say.

"Believe me, this stance would look strange if I *wasn't* kissing you," he replies.

We get to the tree and straight away, he presses my front against it.

"What are you doing?" I ask.

"I'm *doing* that fucking ass baby."

"No, we don't have any lube!" I say, eyes wide.

"Don't worry, you're fucking dripping, I know it," he says, as he dips one hand down the front of my panties, I am indeed, dripping, as he suspected.

He groans into my ear and nips the little bit of skin with his teeth, just below it.

He uses his other hand to free his dick from his jeans and proceeds to wipe my arousal over his tip.

He groans again.

"Relax baby, breathe out…. slowly," he growls, as he pulls my panties over my butt.

As I do what he says and breathe out, *slowly,* as instructed, he pushes into my arse.

I gasp.

We have done this before, but we had lube, a lot of it. This time, it was more uncomfortable, but even discomfort and a bit of pain, when it came to Carter, was thrilling, sexy and exciting and he knows, just how to test my boundaries.

"Are you okay darlin'?" He drawls.

God, I love his southern twang.

I nod my head and push backwards into him, he lets out another growl, this time, not so quiet.

He slips his hand back round my front and puts deep pressure onto my clit, rubbing in circles, bringing me very quickly to climax.

He then pushes two fingers into me, beckoning me to higher places.

"This isn't going to last long baby, your ass is too tight, I'm almost there."

"You had better get working then, haven't you?" I smirk back over my shoulder, at him.

"Challenge accepted," he smiles.

He bites and sucks the side of my neck.

"No, don't mark where people can see," I say.

He ignores me and in between bites and sucks he answers with, "I.want.you.sat.in.that.barn.with.me. spilling.out.of.your.ass.surrounded.by. everyone.you.know."

And with his filthy words being spoken into my ear, his bites, his sucks, his dick pumping in and out of my arse, while his two fingers are hitting my g spot, his thumb strumming my clit and his other hand massaging my breasts and plucking my nipples, I release an *earth-shattering* scream of pleasure.

The hand from my breast quickly whips up to my mouth, muffling my cries as he joins me, with his own orgasm.

Heading back into the barn, looking as neat as we possibly can, we've not done too bad really, but we do look a little dishevelled, we sit back down with the rest of them.

"Where have you two been?" Carl asks.

"By the looks of them, they've been trying to join the baby club," Sara says.

"We've been on the bounce house," Carter adds, quickly.

"Yeah, we've been on the bouncy castle," I say, looking at Carter.

"Have you fuck! You might have been bouncing on *something*, but it's definitely not anything soft," Sara says to me.

We all laugh.

"Oh, shoot me now," my dad says, and my mum puts a soothing hand on his cheek, and smiles.

I look at Carter and he just winks at me, obviously thinking about our sticky, dirty little secret.

Chapter 49.
Carter, 3 months later.

We've been busy getting Buck ready to be ridden by other people.

He will only be suitable for more experienced riders. Sammie has been riding him quite a bit and he is handling it well.

We have had a lot of interest in riding lessons and some of that interest, has been in western style riding.

I don't know if it's because, country and western is extremely popular here, or if it's because people know there's an Alabama cowboy living on the farm.

Buck is ideal for that type of riding, then again, Max is a natural too.

Otis and Flash are doing well with the *less* experienced riders and up to now, Sammie has taken the lead with them, whereas, I have been with the more experienced.

I love watching her teach people how to ride, she's so patient and passionate about it.

Horses are a big part of her soul, and she wants to spread and share her love for them, with others.

We've also had a few events at the barn, we've decided to advertise it as that, *"The Barn"*.

It's simple, to the point and states it's the *only* place to have a country themed event.

Sara has been in charge of the marketing side of it, just like she is in charge of all the business side of the farm now. Her website building skills are pretty impressive.

Last week, we hosted a 50th anniversary there.

It's doing well, the whole farm is doing well, we are even thinking of opening as a petting farm for school field trips, giving kids the opportunity to meet the animals, see how the land works, hear about the circle of life here and ask any questions.

I've also been offering horse training packages, on and off the farm.

Sammie comes over to me and throws her arms around my shoulders, crushing her lips to mine.

"What was that for?" I say, with a smile.

"Well, you're over here, looking all sexy in your hat and I just wanted to feel you," she replies.

"*Deep*!" I say, with a laugh.

"What you thinking about?" She asks.

"Oh, not much, just everything that's happened lately, how much more we are doing on the farm and how much more we have *planned* to do," I reply.

"Yeah, all your ideas. You've really helped my dad an awful lot, we are really grateful you're here and I'm so glad it was you, who got my letter that day."

"Yeah, what's with that, you weirdo, wanting to write to a prisoner?!" I say, with a smile.

She smiles back, "I must like the bad boys," she winks.

We lace our fingers together and walk towards the house, hand in hand.

In the kitchen and every room of the house, lately, we have the same busy, exciting but nervous energy rolling around.

Sara is due any day now, and everyone has their own feelings and thoughts about it.

Sammie is really excited to meet her niece. I'm excited too, not sure I can call her my niece, but close enough, I'm dating her aunt.

Carl is getting nervous now and is often on edge, not daring to leave the farm at all, incase anything happens. I think he thinks that, once she goes into labor, the baby is just goin' to fall out and he will miss it.

Everyone is excited and probably nervous, about having a baby in the house again, but all in all, there's very positive vibes all round.

Until you get to the mom to be of course, she's just *constantly* fucking miserable.

I can imagine, it's hard, wobbling around the place all the time, with swollen ankles, no sleep and back ache, but she does moan!

I smirk.

I do feel bad for her, she looks tired and worn out.

She keeps trying all these different ideas, to hurry things along.

I've asked if she wants Sammie and I to put on a show for her, a few times, to bring on her labor, which she seemed all for, but no one else was very happy about it. The excitement and nerves of everyone in the house, also spreads to the other farmers too, they're like one big family and the arrival of the baby, is anticipated by everyone.

Carl comes into the kitchen, just as Sara is coming through, holding the bottom of her back and throwing out a string of cuss words.

"When the fuck is this baby going to come out?" She says, to no one in particular.

"She won't be long now," Sammie replies, with an understanding smile.

"Carter, can I talk to you in the room for a minute," Carl asks me.

I nod and we head towards the den, sitting down, opposite each other, on a couch each.

"What's up?" I look at Carl.

He looks back and takes a deep breath, I frown.

"It's nothing bad," he replies, "I just don't know if you would be up for it."

I look at him and tilt my head.

"Sara and I," he looks at me, his brow furrowed, "We were wondering if you would be godfather."

My eyes widen.

"Fucking hell, I thought you was goin' to ask for a fucking threesome," I laugh.

"You're a pervert!" He says.

"I know, your sister keeps telling me," I reply.

I look down at my feet and then back up at him again.

"I would have thought you would ask Jake. Why would you ask me?"

"Jake and I are friends, but we will never be like we were before, since the way he was with Sammie that time, I've had to forgive him, but I'll never forget. But Sammie is Victoria's auntie, and you are with her, you treat her well, you protect her, and I think you are likely to love and protect Victoria too. Besides, you're more or less my brother, so who else would I ever prefer to ask?" He says.

Shit I don't cry, but I feel like I might right now!
So, I clear my throat and say, "I would be honored!"

≈≈≈≈≈≈≈≈≈≈≈≈

Later that evening, after everything on the farm was complete, the stables and horses were sorted and we had all eaten dinner, we are sat in the den as a family, and I really do feel like a part of the family.
I have done for a while, but that moment today, with Carl, made me *really* feel it.
I've never felt so welcome, even with Pops, yeah, he loved me and I loved him, but it was a hard relationship, and it was always work work work, we didn't really get these family times, like we have here.
Carl is sat on one couch, next to Clara and he has Sara's head in his lap, while her legs are over Clara's lap.
She's having her legs and ankles rubbed and reading a baby and birthing book.
Sammie, Frank, Elsa and I, are on the other couch and there is a lot of conversation about babies goin' on, around the room.
At the moment, the women are talking about birth and trying to calm Sara down after reading something very graphic in the book.
"Stop reading it!" I say, "You're only upsetting yourself and quite frankly, my balls, have crept up inside my stomach!"
That makes her and everyone else laugh.

"I'm getting tired, I think I'll head off to bed," Sara says, as Sammie gets off the couch, to help her stand up from the laying position.

I smile at them both, they're so close.

It's great, that she's going to be an actual auntie, to one of her best friend's baby.

Just then, everyone else follows suit and agrees, we are all ready to head off to bed.

We go upstairs, as Frank and Elsa turn off all the lights, let the dogs out and lock all the doors, as usual.

Sammie lays on top of the bed sheets and sighs.

"She's getting bigger every second," she says.

"In my experience, women don't like to hear things like that, so with her hormones and everything, it might be best not to say that to her!" I reply.

She kneels up on the bed, looks at me and shakes her head.

I smile.

"Hey Carter!" she says.

"What baby girl?" I reply.

She rolls her lips and lifts her t-shirt, up over her head, my eyes bounce down to her tits, pushed up by a lacy green bra, and back up to her face.

"Make love to me!" She says.

I walk towards her.

"No kinky stuff, no roughness, no bruises, bites or marks," she carries on.

I get to the bed and lean over to kiss her, softly.

"Don't cotton to that now?" I ask.

"I love you taking over me, pushing me, making me feel confident and sexy, owning me, but making me feel needed at the same time. It's hot as hell!"

She looks into my eyes, "But tonight, I want soft, loving, smooth, emotional."

"I'll do whatever you want baby," I say, while climbing onto the bed and pulling her towards me, not allowing a slither of light between us.

All night long, I do as she asks. I hold her close, I kiss every part of her body, I gently caress her skin, leaving goosebumps in my trace, gently pumping in and out of her, until we are both sexually satisfied.

Then she lays in my arms, and I hold her close, as we drift off to sleep.

Chapter 50.
Sammie.

Victoria is here now, she's a week old and is so perfect.
She has a full head of dark hair, pink skin and blue
eyes.
Sara and Carl are besotted too, I've never seen Carl like
this.
Even with Sara, obviously he loves her, but their
relationship often looks like how mine and Jake's did,
he's not overly affectionate, but the moment Victoria
came into the picture, he was a big melted, pile of
mush.
      I'm laid on the rug, on the living room floor,
looking at the baby, in her little baby rocking chair.
She sleeps well through the day, but at night she's a
terror.
Screaming the house down. No one has had any sleep
in the last week, and we are all walking around, trying
to run the farm, with all the extras, like zombies.
I look up to the sofa and Sara is drifting off to sleep. I
gently nudge her leg,
"Why don't you go to bed for a bit?" I say.
"I'm okay, she might need something," she answers.
"Well, I'm here, her dad is outside, and my mum and
gran are around," I reply.
She looks at me.
"Just go get an hour or so, to yourself, she will be fine
and if we need you, you're only upstairs," I say.

She smiles and stands up, kisses me on the head, kisses Victoria and walks off out of the room.

I look back at Victoria, who starts to stir a bit.
I lift her out of her chair, before she can start crying and have her mum come back downstairs.

"Come on chick, let's have a cuddle," I say, as I sit down on the couch with her in my arms.
She settles back down for a snuggle.
Carter comes in the room, from being up at the stables.
"Hey baby," he sits down next to me and kisses me, then he bends and kisses Victoria's hand.
I love how he is with her, I just know he would do *anything* for her.
Then with Carl and Sara, wanting him to be her godfather, too. That meant a lot to both of us.

"You want a hold?" I ask him.

"Sure," he says.

"Have you washed your hands?" I reply.

"Of course I have," he says.

I hand Victoria over to him and she looks even smaller in his arms.

My ovaries have just exploded.

"So, you think we should do a Halloween party in the barn?" I ask Carter.

"Sounds good. I used to love Halloween, it's a big deal over in the States." He replies.

"I like Halloween too, it's no Christmas, but I do like it, and I love the farm in Autumn, although I love the farm in all seasons," I tell him.

"It's better than Christmas," he says.

I look at him, like he's from a different planet.

He laughs, "I take it you're Christmas mad then."
I nod.
"Are you okay?" I ask Carter.
"Yeah, just a bit tired today, but I think we all are, due to this monkey," he looks down at the baby.
I smile, "Yeah, she's a little shit!"
We both laugh quietly.
I sit and watch him with Victoria, he's just sat with her in his arms, looking down at her and I love him even more.
"You want a drink?" I ask.
"No babe, I'm good thanks."
         I get up, to go get a drink for myself.
"Where's the baby?" My mum asks.
"She's with Carter in the room, I need a drink," I reply.
"He's good with her, isn't he?" My gran says.
"Yeah, he's making me want a baby."
They both look at me, worried.
"Don't worry," I laugh, "I'm not going to have a baby, not anytime soon anyway."
I sit down at the table and drink my coffee, leaving Carter to sit with Victoria for a bit.
"I think we are all tired at the minute, I barely know which way is up," I say.
"Yeah, it's strange having a baby back in the house, it's going to take some getting used to again," my mum replies.
"She's beautiful though, isn't she? Imagine what it's going to be like when she has a little personality of her own, running round, making a mess," gran adds.

"Making a mess?" I say, "Never mind making a mess, I'm having her up cleaning out the stables, keeping her own horse as soon as she can walk, remember, Flash is hers, I'm not going to look after her forever!"
We all chuckle.

≈≈≈≈≈≈≈≈≈≈≈

Sara comes back downstairs, a little while later and joins us all in the lounge.
My mum is cuddling the baby.
"You're not having her yet," she says, "I've only just got her."
Sara smiles and sits down next to Carl.
"You need to get a shower before you go near the baby, you stink," she says to him.
"Thanks!" He replies and stands up, to go get a shower.
"Farmers!" she says.
        "Carter and I were saying earlier that we could do a Halloween party in the barn, Victoria's first Halloween needs to be epic," I say.
"Halloween is massive in America, isn't it?" My dad says.
"Yeah, it's as big as Christmas, maybe even bigger. We go all out for it. I've always been into the darker side of things anyway. Didn't go down well, in my family of Christians, that's for sure," Carter replies.
"We are Christian," my gran says.
"Yeah, I know, that's why I'm not goin' to tell y'all what I used to do," he says.

We all look round at each other, looking slightly worried.

≈≈≈≈≈≈≈≈≈≈≈

It's time to go up to bed and we are all hoping to get a little sleep tonight.

"You wanna join me in the shower?" I ask Carter.

"Fuck yeah," he says and I laugh.

We head into the bathroom and as soon as the door shuts, he kisses me, trailing his lips from my mouth to my jawline, down my neck and along my collarbone.

He takes my top off and kisses down my chest, while he removes my bra, biting my breasts gently, and taking my nipples into his mouth, alternately.

Removing the rest of my clothes and then his own, he walks us into the shower, while we are still kissing and turns the water on, a little hotter than usual.

"Carter," I gasp, "It's a bit hot!"

"You'll get used to it," he says, as he soaps up his hands and runs them all over my body.

I breathe out and then suddenly, he's changing the water to cold, I take a deep, sharp breath in and slap him.

"What are you doing?" I whisper-shout at him.

He chuckles, "Heightening your senses," he replies.

I push him back against the wall, into the water, so it's pounding straight onto the top of his head and down his face, then I push my body against his and reach up to kiss him, as he laughs against my lips.

I run my hands through his wet hair and over his dripping body, words can't describe how hot he looks, naked, wet, tall and strong, perfect!

We carry on kissing, passionately, allowing our tongues to tangle together and it's incredibly seductive, but there's no plans for sex, we are all like the walking dead right now and need to sleep, so it doesn't go any further than that.

It seems he was just in a silly, playful mood tonight, whilst trying to scold me and freeze me half to death, fucking idiot!

We head back into the bedroom, wearing just towels and as the bedroom door closes behind us, he laughs like a damn child.

I hit him again, "What the hell was that?" I say.

"I was just playing," he says, while removing his towel, with a smirk and getting into bed.

I shake my head at him and do the same, joining him in bed.

We cuddle up to each other and I put my head on his chest.

Looking up at him, I say, "So, I'm curious, what did your family of Christians not like?"

"Oh, nothing really, I used to like joining in with a few different practices, an ex-girlfriend thought she was the devil, used to have a ouija board et cetera," he replies.

My blood runs cold.

"You don't do any of that anymore though?" I ask.

He looks down at me, "I'm still fascinated by it all and find it interesting, but no, not anymore. Don't worry, I will never be involved in anything like that here, especially if you find it uncomfortable," he says.

I put my head back down on his chest and we just lay there silently.

I'm listening to the steady drum of his heartbeat, as we finally fall off to sleep, without having sex, for the first time since we started.

Chapter 51.
Carter.

It's Halloween, and we have the party tonight, in the barn.

Just like for the baby shower, Sammie has invited *everyone,* and a lot of people are coming out. It's family friendly, but it is on an evening, so if any adults want to have a bit of fun later, kids will have to be here at their parent's discretion.

We set up the barn this morning, after jobs on the farm had been completed and it's gone from being all light, white and airy, to dark, sinister and creepy.

The only lights we are using, are the string lights and the candles in the jack o lanterns, so it stays pretty dark.

All the tables are covered with black linen and orange confetti, with black sashes on the backs of the chairs.

The arch is decorated, this time, with black and orange balloons and we have fake cobweb stretched everywhere we could put it, with giant fake spiders tangled in them and giant jack o lanterns in the centre of each table, with candlelight inside.

We have skeletons, scary clowns and ghosts hanging from the ceiling, all around the room.

Halloween themed food, candy and sodas are on a stretch of tables, down one side of the room, opposite the bar.

The bar is fully stocked, for anyone wanting alcohol.

It's looking pretty good and ready to go, with added ambiance, thanks to the smoke machine by the door and the Halloween music being played through the speakers.

We have also hired someone, to do face painting for the kids, or adults if they want. She's only staying for the first two hours of the party.

We are all getting ready and I can't wait to see Sammie in her costume.

She has gone for a horny devil; with a red, latex romper, red stockings and suspenders, black stilettos and a black choker to match, complete with a red devil tail and a pair of horns.

Just thinking about it makes my cock strain, begging for freedom.

We are in the bedroom, while I'm putting on my costume. Mine is pretty boring, I'm a vampire, so I just have black trousers, a white shirt with the sleeves rolled up and extremely shiny, black dress shoes.

Sammie has put this white shit all over the top half of my body and face, to make me look pale and she's put some grey stuff on my face, something she said was *"contour"*. She's also put something called *"lip stain"* on, and around my lips, so I look blood stained, finished off, with an actual bucket of hair gel on my hair, pushing it sleek back, making it look wet and dark.

She's sat at her mirror, doing her makeup, wearing only red, lace underwear.

When I look over at her, she looks back at me, through the mirror and says, "You look hot, I love me a vampire."

I walk towards her and *roughly* pull her up, off her stool and her eyes widen.

I put my hand into her hair, that's styled into big, flowing curls and pull her head back towards me, she leans back onto my shoulder and whispers, "Don't ruin my hair and makeup, I don't have time to redo it."

I smirk, and bite her neck hard enough to draw blood, then suck her clean and lick the trace.

"The last time I tasted your blood, you freaked out, now you say you like a vampire. Make your mind up!"

"Nothing about you surprises or shocks me anymore," she replies and I smile.

I look at her in the mirror, from behind.

"That red lipstick on your plump, perfectly formed lips should be fucking illegal."

"Things being illegal doesn't stop you." She looks back at me, in the mirror, with a cheeky glint in her eyes and I fucking love her giving me cheek, having the confidence to challenge me, she is goin' to be the death of me.

"That's 100% true darlin'," I say, as I push her forward, so her hands are flat on her vanity and she's looking at me through the reflection.

After I unbutton my trousers, and pull her panties off her completely, I lick my way up the inside of her stocking clad leg and eat her pussy from behind.

"Oh, Carter!! Oh yeah!" She moans, sending me savage.

I suddenly, *painstakingly* pull my tongue out of her fucking delectable slit and stand up behind her, looking at her reflection.

"Do not take your eyes off of that mirror, for one second!"

"Yes sir," she replies.

My eyes flash to hers and I wrap my hand around her throat, both of us looking at the rose tattoo that is now acting as her choker.

Her lips part and I growl a low, guttural noise.

"We need to be quick baby, we are going to be late," I say, before I roughly shove my cock inside of her, from behind.

She puts her head back on my shoulder, as I push deep into her pussy.

"Eyes on the mirror baby," I whisper.

She looks back into the mirror, "I love the look of your hand round my throat," she pants, as I'm driving into her and pulling all the way back out again, over and over.

All I can do, is moan back, because the sensation of coming out of her and re-entering each time, is too much for me to be able to speak, or even think up words.

I tighten my grip and feel her throat, flex under my palm.

Putting my other hand around the front of her, I rub circular, high pressure movements on her clit, as she moans loudly, through my hand.

It's sexy a fuck, us both watching in the mirror, as I screw her from behind, with one hand around her throat and one hand on her pussy, stimulating her little mound of nerves, looking into her hooded, emerald green eyes.

My thrusts get deeper and faster, while I get us both there quickly, so we can have time to neaten ourselves up for the party, which I'm sure people must be arriving at already.

Sammie has managed a few orgasms already, but I want to give her at least one more before I come.

I apply more pressure to her clit, while I fuck her harder.

She screams, her legs shaking beneath her and I move my hands to her waist, to hold her upright, while I plough my way to my own shattering.

Exploding my release into her pussy, I slowly pull out, holding us both up, which is difficult at the minute, seeing as we are both feeling like a wobbly mess.

I finally step back from her, and a trail of me, is spilling down the inside of her leg.

I look at her in the mirror, while I wipe my cum from her leg with my finger, and she watches my every move.

"Do you want this pushing back into your pussy baby, or do you want it on your tongue?" I ask, with a smirk.

She turns her head over her shoulder to me, and grabs my wrist, moving my hand to her lips and putting my finger in her mouth, sucking it clean with a little pop.

After making ourselves look presentable, well, Sammie looks like a walking wet dream, but we straighten ourselves up, so we don't look like we've actually just fucked in a mirror, we head downstairs and out over to the barn.

Everyone else in the house has left already.

Entering the barn, we see that we are probably one of the last people here and everyone seems to be having a great time.

All the kids have lined up to get their face painted by the face artist and the music is well and truly pumping, with a few people doing the *Michael Jackson Thriller* dance on the dance floor.

Sammie and I look at each other and she just looks incredibly sexy. I love every single bit of her, and I love her more, every time I look at her or think about her. She holds my hand and smiles at me, then we walk towards the family.

Everyone looks fantastic.

We have Frank and Elsa as Gomez and Morticia Addams, Clara as Lily Munster, Carl and Sara are Edward and Bella Cullen, Victoria is the cutest jack o lantern I've ever seen and just then, Sammie shrieks and coos, grabbing her and squeezing the life out of her.

"She's goin' to suffocate your child," I say to Sara.

"I don't care, I'm having a night off," she replies, holding up a glass of champagne.

We all laugh.

Jake and Louise come over, dressed as the Joker and Harley Quinn.

"That's a very couple like costume choice," says Sara and we all look at them.

"Couple?" answers Louise, "It's just costumes."

Sammie looks at Jake and he blushes a little.

I go and grab us a drink, and Carl comes over to me at the bar.

"What you think is going on with them?" He asks, gesturing to Louise and Jake.

"Not sure, looks like they're here together, but it's no one else's business, is it?"

Carl looks at me, "You in a mood? You seem like you might be bothered by them being together."

I frown at Carl, "Why would I be bothered?"

"Because you and Louise had a thing," he says.

"Don't be stupid, I don't care what Louise does, it's nothing to do with me, she doesn't mean anything to me in that way, I just hope he doesn't hurt her, like he could have hurt Sammie," I reply, before grabbing Sammie a champagne, me a whiskey and walking away.

I walk back over to everyone else, who are all now sat at a table and sit down next to Sammie, handing her the champagne.

"Oh! Thank you!" She says and kisses me.

I could kiss her every second for the rest of my life.

"Do you think they're here together?" She asks, suddenly.

"Jake and Louise?"

"Yeah."

"Probably, they're in a couple costume and they're not leaving each other's side, does it bother you?" I ask her.

"No, why would it bother me?"

"You were with Jake for two years and she's one of your friends."

"As long as they're happy, that's all that matters, because I'm the happiest I've ever been and it just gets better every day," she smiles at me.

"Me too baby," I kiss her, softly and slowly.

"Another successful event in the barn, it looks like," Sammie says.

"Yeah, looks that way," I reply.

"Isn't there any romantic, slow dance, Halloween songs?" she asks and I laugh, then think about it for a while, before saying, "No, I doubt it."

"You forgot your teeth," she says.

"I can't talk, eat or drink with them fuckers stuck to my teeth," I reply.

"But I wanted to kiss you, with them in."

"I'll be right back," I say, while heading out of the barn, back to the house to look for the teeth.

≈≈≈≈≈≈≈≈≈≈≈

I never went back to the barn, I'm just sat on the bed, in shock, when Sammie comes into the bedroom.

It's been hours and I know the party is over now, I can hear everyone leaving.

Sammie comes in, "Hey, I thought you had fallen asleep, why didn't you come back?"

She looks down at me and I look back up at her, with pure confusion, not knowing what to do, or how to feel.

She quickly comes over and gets down on her knees, in front of me,

"Hey!"

I look into her eyes, and she looks back into mine, putting her hands on mine.

"What's happened? What is it?"

"I don't know how she got my number, but she has, she's found out where I am and I have a message from her, she's called me and left a message, wants me to call her tomorrow," I say, quickly, pushing the words out as though they're in a *race* against each other.

"Carter, slow down, who has called you?"

I look at her, frowning, realizing I'm not making sense.

"My mom."

Chapter 52.
Sammie, Christmas on the Farm.

I'm stood at the kitchen window, watching all the men moving the cows.

It's coming up to Christmas now and it's been fairly mild, but it's getting colder.

We have the barn and parlour, which are great, but when it's deep Winter, the cows need to be housed indoors, and we don't have the accommodations for that.

In previous years, we have moved the cows to another farm, who can help out and house them for us over Winter and we have always shut down, but now, we have other things to be doing on the farm, while the cows are away.

I catch sight of Carter, who is herding them in true cowboy style, mounted.

I smile.

His mum got in touch with him a couple of month ago. He phoned her on speaker, in front of us all in the kitchen one morning, and at first, it was civil, she said they missed him and wanted him to go home.

I'm not going to lie, I wanted to be sick at the thought he might have left.

By the end of the conversation, it came to light, that she only wanted him home, because they were struggling and the ranch was going under.

They had no idea what they were doing and everything his grandad had worked for, they were losing and would soon have no money.

She ended up telling him, that he was dead to her and she didn't care what happens to him.

He acts as though he isn't bothered by any of it, like he's some big tough guy, but someone with a heart like his, isn't that tough really.

I think we all wanted to cry, when he finished the conversation with, *"mom, that's nothing new to me"* before putting the phone down on her.

If that woman had been in front of me, I would have put my fist down her neck.

I look at him, doing his thing and my heart aches, it aches knowing the person he is under the rough exterior, people think he's unbreakable, the way he gets on with things and fights his way through, helping others, no matter what is going on in his own head.

He's a big, strong man, but his heart is even bigger, and whatever his scum of a mum thinks, he is someone to be proud of.

He looks at me through the window and we smile at each other, then he turns Buck around and follows the trucks and trailers on horseback.

Watching them all leave the farm, with the cattle, moving on up the snow-covered pathway, my eyes scan across the whole of the farm, as far as I can see, a blanket of glittery, pure, clean white snow.

The trees have all lost their leaves and are also covered with snow.

We very rarely get it at Christmas, but it looks like we may still have it for Christmas Day.

Even though the cattle have gone for the Winter, we still have the chickens and horses to take care of, and we are still offering lessons and training, as long as it's not icy.

We also have four events booked in the barn before Christmas. They're DIY events though, so we don't dress the room up or anything, they do what they want in the barn, as long as there are no drugs, smoking and they clean up after themselves.

They also have to stick to the barn, they aren't allowed to trespass the rest of the land.

We will be putting up a tree in there, before the first event though.

Carter and I are going to do that at some point.

Even though I have had a boyfriend before, we have never trimmed up a Christmas tree together and it's something I've always wanted to do, so I'm roping Carter into it.

"What are you looking at love?" My mum asks.

"I was just looking at the snow, the farm, thinking about the things we have going on over the Winter, which we wouldn't usually have. Also watched the men take the cows out." I turn round to face her.

"It's going to be an exciting Christmas this year, with Victoria being here," I say.

"Yeah, I can't wait," she replies.

I sigh.

"Everything okay?" My mum asks.

"Yeah, I was thinking about Carter's mum, what she was like to him on the phone. I wonder if he thinks about it."

"She was a nasty piece of work," she says.

I nod.

"What is gran doing today?"

"I think she's helping at the church today," she replies.

"I think I'll go tack Max up, go for a ride when Carter gets back."

"Okay love, be careful."

"Always am," I reply.

I get my wellies and coat on and walk up to the stables.

I swap the horses over, to a clean stall each, and clean out the used stalls, putting out clean water and food for all four of them.

I tack up Max and take him out of the yard.

We stick to the grass, with thicker fresh snow, so there is lower risk of an accident. Just having a slow walk around the farm, waiting for Carter to get home.

"Oh Max, I don't know what is wrong with me today. I'm feeling a bit down."

I lean over and stroke his neck.

Just then, I see the trucks, coming back down the drive and then I see my cowboy, coming up the back, round the side and my heart skips a beat, like it does *every* time I see him.

"This isn't healthy," I say to Max, "I'm not supposed to feel this strongly for someone, he is right there, I can see him and yet, I miss him."

"Come on,"

I squeeze Max to walk a little faster over in Carter's direction.

Reaching Carter, he says, "Hey baby, what are you doing, riding on your own in this weather? It's not safe."

"I'm fine, I just thought, I would come wait for you and we could go for a little ride, I've done all the stalls." I say.

"Sure, let's go."

We both head off, toward the trees at the top end of the farm.

"Everything go okay with the cows?" I ask.

"Yeah, all good, they're going to be nice and warm there, compared to here."

"Carter? Are you okay?" I ask.

"Yeah baby, course I am, why wouldn't I be?"

"Just checking." I smile.

We ride on for a while, in silence, just looking out, over the beautiful Winter scene.

"We need to put a tree up in the barn, for those Christmas parties, that are getting held there."

He nods in reply.

"Shall we do it tonight?" I ask.

"Do you want to do it tomorrow instead? I'm a bit tired today and I just really want to sleep, if I'm honest," he replies.

"Sure. We will get an early night and get some sleep. Victoria is still keeping people awake, isn't she?" I smile.

He smiles back.

"Do you want to head back?" I ask.

"Yeah, okay," he replies, and we head back to the stable. Locking the horses up securely, we head back to the farmhouse to get warm.

≈≈≈≈≈≈≈≈≈≈≈

I say goodnight to everyone and go upstairs, to see Carter sitting on the bed, in the same way I walked in and saw him at Halloween, when he had heard from his mum.

He says he's not bothered by things, but he's been a bit quiet since he spoke to her.
"Hey," I say.
"Hey," he yawns.
"I'm just gunna get a shower," he says.
"Do you want me to join you?" I ask.
"If you want."
He walks into the bathroom, and I watch him, wondering whether I actually should or not.
We've had sex, as normal and he's been working hard, but he has been distant since that day and I don't know if he actually wants to be bothered, or if he would rather be left alone.

I decide to go to the bathroom with him, but not to make it a sexual thing, just be there for him.
We go to the shower and get undressed, quite robotically.
He steps in the shower first and puts his head and face under the water.
I watch him for a bit, before I get in behind him.

Grabbing the body wash, I lather some up in my hands and stroke it, up over his back and shoulders, moving my hands to massage his shoulder muscles.

He lets his head relax and fall forward and I step in closer to him, running my hands down his biceps and wrapping my arms round his waist, locking my hands onto his abs, and putting my forehead on his back.

"What's wrong?" I ask.

"I'm just tired," he says.

"Would you rather go back to Alabama? Because if you want to go home, I understand."

He turns round to face me, looking down at me, he says, "No, that's not what I want. I really am just tired." I nod.

He leans down, to kiss me and we spend the next half an hour in the shower, just using the soap to stroke and explore each other's bodies, *"washing"* them in silence, no sex, just intimacy, finishing off the shower with a close, soapy, warm cuddle.

≈≈≈≈≈≈≈≈≈≈≈

Now that the cattle are off the farm, there isn't much for us to do, so we spend Winter, especially Christmas season, as a family.

We get a bit of a lay in too, well a lot of a lay in, really.

"When are we putting the decorations up?" I ask my mum.

"Whenever you want! We want to be doing it early really, with it being Victoria's first Christmas," she says.

I smile.

"Are we going to do the one in the barn today? So that it's up, for the events people are renting it out for?" I say to Carter.

He nods, while he has his coffee.

Sara brings Victoria downstairs, she's being a bit whiny today.

"Uh oh! What's wrong with madam?" My mum says.

"Oh, she won't stop moaning, could she be teething this early?" She asks.

"Some do," my mum says, "So it's not unheard of."

She sees Carter and her eyes light up.

Whoever she is with at the time, if she sees Carter, she always wants him. She's his biggest fan.

"Look at her!! Little tart!" I say and everyone laughs.

She's leaning away from Sara, holding her arms out to him.

He puts his arms out for her and she more or less, nose dives into him.

I walk over to her, grab her face and kiss her head,

"You're a tart like your mother!" I say.

"Charming!" Calls Sara as I walk out, to go to the barn.

≈≈≈≈≈≈≈≈≈≈≈

I'm down at the barn, setting the tree up, waiting for Carter to be free of his latest and youngest fan.

He comes in when I'm halfway through doing the branches.

"How much did she cry when you left?" I laugh.

"Not that much, Carl came in. She's definitely into the males."

"I'm just doing the tree branches, do you want to bring the garlands and other decorations in? they're in the van outside," I ask Carter.

"Sure," he says.

He brings the last box in and I'm just trying to sort the top branches out, but I'm not tall enough.

He looks at me.

"You okay there?" He says.

"Not really."

He walks over to me and sorts the top branches out.

"Why don't you have a real tree?" He asks.

"We've never been able to have a real tree, because of the dogs and now, because of Victoria, with the pine needles dropping off and everything."

He lifts his chin.

"You're still a bit quiet, you still tired?"

I'm trying to tread carefully.

He sits down on the stage. The tree is being set up, to the side of the stage.

"I'm okay, I just feel a bit strange for some reason, not sure why."

"Is it your mum?" I ask.

He shrugs his shoulders.

I walk over to him and straddle his legs, wrapping my arms around his shoulders and he squeezes me.

We just sit there, like that, for a good 10 minutes.

"Come on," I tap him on the back, "Let's get festive and do this tree, just think about happy things."

I walk over to the music centre and put some Christmas music on.

"Rocking around the Christmas Tree" plays and we walk over to the tree and start by putting the lights on it. It's going to need a few thousand lights on this tree, it's quite a size, but it's going to look beautiful.

We put the lights on together, wrapping them all the way round, warm white and twinkling fairy lights. They match the ones, that are installed on the walls, perfectly.

Because the barn colours are like a white grey, with lots of white furnishing et cetera, we've gone with white lights on a dark green tree, with silver and white baubles. Some plain, some shiny, some glittery and others fluffy.

With thin, silver lametta, because I'm not a fan of tinsel, and a white star with flecks of silver in it.

≈≈≈≈≈≈≈≈≈≈≈

It takes a few hours to finish, so that it looks designer and professional and it's amazing, with a large barn window behind it, complete with a perfect, Winter snow scene.

It's like something out of a movie, or from the front of a Christmas card.

We have listened to some great music, the lights on the tree and around the walls are twinkling and we are just wrapping fake presents, sat on the floor in front of the tree.

It's a nice warm feeling.

Carter gets up, to walk over to the bar and gets us a drink each, while we wrap the boxes, that will sit under the tree, in silver and white paper and ribbons.

As he's pouring our drinks, I ask, "What's your favourite Christmas memory?"

He looks at me, grabs the glasses and walks back over.

"Thanks," I take one of the drinks and he sits next to me again.

"This," he says, in reply.

I look at him, "No childhood Christmas memories?" I ask.

"Not particularly no, I used to like how the ranch looked, with the tree and everything, but no particular memories that stand out or anything."

I feel sad, but I don't show it and I don't tell him mine.

"Please come home for Christmas" by Jon Bon Jovi comes on.

"Dance with me?" I say, in a half question.

He stands up and pulls me up too.

We dance, the way he danced with Louise, at the Honky Tonk.

One of my hands on his shoulder, one of his hands on my back and our other hands interlocked, with space between us, so we can look at each other and talk et cetera.

"I've always wanted to dance like this… properly," I say.

He smiles, "Properly?"

"Yeah, rather than just hugging and swaying on the dance floor, like everyone does these days. This is a *proper* dance," I say to him.

He smiles at me.

"I'm sorry I've been quiet lately," he says.

"No, it's okay, just know that you can talk to me, if something is wrong. You don't have to bottle it up. It's not good to do that," I reply.

He nods.

At the end of the song, he leans down to kiss me, and we sink into it pretty desperately.

Going from romantic, to urgent.

We slide down to the floor and start pulling at each other's clothes.

Within seconds, we are naked and he's pulling me close to him.

I push him back and start to kiss down his body, going really quite quickly, because I have the need to taste him.

Taking his dick in my mouth, I swirl my tongue around the head and glide it down the length of him.

He moans and puts his hands, in my hair, bobbing my head up and down a little, but before he can get too carried away, he gently pulls my hair up, so I know to stop.

"What?" I say, as he's pulling my body, up his body, until I'm more or less sitting on his chest.

"Higher!" He growls, "Sit on my face."

"Oh, I don't know if I'm com—"

He pulls my body up and lowers me onto his face, before I can finish my objection.

Pushing his tongue right into me, he wraps his arms around my thighs, pulling me flush against him, so I can't shy away. I have to be there and enjoy it.

Before long, I can't take it anymore, I have to chase the orgasm that is brewing inside of me, so I roll my hips, I grind and roll my hips on his *face*, and I don't even feel shy.

Where is Sammie? Because I don't know who this woman is.

His moans are sending vibrations to my clit, while his tongue is *actually* fucking me.

I can feel the pressure building and I'm almost there, I'm almost going to…. oh fuck! It happens again, I scream his name, shaking and soaking him through, but knowing how turned on he was by it, the last time it happened, I don't feel anxious, embarrassed or ashamed. *I feel empowered and he loves it.*

≈≈≈≈≈≈≈≈≈≈≈

It's Christmas morning and we have all been enjoying some family time, round the tree in the living room, with hot chocolate.

The tree in the farmhouse has the colour scheme of creams, browns and golds, to match the decor or the room.

A warmer look, than the one in the barn.

We have swapped gifts and got loads of pictures, of Victoria in her Christmas outfit and opening her presents.

She was more interested in the wrapping paper, and now we are all helping prepare dinner, apart from Carter, who has gone to do what's needed with the horses for the day.

It's a big job to prep this food, because there's so much of it, so we are getting stuck in.

We are having Christmas dinner at the barn this year, because we have a lot of people coming to join us. With it being Victoria's first Christmas, we wanted to bring all the families and important people, together.

I break off, from helping with the dinner, for a little while, to set up the tables and make sure all the lights are lit, for when people walk into the barn. So, while the rest of them, finish sorting dinner and Carter is busy with things at the stable, I head to the barn.

I put the white tablecloths on the tables, with silver runners down the centre and in the middle of the tables, I place a candle, surrounded by white and silver berries. I set out the plates, cutlery, glasses and napkins, all white and silver themed and looking very inviting. Then I turn on all the lights, the wall fairy lights, the tree lights and the chandelier, because it's quickly getting dark outside.

Inside the barn, right now, looks like a warm, welcoming Winter wonderland.

The last job to do, before the food starts to get carted over, with the guests, is to write the place cards. Attending we have; Frank, Elsa, Clara, Carl, Sara, Victoria, (although she will probably stay in her pram), Giles and Sue (Sara's parents), Sammie, Carter, Miles, Jake, Louise, Mark and Josie (Louise's parents).

≈≈≈≈≈≈≈≈≈≈≈

We sit down, to the feast that has been prepared, the food looks great, the barn looks beautiful, the people are happy, it's Christmas Day and I am *madly, head over heels in love.*
The snow starts to fall again, just as Bing, croons at us through the speakers.
"Merry Christmas Everyone," I say, and everybody lifts their glasses, replying in unison, "Merry Christmas!"

Chapter 53.
Carter.

Spring is here again on the farm, and we have the cattle back, so things are in full swing.

We also have, two new Geldings in the stables, on a full livery package, where the owners don't do the everyday upkeep. They just come and ride them when they have time.

Part of their contract is that we can use the horses for riding lessons, if needed.

The owners were all for that, because it meant the horses are getting good exercise, if they can't get up to ride them, themselves.

The riding school is doing well, and Sammie has a steady diary flowing.

I am training two horses off farm at the moment, but we are hoping to fence off an area, a bit further away from the main stable and paddock, for the horses to come to us, to be trained. Makes it easier, when I have other things to do here, and I don't have to keep leaving.

As part of that new development, we want to build a small, three stall stable to keep the horses that I'm training in, so eventually they will come, stay here to be trained and then go home, when the program is complete.

It's actually coming up to a year, since I came to the UK.

A lot has happened in that time, I don't even feel like the same person anymore, I even use some UK language now, I tend to say pounds instead of dollars and there's a few more words and phrases creeping in.

I've definitely calmed down, that's for sure. I think I've only punched somebody once.

Speaking of that, Jake is actually dating Louise.

We knew they were seeing each other, but they kept trying to hide it.

It was obvious that something was goin' on at Halloween, coming in a couple costume and not leaving each other's side all night. I caught them, last month, kissing in the stables.

Louise had given Flash to Victoria, before she was even born, but she comes to see her whenever she's at the farm and there they were, what do they call it? Snogging? In the stable. Full on making out.

Not a good move, when you're trying to hide, something from the people who work there.

I can still see the shock on their faces when I walked into Flash's stall and he had her pinned up against the wall.

Seems he might have a bit of passion in him, after all.

Talking of dating, Clara has a *"companion"* they are calling him. I call him a fuck buddy, much to everyone's disgust, apart from Sara obviously, she loves it.

I think they all love it really, but I do it either way and I'm not goin' to stop.

It's entertaining watching them all die inside.

We have a couple of birthday celebrations coming up in the barn, one of which, they have asked me to be the entertainment.

Sammie wasn't impressed, because she thought it was stripping, they wanted me to do, her mind is always in the gutter lately.

But no, they had seen Sammie and I, singing at the Honky Tonk and said that the party is country themed, and wanted me to sing country. They were gunna pay an extra 200, so I might as well.

Any money we make, goin' into the farm, is a bonus.

Victoria is almost six months old and is a right little character.

She shuffles between rooms, on her ass, grinning at everyone. She has three teeth at the front of her mouth, so when she looks up at us grinning, it looks cute as fuck and you can't help, but to laugh. Then she laughs. She actually copies a lot of noises we make, she blows raspberries a lot, which I know is a big thing with babies, but she does it right after I've blown them on her stomach.

Her giggle is infectious, and she finds it funny, to take my hat off and throw it on the floor.

The rules can be broken for her, it's fine, she's too cute at the moment, to say no to, probably always will wrap us all around her little finger.

She's a *perfect* mix of her mom and dad, with Carl's black hair and Sara's blue eyes and pale porcelain skin. Sammie calls her, *"My English Rose"*.

She also has a mix of their personalities too, cheeky like her mom and miserable as fuck sometimes, like her dad.

She's definitely goin' to break some hearts, well that's if the army of people behind her, don't break their legs first.

She's still Uncle Carter's girl though, I'll do anything for that little monkey.

We are all having breakfast together in the kitchen, the usual big feast that Elsa and Clara put on for the family and all the workers, but now Clara's bit on the side is joining us, they're going to church today. *Hypocrites,* they're not even married and they're sleeping in the same bed!

I smile to myself.

"What are you smiling at?" Asks Sammie.

"I can't tell you, you'll think I'm a pervert," I answer.

"We all know you are," she says, as I sit down next to her and grab her knee under the table with a firm squeeze.

She giggles.

As soon as I sit down, Victoria is trying to reach over to sit on my lap.

I put my arms out for her and Sara hands her over. Sammie gives her a bit of toast to chomp on, and she has a go at it for a while, before putting the soggy, chewed up piece of mush right onto my plate.

Everyone laughs, which then makes her laugh.

I turn her around to face me, holding her up in the air, "Thanks kid. It's a good job you're cute!" I say to her, before sitting her back down on my lap.

I look at Sammie, who smiles at me.

She smiles at me a lot, obviously, but when I am doing anything to do with Victoria, her smile is a different kind of smile. It's all mushy and shit.

"Are you training today?" Frank asks me.

"No, not today. I went yesterday. It's ideal to do it daily, but they don't want it, I just told them it will take longer to get a result. It will be better when we can house them here, while I carry out the full program," I reply.

"What about lessons?" Frank asks Sammie.

"Not got one booked until 11am, I'll need to get them all in the paddock while I muck out, then get them tacked up to start, so I'm going up there after breakfast."

Frank nods. "Anything going on in the barn?" He asks.

"There are two events booked this month, one of which, they want entertainment, but that's it. Nothing today," says Sara, who deals with bookings.

"They want us to sort entertainment?" Elsa asks.

"Yeah, well they were at that country night we all went to, *wow,* so much has happened since then!!… And they want a country singer, they've asked Carter to do it," Sara says.

They all look at me.

Chapter 54.
Carter.

"They want you to sing?" asks Clara.

"What? You think I can't do it?" I say.

"Not at all, but apart from that night on karaoke, have you done it before?" Frank asks.

"It's not unusual, to do that sort of thing over in the States, people were always doing shows at country bars, I've done it loads of times," I reply.

"He plays instruments and everything!" says Sammie.

I smile.

"Are you using Buck today?" I look at Sammie.

"Yeah, I'm going to ride him, unless you need him?" She replies.

"No, but just be careful, Spring is here again and pretty soon, Flash is goin' to be in season, so he might start getting a bit touchy," I say, "If his behavior changes at all, don't try and stop him, just call me."

She nods, looking a little nervous.

"Okay, so once breakfast is done, we need to get the cows to the parlor and Sammie is working at the stable, so she won't be available. Carter are you half available?" Frank asks.

"Yeah, I'm around, but need to be ready for having to sort Buck out. Speaking of horny males, when are you weaning that bull?" I reply.

"Any day now, you're right, he needs to be separated from the cows, he's coming up to sexual maturity and we don't want any unplanned pregnancies," he says.

I nod.

We finish our food and drink and get up to start the day, leaving Elsa, Clara and Dave, Clara's lover, to clean up after breakfast.

Sara heads upstairs to her office with Victoria, while Victoria waves at us all frantically.

God, she's cute.

≈≈≈≈≈≈≈≈≈≈≈≈

We are getting the cattle to the parlor for milking, when my phone rings, it's Sammie, *fuck!*

"Yeah?" I answer and all the farmers roll their eyes at me, it's now a thing to take the piss out of how I answer a phone.

"Hello is the word you're looking for," she says on the other end of the line.

"Whatever, what's wrong?" I reply.

"Are you busy? Can you come up here? Buck is being a dickhead," she says.

"I'm on my way."

I end the call and head up, over to the stables.

When I get there, Sammie is just sat on a bench looking annoyed, the rest of the horses are in the paddock.

"What's wrong?" I say, I can hear Buck kicking off in the stables.

"He bit me, the little fucker! I've never been bitten by a horse!" She says.

"He bit you?" I ask, walking over to her quickly to check the bite.

"It's just a bruise," she says, "It's not broken, he's just bruised me, but I'm not impressed with him, I was only trying to get him out into the paddock. Little fucker, can stay in there sulking now, *fuck him!*" She says, and I can't help myself but to smile.

"It's not funny!" She glares at me.

"It's not baby, no," I say, as I touch the side of her head on my way past her, into the stable.

When I get in to Buck, he glares at me, his ears pinned back and nostrils flaring. *Fuck!*

"Shhhh," I say, while holding my forearm out to him, down the length of his face.

Keeping my tone, steady and quiet I tell him, "It's okay, I know what women do to us, I understand. Looks like Flash might be ready to be having a baby, huh? But it's fine, we won't torment you, we will find somewhere for you, until we figure out what to do. But if you bite my girlfriend again, that place for you, will be a horse burger."

By this time, he is allowing me to touch him.

I gently stroke over his eyes, to test his trust and hold my hand flat on his muzzle, to be sure his nipping has calmed down.

I come out to Sammie, who's still on the bench, and I sit next to her.

"Has he calmed down?" She says.

"Yeah, he has a case of blue balls syndrome."

She laughs.

"I need to do his stall, but he won't let me in," she replies.

"I'll take him out, you do the stall. I'll take him away from the others for a little while, let him work off some energy on a run. If you want to get the horses tacked up afterwards and then go home, I'll take the lesson, I don't want you riding him until we can figure out what we are goin' to do with him."

She nods and I kiss her, before goin' to lead Buck and get him ready to leave.

≈≈≈≈≈≈≈≈≈≈≈

When I get back from the ride, all the stalls are clean and replenished, the water and food buckets are replaced and the five other horses are tacked up, in the paddock waiting for the lessons to start.

The lesson goes well, Buck behaves himself to a point and I manage to keep him steered away from Flash, but we are going to have to sort something, this isn't fair on him.

Sammie is back at the house now, so I finish off up here, by grooming the horses after the lesson and putting them all in their stalls.

It's not a large stable, with only six stalls, three on each side, but I try to keep Flash and Buck, the furthest away from each other.

After sweeping and hosing the main stable and yard down to finish, I lock it all up and head for the farmhouse.

I walk into the kitchen, where everyone is sat having a coffee and like clockwork, Victoria is shuffling towards me.

"Someone needs to pick her up, I don't want to reject her, but I stink, I need a shower first."

Sammie picks her up and says, "Uncle Carter is a smelly boy, let's go in the room and watch Peppa pig."

I smile.

"I need to talk about a few things when I come down," I say to them all, as I head upstairs for a quick shower.

When I come back down, everyone looks up at me, as though they have been waiting there, to hear what I wanted to say.

I frown at them.

"What was it you needed to talk about?" Frank asks, "We have some work to do on the land."

I get to the bottom of the stairs and head to the table, to sit down with them all.

"Flash is coming into season, she's likely to stay in, until the end of Summer, it's not fair on Buck to be kept with her. We either need to find somewhere else to house him, whilst she's in season, mate them or get him Gelded. He's bitten Sammie today, because he's horny and tormented, so we need to help him," I say.

"Do we have the finances to build the training stables now? that way, we can at least keep Buck on the farm in one of the stalls there and keep him separate on the land too," Frank asks Sara.

She nods, "We have more than enough money to get that started, I can get looking round for builders now if you want?"

"No! I can do it, just get me a budget and I'll sort it out, I've built many stables, we can all do it here, as part of the land work," I say.

"We haven't built stables," says Carl.

"You'll learn," I reply,

"We don't need to pay builders, I just need a material budget, and we can all pull together and get it done between us."

They all look worried, but I know we can do it.

Sara nods, "I'll sort it," she says.

"In the meantime, I'm goin' to pay for someone to house him, someone who only keeps males, it will take a while to build something sturdy here and he is really struggling and is a danger to the other horses."

Frank nods.

"We will make, the fencing of a new training area, part of the groundwork this week, so at least that's done," he says.

"Thanks," I reply.

Sammie comes into the kitchen with Victoria and as usual, straight away she's reaching out to me.

Everyone laughs.

"No one gets a look in when you're around," Jake says.

I smile and kiss Victoria on the cheek.

I look over at Sammie, "What are you doing later?" I ask.

"Tonight?" She says.

"Yeah, early evening."

"Nothing I don't think, why?" She asks.

"We are goin' on a date, you don't have to get dressed up, it's not that kind of date, it's a typical cowboy date, wear something warm," I say, as we all get up to go do the groundwork on the farm.

≈≈≈≈≈≈≈≈≈≈≈

All the work is finished, and Sammie and I are upstairs, getting a shower.

We are just enjoying being together this way, no sex, just rubbing soap over each other, kissing, talking and she loves it when I wash her hair.

"Where are we going?" She asks.

"Nowhere in particular," I say.

"How can we be going somewhere but going nowhere in particular?" she frowns at me, and I chuckle.

"You'll see," I reply, as I run my hands down her hair, gently tugging it back to kiss her.

We get dressed, just into something warm, it's not particularly cold right now, but it does cool down at night, in March.

She dries her hair and ties it up, as I sit on the bed and watch her, she then puts mascara and lip oil on, she does that every day, without fail.

Heading downstairs, I grab the keys to one of the trucks.

I already set everything up earlier on, putting sheets, pillows and sleeping bags, into the truck bed, along with a portable stereo for the ambience music.

While we were getting ready, I had asked Elsa to prepare a picnic basket for us, and put it in the truck bed, so that Sammie didn't know about it.

I've also placed a string of lights, across the bed, to light up, when we get to where I'm taking us.

When I was out on a ride once, I came across, what we would call a *lookout*, and I just knew, because there was no light pollution and it was so open, that there would be a blanket of stars.

Tonight, there is no cloud covering, so it's *perfect*

Chapter 55.
Carter.

We head to the truck, hand in hand and she aims for the passenger side, I quickly put my arm past her, so I can open the door for her, she looks at me and smiles.
I close the door after her and walk around to the driver's side.

"Why do you always do that?" She asks, when I get into the truck.
"Do what?"
"Open the door for me, whether it's a car, the stable, the house, you always open the door for me."
I smile, "If you're goin' to tell me, you're one of these women that doesn't think men should open their doors and pull out their chairs, we aint goin' to work."
"Oh no, we are going to work," she smiles back at me.
I put one hand on her knee, for the entire drive, up into the Yorkshire moors.

"Where are we going? Is this where I never see my family again," she laughs.
"Maybe," I reply.
I back into the spot, over looking nothing but fields...
dark fields, which we know, in daylight, are all different shades of green, but right now, they're purples, greys, blacks.
She looks at me, "Okay, but the view is at the back, why have you backed in?"

"Because we're not sitting in the front seats, we are goin' round to the truck bed," I answer, turning, to get out of the vehicle.

I walk around, to open her door and take her hand, as she steps out.

We head towards the back of the truck, and I drop the tailgate, stepping up onto the bed and holding out my hands, to help her up.

She takes my hands and steps on, then sits down, on the blankets, that are all laid out.

I switch on the string of lights and prop up all the pillows so we can lean against them, she just sits watching me.

I then grab the stereo, and tune it into some country music, putting it on top of the truck, out of the way and so we can hear it wherever we are.

I look at her and she rolls her lips but doesn't say anything.

Grabbing the picnic basket, that Elsa packed for us, I open it up, I've no idea what's inside, but I don't let Sammie know that.

She's done us proud, there's home baked bread, the Dairy's own butter, spreads, jelly, peanut butter *(I smile at that)*, a selection of meats and cheeses, fruit salad, a bottle of wine, low alcohol because I'm driving *(again, I smile at that)*, two plates and two wine glasses.

Everything is packed in separate little tubs, and I know, from what she's put in here and how it's set out, that she really wants us to enjoy ourselves and that she approves of us being together, which means a lot to me.

"Wow," she says, "You've thought of everything."

Naw I can't do it.

"I had some help," I say.

She smiles and looks around at the view, and up to the stars, as I pour us both a drink and set everything out for us to tuck in.

"So, this is a cowboy date then?" She asks.

"Yes ma'am," I say, as I tip my hat.

She smiles and pops a grape into her mouth.

"How did you know about this place?"

"I was riding and came across it, there's water down there," I point outwards, "It's where we went to break in Buck."

"Oh, is it?" She replies, looking, even though she can't see it.

"Wow, the stars are like diamonds," she says, while tipping her head back and looking up.

I lean forward and kiss her neck, just at the column of her throat.

She looks at me and we both smile.

"I've been here, nearly a year now," I say, as we are eating the amazing spread, Elsa has put together.

"A year?"

"Yeah, next month, couple of weeks."

"How have you found it?" She smiles, "We worked you hard enough?"

"*You* have," I reply, "Not sure about anyone else."

She laughs, "Well, you've sparked something in me, that I didn't know was there."

I look at her, "I love you," I say.

She smiles, "I love you too."

Josh Turner's *"your man"* comes on the stereo.

"The last time this song played, I wanted to dance with you, but you were with Jake, and I was sort of with Louise, although she knew I belonged with you."

I jump down off the truck bed and hold out my hand for her to dance.

She smiles and takes my hand, jumping down to the floor and I walk us, towards the front of the truck.

"What are we doing? Why don't we just dance over there?" She asks.

I don't answer, I just open the driver door, turn the headlights on and walk her around the front, pulling her towards me.

"Because we are dancing in the headlights," I say.

I sing the words to the song in her ear, as we slowly sway together.

I'm running my hands through her hair, over her cheeks, her neck, her arms, her waist, hips and ass and I can't touch her enough.

"I'm touching you and I don't feel like I'm touching you enough, I need more."

She laughs, "Sounds like when I am looking at you, you're actually there, yet I'm missing you."

I look into her eyes.

"Do you think that's healthy?" She asks.

"Probably not, but everything that isn't healthy, is always addictive," I reply.

≈≈≈≈≈≈≈≈≈≈≈

Before long, we are back in the truck bed, ripping our clothes off and frantically making out.

Kissing my way down her body, I am making sure, my lips and tongue, touch every bit of her! I can't get enough and knowing she feels the same, is just incredible.

I've never felt this before, I've had women, I've had a *lot* of women, but it's never been a *need* like this, not for one person anyway.

The need I have now, is for Sammie, not for just the act of sex, but for her as a person.

I pull her thighs up, around my head and drag my tongue, the length of her slit, sucking at her clit, while pushing my fingers into her, to feel her shatter almost instantly around them, soaking my hand through.

She pushes my head away and looks down at me, "I need a minute," she says.

I kiss my way, back up her body and when my face is level with hers, I put my fingers in my mouth, sucking her arousal from them, before then, forcing them into her mouth.

"Taste yourself, taste how fucking sweet you are!" I demand.

She keeps her eyes on mine, as she sucks my fingers, hard.

I pull her up onto her knees and stand in front of her.

"Put those lips, around my cock and suck like you did just then!" I say.

She looks up at me and smiles.

Keeping our gazes locked, she brings her head forward and licks around the head of my dick.

She then, starts to take me into her wet, warm mouth, edging forward bit by bit, teasing me with how little she takes, but she does as I said and she's sucking, like her life depends on it.

It's fucking torture, trying not to choke her.

She keeps her eyes on mine, as she takes me in, slowly sucking her way down my shaft, until she's almost reaching the base, then she glides her lips back down to the tip, until I am totally free of her mouth.

I'm panting desperately, needing to be back in there.

She holds my dick in her hand, while slowly gliding her tongue on the underside, like it's a fucking popsicle.

I can't take it anymore, I put a hand on either side of her face and force my cock past her pouty little lips and down her throat, watching her gag, and the tears spring, to her beautiful shining fucking, jewel eyes.

I grab her hair, pushing as far back in her throat as she can take, before feeling the need to come, but I don't want to finish in her mouth.

I pull out and flip her over, pushing her top half down onto the pillows and dragging her hips up, into doggy position.

Sliding into her tight little pussy, from behind, I whisper in her ear, "This cunt, is goin' to be, the fucking death of me, but I'll die a very happy man."

I'm pounding deep into her, hard, while I put one of my hands around her front to stimulate her clit, with lots of pressured rubs and a few nips, causing her screams to get loud.

We don't have to be quiet up here, no one can hear us, and we are both, taking advantage of that.

I spit onto her ass, holding her ass cheeks apart, letting my saliva act as a lube for her tight little ring, then I gently insert my thumb, and she gasps, looking back, over her shoulder at me.

"Relax, I've been up there before," I say and she blushes.

≈≈≈≈≈≈≈≈≈≈≈≈

With the multiple stimulations going on, she doesn't take long to come apart, a few more times, before I can feel my own orgasm building up.

She reaches her hand, around the back of her and grabs my balls, to stroke and massage them, which only spurs things on, because a couple more rough thrusts and I'm roaring out my spill, like a fucking wild animal.

I fall to the side of her, and she turns her head to look at me, both of us panting like we have just completed a damn marathon.

Our skin pink, our hair stuck to our heads and sweat dripping over our bodies, we laugh and kiss, wrapping ourselves up into each other, covered lightly with one of the sheets.

We just lay there, in each other's arms, naked, satisfied, in a truck bed and under the stars.

We both sigh.

≈≈≈≈≈≈≈≈≈≈≈

"I remember, the first time I saw you when you arrived, the way you looked, I wasn't expecting it, you were so fucking hot," she says, after a while of us laying in silence.

"I wanted to bend you over that table, there and then," I reply.

"I wanted that too," she laughs.

"You were a nightmare!" I say.

She laughs again, "I didn't *mean* it, I was trying not to like you, trying to convince myself that, if I was mean to you, we would hate each other."

"That was never goin' to happen," I reply.

"How do you know?" She looks up at me.

I look down at her, letting my gaze bounce between her beautiful, striking green eyes, that hooked me from the moment I saw them and her sexy fucking lips that drove me wild with every bite, lick and roll, she tortured me with, just thinking in silence.

Then I answer with, "Because from the first letter, I knew I couldn't be without you, I knew there was something there, your letters were the *only* thing that I looked forward to and as time went on, I had to meet you, I *had* to be near you. I was *hooked*,"

I kiss her and carry on, "Then, when I saw you there, in your kitchen, the most beautiful woman I had *ever* seen, knowing already, how much of a beautiful person you were, I knew, not only that I *loved* you, not only that I can't live without you, but that I *wanted* to love you forever, I didn't *want* to live without you" I kiss her again, "You were a choice *and* a need. You are *everything* to me, my only reason for living, the one thing tying me to this world. It's not oxygen keeping me alive, it's not gravity keeping me on this earth, it's *you*! I want, more than anything, to spend the rest of my life with you. I want you to be mine, *forever*"

Epilogue.
Carter, 18 months later.

The barn is set up ready for today.

On the stage, there is the arch, which is decorated, this time, with warm white string lights, green vines and white roses, trailing all around it. Underneath that, a bale of hay. That's for sentimental reasons, as well as a touch of country.

The lights around the barn walls, are twinkling with the others and because the sky is at twilight outside, they're pretty noticeable indoors, giving a warm, welcoming glow.

Leading down from the stage area, going the full length, of the middle of the barn, all the way to the entrance doors at the back, there is a white runner.

Chairs, that are decorated, with white lace sashes, white roses and green vines and that are filled, with everyone we know, just like at the baby shower and the Halloween party, are set out in rows, on both sides of the runner, facing the stage, the arch, the hay bale, a vicar..and *me*.

I'm stood at the front, in a full white suit and a white cowboy hat.

Accompanied by Carl, who is in a light beige suit, a white shirt and a caramel colored tie.

Apparently, Frank has the same outfit, and the ties match the bridesmaid dresses.

"How you feeling?" Carl asks.

"Ready," I reply.

I had proposed to Sammie, in the truck on our date, I wasn't even planning it, but it was the best decision I had ever made.

The hay bale is present, because we had our first kiss in the hay barn.
The room is buzzing with emotion and excitement, and everyone is waiting to get a glimpse of the bride.
No one, more so than me.
Everyone is dressed in outfits, that match the color scheme perfectly and it all looks like, the perfect country celebration of love.
Exactly the type of thing I envisioned, when I suggested doing this to the barn.

"Nearly time," says Carl.
I nod, now getting nervous.
The doors open and *"I'm gonna love you"* by Cody Johnson and Carrie Underwood sounds through the speakers, the song Sammie and I sang together on karaoke at the Honky Tonk.
First down the aisle, in a caramel colored, floor length, satin dress, is Louise, I see the little wink she gives Jake, who is sat in one of the chairs, on her way down towards the stage.
She looks at me and we give each other a warm smile.

Next down the aisle is Sara, wearing the same as Louise, even their hairstyle is the same, but the only difference is, she's holding hands with Victoria, who's wearing a fluffy little white dress with a sash across her middle, a sash that matches the bridesmaid dresses and the men's ties, she's also holding a little beige basket, filled with red rose petals, which she's meant to be

throwing on the white runner, but she's throwing them at the people sat down.
Everyone laughs.

Then suddenly everybody stands, and Frank and Sammie arrive at the doors and I audibly gasp.
She always looks good, but she looks like a fucking angel right now.
Her makeup very light and natural, her hair is in soft loose waves, with a trail of flowers running through it.
She's holding a simple wildflower bouquet, with one hand and the other hand is clung to her dad's arm.
The dress she has gone with, is a slim fitting, flowing, lace dress in ivory, skimming over her curves perfectly, swaying, as she makes her way towards me.
Country, whimsical, feminine.
She looks absolutely incredible and…
Do I have tears in my eyes? Do not fucking fall down my face!
I swallow.

They get to the front and Frank hands his daughter over to me, I'm not even a dad, but I love her too and I know how *painful* that must have felt, and I notice, he also has tears in his eyes.
I shake his hand and take Sammie's hand, as she makes the last step with me, onto the stage, with the vicar.
"Are you crying?" She whispers.
"Nearly," I smile.
She smiles back.

It's time to declare our love.

"I, Carter Nelson, take you, Sammie Jenkins, to be my wife, to have and to hold, from this day forward, for better, for worse, for richer, for poorer, in sickness and in health, to love and to cherish, till death us do part, according to God's holy law. In the presence of God, I make this vow"

After we both, exchange vows and rings, It is announced that we are now man and wife.

I take off my hat, putting it on my Wife's head, for the *first* time, earning me the *biggest* grin, before I crush my lips to hers, while the room erupts into cheers and claps.

"I love you," she whispers.

"I love you more," I whisper back.

The End

Acknowledgements.

I would like to say, a big thank you to a few people.
Firstly, my mum.
She has always believed in me and, if it wasn't for her,
working hard for me and being the amazing person she
is, I wouldn't be who I am today.

Secondly, my girls.
Zaz, Steph, Jen, Jay, Willow and Nagin.
Always checking in and asking how things are going,
whilst I have been writing. Thank you, for being my
cheerleaders.

Last, but in no way, least, my little Booktok family.
The people I have met on social media, have been
amongst the best folk and the biggest support.
I really appreciate you all.

Printed in Dunstable, United Kingdom

66906248R00228